A deadly search for sour grapes . . .

Norrie Ellington is a successful screenwriter living in New York City. She's also been a silent partner for her family's winery upstate—until her sister and brother-in-law take a year-long sabbatical. With an experienced staff doing the work, Norrie figures Two Witches Winery will run itself while she enjoys the countryside and writes in peace and quiet.

Unfortunately, there's a sour grape in the village of Penn Yan who doesn't care for vineyards. Bed and breakfast owner Elsbeth Waters complains to everyone who'll listen that the local wineries are bad for her business. But when Elsbeth's body is found on Norrie's property, the victim of foul play, the screenwriter-turned-vintner dons a sleuthing cap to uncover the identity of a killer who told the B&B proprietess to put a cork in it—permanently . . .

Visit us at www.kensingtonbooks.com

Books by J.C. Eaton

The Sophie Kimball Mysteries
Booked 4 Murder
Ditched 4 Murder

And coming soon:
Staged 4 Murder (July 2018)

And in E-Book
The Wine Trail Mysteries
A Riesling to Die

Published by Kensington Publishing Corporation

A Riesling to Die

J.C. Eaton

LYRICAL PRESS
Kensington Publishing Corp.
www.kensingtonbooks.com

First Electronic Edition: March 2018
eISBN-13: 978-1-5161-0798-8
eISBN-10: 1-5161-0798-5

First Print Edition: March 2018
ISBN-13: 978-1-5161-0801-5
ISBN-10: 1-5161-0801-9

Printed in the United States of America

To all of the amazing wineries on New York's Seneca Lake Wine Trail, this mystery is for you. And to our friends and former employers at Anthony Road Wine Company and Fox Run Vineyards, we thank you for teaching us so much and giving us so many terrific memories. You folks were the inspiration for this cozy mystery series. May it always be a good year!

Acknowledgments

Our grapes would die on the vine if it wasn't for our amazing support team of readers, critics, hand-holders, coaches, cheerleaders and computer gurus who jumped at the opportunity to embrace another J.C. Eaton cozy mystery series. (Okay, maybe not jumped, but certainly signed on!) Thank you Beth Cornell, Larry Finkelstein, Gale Leach, Ellen Lynes, Susan Morrow, Susan Schwartz and Suzanne Scher.

If it wasn't for our agent Dawn Dowdle from Blue Ridge Literary Agency and our editor, Tara Gavin from Kensington Publishing, none of this would have been possible. You are indeed, "the best of the best" and we are so fortunate and grateful that you took us on. And a very special thanks to Robin Cook, our production editor, who has to suffer through all those pesky errors we make.

Finally, thank you, Camille Figueroa from Anthony Road Wine Company in Penn Yan, New York, for serving as our inspiration for this series. Your knowledge and enthusiasm about the wine industry was contagious!

Chapter 1

The sign off to my right read Welcome to the Seneca Lake Wine Trail, and I knew in that instant I had lost my mind. What the hell was I thinking? I slowed the car for a split second and then picked up speed. It wasn't that I minded doing favors for people, but they were always on the easy side. Picking up someone's mail while they were gone, feeding a friend's cat or taking a colleague to an appointment because their car broke down. But this? This bordered on insanity.

My older, by one and a half years, sister, Francine, pleaded with me to "oversee" our family winery in Penn Yan, New York, for a year so she and her husband, Jason, who worked for Cornell University's Experiment Station in nearby Geneva, could spend that time researching some godforsaken bug in Costa Rica.

I wished I had never said yes, but Francine could be downright persuasive. Annoying, really. She called me three months ago as I was headed out the door of my tiny Manhattan apartment wedged between Nolita and Little Italy. An apartment I inherited from a great aunt because no one in our family wanted to live in "the city." They equated it with drugs, sex, robberies and lunatics. Unfortunately, they were sort of right. But the advantages to living in a place that didn't shut down at eight o'clock could be mind-blowing. Too bad my sister didn't share my opinion. Her life revolved around that winery and now she wanted mine to do the same.

"Come on, Norrie, you're the only one I trust. It's not as if you have to live in New York City. You're a screenwriter. All you need is a laptop and a phone line. We've got those. Besides, it's only for a year. One year."

"A year? A full year? That's the life span for some species. Can't Mom and Dad do it?"

"You have *got* to be kidding me. The last thing Jason and I want is for them to come back from Myrtle Beach and undo everything we've done in the past five years. I thought Dad would never retire."

"The winery has staff. The winemaker, the vineyard manager, the tasting room manager, the bistro chef, the—"

"Norrie, you don't have to tell me who works for us. That's just the point. They're staff. You're family. And, you're part owner of the winery."

"A silent partner. I like it that way. You know as well as I do I've never been interested in the winery business. Not like you. You have a degree in hospitality and hotel management. Big surprise. Even as a kid you were the one who would go out in the winter to help prune the vines, or badger the winemakers to figure out how they made wine out of grapes. I'm the one who sat in my room writing. Remember?"

"Of course I do."

"For your information, I've made a great career out of it."

"You can still do that. Only from Two Witches Winery instead of Great Aunt Tessie's apartment."

That was another thing. The name. Two Witches Winery. It was located on Two Witches Hill in Penn Yan overlooking Seneca Lake. The hill was named after, you guessed it, two women in the eighteenth century who were thought to be witches. Unfortunately, Francine and I had to go through school with that moniker. Boys teased us relentlessly. "Which witch are you?" "Are you the good witch or the bad witch?" We begged our parents to change the winery name, but they refused. My dad said it reflected the history of the hill.

As far as Francine and I were concerned, it reflected the prior owner's refusal to think up something original and when my parents bought the place when Francine was born, the name stayed. But that didn't mean I had to.

"I'm sorry," I said. "I really can't do this."

"Can't or won't? If it's because you think you're not qualified, don't worry. I'll walk you through everything. Come on, you'll still be able to write those screenplays and maybe living in the Finger Lakes will give you some new ideas."

"I've had twenty-nine years of Finger Lakes living already."

"Great. You can make it thirty. Please, Norrie? Please?"

"I really, really can't."

"Pleeze…pleeze, Norrieee."

The "eez" sounded like the worst whine I'd ever heard and, in a moment of sheer weakness, lunacy, really, I said yes. Now I was less than fifteen miles from Two Witches Winery and it was too late to turn around and go back to the city. I had sublet my apartment for a year and crammed all of my personal belongings into my small Toyota sedan. I took a deep breath and looked off to the right.

Seneca Lake was in its glory. It was early evening in mid-June and its sapphire water, set against the deep green hills, was magnificent. A few sailboats dotted the shore. Time for happy hour at the lake's numerous bars. It was idyllic all right, if a Norman Rockwell painting was what someone had in mind. For me, it was simply the place where I grew up. I picked up speed and continued to drive north, chastising myself for ever agreeing to do such a lamebrain thing.

I was so deep in thought I was halfway up the lake before I knew it and almost missed the turnoff to our winery. A giant sign on the road read "Grey Egret Winery and Two Witches Winery to the right."

Grey Egret sat at the bottom of the hill. It was a small winery owned by the Martinelli family. I wondered which one of their kids got stuck continuing the legacy. Their parking lot was emptying and I glanced at the clock. Five fifteen. Most wineries closed at five. That meant I was spared making an entrance at Two Witches. I'd just head to the house.

The vineyards on either side of the road seemed to stretch on for miles. Some belonged to us, others to Grey Egret. Other than the cars coming down the hill, it was one of those quintessential postcard scenes. I pressed on. Then, out of the corner of my eye, I saw what looked like a llama. Nope. Too fat. What the heck? It was on our property, too. Fenced in with the winery behind it.

I don't care what it is, I'm not taking care of it.

The house was about a half mile past the winery, set back near the woods. I pulled into the long driveway and looked at the vineyards again. I had to admit, based on eyesight alone, Francine and Jason were doing a great job. Last thing they needed was for me to muck it up.

A quick slam of the car door and I walked to the house. Francine must've glanced out the window or, worse yet, had sat there waiting. She hurried toward me. Tall, slender, with ash-colored hair, she had the look of a professional model without all the effort.

"Norrie! Thank goodness. I was beginning to think you had second thoughts."

"I had third and fourth thoughts. Give me a day and the number will exceed ten."

She looked at me doubtfully.

I gave her a hug and smiled. "I sublet the apartment. Even if I wanted to escape out of here, I'd have to wait out the year."

"Good. You won't be sorry. Think of it as an adventure. Something new every day."

"Uh, yeah. Speaking of new, what's that animal in front of the winery? Please don't tell me it belongs to us."

"That's Alvin. He's a Nigerian Dwarf Goat."

"My God! He's a dwarf goat? What do the regular ones look like? Camels?"

"Don't be silly. He's really quite small for his breed. We got him two years ago. Jason thought it might be entertaining for the visitors, and he was right. When word gets out that a winery has great wine and is also a fun place for kids, people are more likely to visit."

"You'd better not tell me I have to feed him and clean out his...his what? A stall? A barn?"

"He has a small house, but the vineyard guys take care of him. You can cross that off your list."

"Whew."

"Come on, you must be hungry. Jason threw a few steaks on the grill and I made some rice and ratatouille. He's got an evening meeting with his colleagues at the station, so we'll have lots of time to chat. Hold on. Let me get him. He can help you with your bags." Francine took one look at my car and winced. "Pioneers crossing the plains didn't take as much stuff. We have blankets and...what's that? Don't tell me you packed a coffeemaker?"

"It's a Keurig. I don't know how to use a real coffeemaker."

"You can relax. We own a Keurig, too. And we have a microwave and Wi-Fi and all sorts of twenty-first century stuff. It's not like when Mom and Dad lived here. We even have satellite TV. No more antenna and three stations."

"Francine Ellington Keane, that's blasphemous."

We both laughed and, for the first time, I didn't feel as if I had made the mistake of a lifetime. Francine shouted for Jason and, after more hugs, the three of us carted my stuff into the house.

"Hope you don't mind," Jason said, "we sort of took down the dorky daisy wallpaper from your old bedroom, removed the furniture, well, sold it, actually, and set up a new, modern guest room. Hey, there's a queen-size bed in there now. That's got to be a plus."

"Uh, sure. I haven't slept in that room in what? Seven? Eight years? It'll be fine."

It wasn't as if I hadn't seen my sister or brother-in-law in all that time. It was just I'd seen them at other locations. Or, to be precise, other events. Our cousin Marianne's wedding in Pennsylvania, our nephew Shane's wedding on Long Island and our uncle Phil's funeral in Ohio.

The one thing that stayed the same was the view from my bedroom window. Since the room was upstairs and at the front of the house, I could see clear across the lake. When I was little and we'd had a blizzard, I used to pretend I was living in the ice house from *Doctor Zhivago.*

Francine and Jason did more than modernize my old bedroom. They totally remodeled the old farm kitchen and re-did the downstairs bathroom. They also added a small en suite to their room but left the old claw tub and turn-of-the- (gasp) twentieth-century bathroom; the one I was to use, as is. At least there was hot and cold running water.

My sister tossed my goose-down pillow on the bed and shrugged. "We've got these, too, but I understand people like to sleep with their own. You can unpack later. Dinner's been ready. What do you say?"

* * * *

I scarfed down a perfectly grilled steak and dove into the fixings she had prepared. It was still warm outside, so we ate on the small deck behind the house. Nothing but woods and the edge of the vineyard. Jason had to rush off to a meeting so that left my sister and me alone to get caught up.

Francine brushed a strand of hair from her forehead and leaned back. "First thing tomorrow, I'll walk you through the winery. I made arrangements with all of the area managers to show you the ropes. Tomorrow you get to work with Cammy in the tasting room."

"Cammy? What happened to Tim McCauley, the prior tasting room manager?"

"He retired over a year ago and moved down south to be near his kids. Cammy Rosinetti's been with us ever since. Her family's from Geneva and she knows the wine business in an indirect way. Her parents used to own Rosinetti's Bar on Exchange Street."

"I thought that name sounded familiar."

"Listen, Norrie, I know things are moving fast and I hope you don't get overwhelmed. Jason and I fly out of Rochester on Friday. That's less than a week."

My voice sounded as if it would crack. "That's three days. Not counting tonight and Friday."

"You're a quick study. You'll have this all under control by the time we head to the airport. Oh, hope you don't mind, but you'll need to drive us. In our car. The Subaru. Four-wheel drive and all. Use it this winter. Walden's Garage will get the snow tires and studs on for you. You remember where that is, don't you?"

"Of course. On Pre-Emption Road. I may have been gone for a while but my memory's still working."

"I'm sorry. I didn't mean to sound—"

"Like Mom?"

"Yeesh. There's more, too, Norrie. I couldn't get into all of it on the phone with you and tonight's not the best time. We'll talk about it tomorrow, okay?"

"Is everything all right? Are you and Jason all right?"

"We're fine. Nothing like that. It's business stuff. The winery. I'll clean up and you should unpack. We've got the whole day tomorrow to talk."

I helped bring the dishes to the kitchen and wiped off the picnic table. "You can tell me anything, you know."

"That's why I needed you to be the one to look after the place."

Chapter 2

Francine had to do some last-minute shopping the next morning so she pointed me in the direction of the tasting room, which I already knew, and told me to introduce myself to Cammy.

Years ago, our tasting room consisted of a loading dock on the back of the winery, but now it was a huge building that resembled a ski lodge. Vaulted ceiling, timber beams, the whole works. A natural-gas fireplace was the centerpiece of the structure, with round tasting tables spaced evenly throughout the room. Large glass-paneled doors opened to the wooded area behind the building and vineyards. To the far left was a witch-themed bistro, what else, that featured sandwiches, paninis and soups. Its arched doorway separated it from the tasting area but still allowed for that "open concept."

The front windows gave visitors an unobstructed view of Alvin. It was impossible, but he looked as if he had grown at least a foot overnight. I was sure the vineyard workers were thrilled beyond belief to be adding him to their to-do list each day.

The winery office was off to the left as visitors entered the building. Nothing special, as I remembered. Some desks, a computer, file cabinets and a printer. Things might've changed, but I doubted it. If this was the spot Francine envisioned me working on a screenplay, she was sadly mistaken. I pictured all sorts of interruptions and not the good kind, either.

"Miss Ellington, can you check on a sewage smell?"

"Miss Ellington, the exterminator says we have termites."

"Miss Ellington, someone dropped a case of our merlot."

Nope, I had my laptop, the house had Wi-Fi, and the winery had staff. End of story.

I opened the door to the tasting room and stepped into the kitchen on the right. I almost didn't recognize it. Two industrial dishwashers took the place of the old clunker we were forced to use. In addition, there were two stainless-steel refrigerator/freezers. The double sink was the same, but the faucets had been replaced. I hadn't really paid much attention to the financials and I wondered if Francine and Jason were in too deep. Was that what she alluded to last night?

I took in the small banquet room behind the kitchen. Other than new tablecloths and window treatments, it looked the same—a warm and cozy spot for bachelorette and engagement parties, meetings, local author book signings and all sorts of events. Lots of wineries, including Two Witches, did that sort of thing to generate extra income and promote the wines. I paused in front of a watercolor a local artist had painted of the winery, then I exited through the banquet room's main door into the tasting room.

We wouldn't open for business for another hour, but I could see the back of a woman whom I assumed was Cammy. Before I could say anything, she spoke.

"Please and thank you for the year."

"Huh?" I stared at the robust brunette with her hair in a bun and an orange winery T-shirt that read, Two Witches Winery–The Spell's On Us.

"It gets crazy around here when we're doing tastings. I don't have time to be saying please and thank you when we're slammed so I like to get it over with right away. Cammy Rosinetti, tasting room manager. You must be Francine's sister."

"Norrie Ellington, screenwriter."

"Uh-huh."

She looked at me as if she thought I was delusional. "Planning on writing an exposé on the winery business? Because if you are, I've got the skinny on stuff you wouldn't believe. Not here, of course, but word gets out."

"Uh, no. I write romances. Maybe you've heard of some of the movies I've adapted from novels or short stories. *Kisses in the Snow, A Hug from the Mountaintop*...mostly TV movies."

"Nope. I don't go in for all that sappy stuff. I understand you're taking over the winery for a year. Doubt you'll have a whole lot of time to be writing about hugs and kisses."

"I'm overseeing the winery. Not actually working, working."

"Uh-huh. We'll see how that goes. Have you ever served customers in a tasting room before?"

I thought back to high school and cringed. "Sort of. It didn't last long. I got a job instead writing up ads for one of the local newspapers."

Again, the "uh-huh" followed by "It's really quite simple. People come in. People taste wine. Hopefully people buy wine. Your job is to get them to buy wine. But without being pushy. The wine sells itself."

"Oh, I'm not going to be doing the tastings. Like I said, I only need to learn *how* to do the tastings. All I remember is white wine first, then red. Always go from dry to sweet."

"That's more than most newbies know. Look, I'll walk you through this anyway. In case."

I didn't like the way she said "in case." I was afraid it was code for "you're on the schedule."

First thing Cammy did was take out a tasting sheet and point to the list of wines. "Each customer gets to taste five wines for five dollars. No double tastings. Keep in mind, it's a taste, not a glass."

Then, as if to prove her point, she took a bottle of water and one of the wineglasses and showed me what she meant. "Some of our customers think wineries are barrooms. We have to remind them this is only a tasting. If they love the wine, they can purchase it. Plus, we deduct two dollars from the cost of the tasting if they buy a bottle."

"Whoa. Sounds like a good deal to me."

"It is. It's also pretty customary around this wine trail."

In the next half hour, she walked me through loading the dishwasher with the filled trays of used wineglasses and restocking the shelves.

"Other than the ones in the bins by the wall, the wines are in the storage room behind that rack of T-shirts. Don't carry out more bottles than you can comfortably handle. Better a dozen trips than one that ends up with broken bottles and wine all over the floor."

"Uh, other than you, who works here?" I asked.

"Lizzie mans the cash register. She's full-time like me but different days. I'm here every day except Sundays and Mondays. Glenda works Sundays, Mondays, Tuesdays and Thursdays. Roger works Wednesdays, Fridays and weekends. Sam works alternate Fridays and weekends. I can get you a schedule if you want."

"Uh, I'm okay for now."

"Oh, forgot to mention this. In the fall, we hire more part-time help for the weekends. The wine trail all but explodes with visitors between September and December."

Explodes. Terrific. I translated that to mean I would be the one responsible for hiring the part-time help. "I suppose there's an application process and all."

"Sure. But most of our hires are from word of mouth or people we recommend."

Finally, I got to see the wine list. Cammy insisted I sip each wine so I'd know the product before I left the tasting room or her reputation would be sullied forever. I didn't argue.

I wasn't really what anyone would call "a drinker." Not even a glass of wine once a week. Pretty unusual coming from a family that owned a winery. But I wasn't a teetotaler either. I'd have a glass of wine now and then at celebrations and I'd been known to enjoy dessert wines after dinners when I had the chance to dine in fancy restaurants.

I picked up the tasting sheet and perused it. I recognized the staples that appeared on most Finger Lakes winery lists—Chardonnay, Riesling, Gewürztraminer, Cabernet Franc, Cayuga, Lemberger, Merlot, Pinot Noir, Pinot Gris and Vignoles—but I was taken back when I saw a new name: Grüner Veltliner.

"What's that?" I asked. "I thought I was pretty familiar with the grapes we grow."

Cammy looked at the list and let out a long, torturous sigh. "It's a white wine with hints of peach and citrus. Very food friendly."

"Then why do you have that awful expression on your face?"

"It's not the wine. It's the grape."

"Huh?"

"Not native to the Finger Lakes and when your sister and the vineyard manager wanted to introduce it, well, let's just say it was a real process. It meant removing the old vines from some of the Chardonnay grapes that had been here forever and planting the new stock."

"I thought that was something vineyards did every fifteen years or so. The vines don't yield the quantity and quality like they used to."

"True, but they always replant the same or similar varieties. The Veltiner is a real risk. Customers are leery of trying something new."

"At least the blends are the same. We still have Cauldron Caper, a mix of Cabernet Franc and Cayuga, and, oh look—Witches Brew. That was Francine's favorite."

"Yeah. It's a top seller, too. Great blend of Riesling, Pinot Gris and Chardonnay. Say, you know more than you're letting on. For someone who says they distanced themselves from the winery, you seem very knowledgeable."

"Uh, like I said, I worked in the tasting room for a while but let's leave it at that."

Cammy shook her head and laughed. "Okay. How many bottles did you break?"

"An entire case. That wasn't the worst of it. It was the last case of some very expensive dessert wine. I kind of tripped over something."

The laugh lines on the side of her mouth got bigger. "Maybe you can help with the gift shop if you feel like it. The gang and I have it pretty much under control when it comes to ordering stock, packing and shipping cartons to buyers and organizing the little events for the banquet room."

Just then the door swung open and a stout gray-haired lady with red lipstick and wide hoop earrings walked in. She took off the light jacket she was wearing, revealing a lime green T-shirt from the winery. "I spoke to Lizzie this morning. She's making the bank deposit and will be in shortly. What'd I miss?"

Cammy motioned her over and stepped back from the table. "Good morning, Glenda. This is Norrie. Francine's sister. She's going to be managing the winery while Francine and Jason go chasing after some bug in Costa Rica."

I could tell by the tone of Cammy's voice she had the same impression of Jason's entomology work that I did.

"Nice to meet you," I said.

"Same here. Hope you plan to do some tastings with us. It's really tremendous fun. Never a dull moment. I thought when I retired from food service at the school I'd never want to work again. This is different. No food fights. No screaming kids. Of course, it does get kind of hairy in the fall, but nothing we can't handle, right, Cammy?"

Cammy puffed out her chest as if she'd been awarded a medal of honor. "We've got it all under control. Oh, before I forget, there's something you need to know."

"What's that?"

"Whatever you do, do *not* let Charlie in the tasting room. To begin with, he usually smells bad. But that's not the worst of it. He passes gas. It's horrible. It drives the customers away. Here we are serving wonderful wine with crackers and all of a sudden it's like the Ovid dump moved next door."

"Uh, how will I recognize him?"

"He's medium size and tan."

"Is he one of the vineyard workers?"

Cammy and Glenda exploded with laughter and I stood there wondering what the joke was.

Finally Cammy spoke. "I guess he wasn't at your house last night. He does that. Disappears from time to time. Probably out hunting raccoons or rabbits."

Whoever that Charlie guy was, I had him pegged for a really unreliable worker and wondered why on earth he'd be at my sister's house. "I don't get it. What's so funny?"

Glenda crinkled her nose and laughed again. "Charlie's a brindle Plott Hound. He showed up last year and never left. The guys in the winery building feed him, as well as your sister. He's kind of the unofficial ambassador around here."

"I take it he's friendly."

Both ladies nodded. "Oh yeah. Very friendly. And not to worry. He's fixed and has had all his shots. The vet estimated he's about two."

"I guess with all the hubbub last night, Francine and Jason forgot to mention him. Although, I did get the lowdown on Alvin."

"Yeah," Glenda said. "That goat's a real attraction for families. Well, I suppose I'd better get my station set up. Doors open in twenty minutes. Fred should be here any minute to get the bistro going."

I couldn't believe the time had slipped by so quickly. I glanced at the bistro and read the list of sandwiches from the chalkboard. "I think I've found my new lunch spot."

Suddenly, a tall pencil-thin lady with white slacks and a light pink button-down shirt walked into the tasting room, clicking her heels on the tile floor as she approached us. Her short dark hair framed her face and I estimated her to be in her late forties or maybe early fifties.

"Is Francine Keane in? I need to speak with her immediately." She ran her fingers through the fringe of her plum-colored scarf as she spoke.

Cammy gave me a sideways glance and I cleared my throat. "Uh, she's out running errands. I'm her sister, Norrie. Maybe I can help you. I'm going to be overseeing the winery while she and my brother-in-law are in Costa Rica for a year."

The woman's stone-cold stare was menacing. "If they know what's good for them, they'll stay in Costa Rica."

I swallowed and rubbed my hands together. One word came to mind but we spell it with a W at the winery. "Maybe I can take a message."

"Tell your sister this isn't over. I've registered a complaint with the county. I want those cannons to cease and desist immediately. This morning I all but fell out of my bed when the first one went off. This isn't the Civil War, you know. We don't have to put up with it. I already spoke to those two gentlemen at the Grey Egret and told them the same thing."

She pronounced *gentlemen* as if it was a curse word. I bit my lower lip and kept my calm. "And you are…?"

"Elsbeth Waters. I own the Peaceful Pines bed and breakfast on the next hill over. Your sister is quite familiar with me."

I'm sure she is.

With that, Elsbeth Waters clicked her heels and exited the tasting room.

"Whoa," I said. "Maybe she should rename her B & B to The Third Witch."

"You haven't seen anything yet," Cammy said. "At least this was a short visit."

Chapter 3

Francine was home by noon and made us chicken salad sandwiches. We sat at the round oak table in her kitchen and watched the visitors going in and out of the tasting room building.

I helped myself to a few potato chips and took a sip of iced tea. "I met your neighbor Elsbeth Waters. It didn't go over too well. What's going on? Other than her complaining about the cannon noise."

"It's always something with her. The woman's been a misery ever since she bought the old Tyler place and converted it to a bed and breakfast. She knew about the cannons and the birds-in-distress calls when she purchased the property. Right now we're only testing the propane cannons. They usually run from August to the beginning of October. Elsbeth was informed. Hank Langley, the realtor, told me it was on the disclosure statement from the seller. If we didn't make those noises, we wouldn't have any grapes. The birds, deer, rabbits and foxes would get them all. Not to mention coyotes."

"You don't have to tell me. I counted on those propane cannons to wake me up. It was better than Mom screaming 'You'll miss the bus.' After October, I had to get used to her screaming again and couldn't wait until harvest time rolled around once more. Funny, but I got the feeling something else was gnawing at Elsbeth Waters. That wasn't the issue you wanted to talk with me about, was it?"

Francine shook her head and put the used plates in the sink. I grabbed a dishtowel and wiped the table as she spoke.

"A big developer is trying to buy out the small wineries on the west side of the lake so his company can build a mega-winery between Geneva and Penn Yan. The wine trail would become some bland commercial business and lose all of its charm. They've been pressing the smaller wineries to sell and some have agreed. It's the last thing Jason and I want to do."

"Can't you just say no? I think that was actually an anti-drug campaign some first lady came up with."

"Nancy Reagan and it's not that simple."

"What do you mean?"

"We can't prove it, but we think they're resorting to dirty tricks. Small things like finding dead animals on winery doorsteps and in mailboxes. One winery owner came to work in the morning and wondered why there were no visitors. He drove down the road to find a closed sign had been placed over his entrance marque."

"That doesn't sound trivial to me."

"It is, compared to what they could do. That's why you have to be on your guard. In case it escalates. Oh, Norrie, this is the worst possible time for us to be going to Costa Rica, but Jason's grant was very specific about the time frame. I'm really sorry to be throwing this at you, but at least you'll have some support from Theo and Don. They own the Grey Egret and are good friends of ours. They bought the winery from the Martinellis five or six years ago and have done wonders with the old place."

"Uh, yeah. The *gentlemen*. That's how Elsbeth Waters pronounced it when she mentioned them."

"Ugh. She's a piece of work, that Elsbeth. Theo and Don are more than winery partners. They're life partners and Elsbeth seems to take issue with that."

"Elsbeth should step out of the middle ages."

"Tell her that. Anyway, as I was saying, all of us on the west side are rattled, but we're not caving."

"If I run into anything awful…I mean, truly awful, I'll call you."

"Um, about that… It won't be so easy. The places we're going to are off the grid. Rainforests. No cellular service. Jason and I will keep in touch as best we can. Listen, Theo and Don know what they're doing and you'll be fine. You can also reach out to Henry Speltmore at the Speltmore Estates a few miles up. He's president of the wine association and a decent guy. Don't look so panicked. Our staff's been around for a long time and everything's routine to them. Even normal winery emergencies."

"I'll keep that in mind when I climb to the roof and wave a white towel over my head."

"John Grishner and his crew will be done by three. I asked him to stop over and give you a rundown on their operation."

"John. Thank goodness. At least it's the same vineyard manager we've had for decades."

"*Had's* the right word. He'll be retiring next summer. The assistant manager is being groomed to take over. Peter Groff. Nice guy. Graduated from the state university at Cobleskill with a specialty in plant science and got his grad degree at UC Davis. Worked for a big winery in California, too, before coming back east."

I put the iced tea in the fridge and nodded. "Good to know."

"He's single, too. Not bad looking."

"Not interested. Don't even think it. I'm here for one year and back to Manhattan. I have no intention of spending my life tucked away in Norman Rockwell land. No offense."

"Okay, okay. I won't pester you. You'll have enough on your plate."

"What I want on my plate is lots of time to work on my next screenplay. I've got a contract with Paramour Productions in Toronto, and I don't plan on blowing it." I tucked a strand of hair behind my ear and caught my reflection in the window glass. I wasn't bad looking either. Shoulder-length auburn hair, light freckles, one dimple (I definitely got gypped) and a decent figure as a result of my exercise program—walking instead of hailing a cab.

Francine rinsed the plates and sat down, motioning for me to do the same. "How did you get on with Cammy?"

"Really liked her. And Glenda, too."

"Wait 'till you meet Lizzie and the rest of the crew. Feel free to pop in and out of the tasting room. Tomorrow I'm having you spend the day with Franz Johannas and his assistants. He'll introduce you. He's the winemaker we hired four years ago when Rhinehart opened his own winery in Ithaca. He still consults with us when we need him. He's married and has two children now. Can you believe it?"

I shuddered. "He was a kid when Mom and Dad hired him. Geez. I feel like I'm the only one who hasn't aged."

"Your braces are gone and you've gotten taller. You've aged."

"Thanks a heap. If you don't mind, I'm going to take a stroll around the place. Yesterday was a blur. I'll be back before John gets here."

"Have fun!"

I slipped out of the kitchen and walked past the tasting room building, pausing to watch a little girl in a pink and white smock pet Alvin. The gravel parking lot had a dozen or so cars in it with more New Jersey and Pennsylvania license plates than New York. A few yards to my left stood the winery building. A black Mercedes coupe and a red Chevy Silverado were parked in the small dirt lot next to the side door. Closer to the entrance was a bright silver Volvo sedan and a few feet from that, an older Volkswagen Golf.

"Like hell you will," someone shouted as two men argued by the door. Too bad I couldn't get a close enough look. I turned the other way, pretending to take an interest in the Riesling grapes that were in the adjacent vineyard.

"If you know what's good for you, you'll do it."

Next thing I knew, the owner of the Mercedes got into his car and took off, spewing enough dust to rival a small dirt devil. I couldn't read the license plate, but its distinct orange and black colors left no doubt it was New York. Another interference from that mega company or something else? Maybe John knew and would mention it to Francine when we all convened later. I kept walking.

I was no expert, but our vineyards looked darn good to me. Verdant green and healthy. Not too bushy. Of course, it was only June and a lot could happen weather-wise that would turn a thriving vineyard into a veritable wasteland. *Not on my watch, please.*

I stood in the middle of the road and admired the rows of Gewürztraminer. A sharp honk and I jumped. It was a small white Toyota pickup and the guy was in a hurry. I moved to the left and nearly lost my balance on the rutted vineyard pathway.

"You okay?" the driver asked. "I didn't mean to startle you."

In the background, it sounded like one of those "learn a language" tapes. Spanish, maybe? He clicked it off.

"Then you shouldn't've honked."

The guy looked annoyed. "I couldn't very well sit in the driveway and wait while you took a selfie or whatever it was you were doing."

"For your information, I was studying the vineyards."

"Studying?"

"Okay. Looking at them. Never mind. Enjoy your visit." That was the moment I got a really good look at the driver. Cowboy cute was the first thought that came to mind and I made a mental note to remember what he looked like so I could use him in one of my screenplays, even if he was a jerk. Average height, from what I could tell with him behind the wheel, and the biggest brown eyes that matched his wavy dark hair. Great screenplay material. I waved him on and continued down the driveway.

The Grey Egret Winery was off to my right and their parking lot also had about a dozen cars. Probably the ones that left our tasting room earlier or cars that hopefully would continue up the hill. I took out my iPhone and looked at the screen. Plenty of time to pay the Grey Egret a visit.

Their building was similar to ours, with that woodsy lodge thing going for it, but instead of tan and brown wood stain, they'd opted for teal and gray. It worked. The place reminded me of a nature museum, and I pictured all sorts of stuffed water fowl on the walls. I wasn't too far off.

Like our winery, their production area was housed in another building behind the tasting room. Their operation was much smaller than ours, according to Francine, but they were growing. Small pine trees framed the entrance and the subtle scent of pine wafted in the air. I opened the door and stepped inside.

"Hi! Welcome to the Grey Egret Winery!" came a man's voice from behind the counter. "Come join us for a tasting."

The counter spanned the entire length of the building, with twenty or so bistro chairs for customers. In the middle of the floor were bins with wines for purchase and T-shirts. No bistro café but a small vending machine with snacks.

"I'm not really here to taste wines," I said. "I stopped by to say hello. I'm Norrie Ellington, Francine Keane's sister. Or, if you'd prefer, witch number two."

The man excused himself from the customers he was serving and walked around the counter. He extended his hand and gave me a big smile. "Theo Buchman. It's a pleasure to meet you. Don, my partner, just got off the phone with your sister. We invited all of you to have dinner with us tomorrow night. Nothing special. Don will probably whip up a lasagna or some sort of Italian meal I can't pronounce. He's the chef around here. But I have all the carryout places on speed dial."

I could see why Francine liked these guys. Well, at least judging from my first impression of Theo. "That's great. And by the way, I can't cook either. I'll be buying Wegmans's takeout if I plan to survive."

Wegmans was the giant food chain in upstate New York and the one place I really did miss in spite of having lots of culinary choices in the city.

Theo laughed and walked back behind the counter. "Feel free to look around. Sure you don't want to try any of our wines?"

"Oh, I do. I really do, but another day. I spent the morning getting acquainted with our own wines. It's been a while."

Just then, a balding portly guy who appeared to be in his thirties came in from another room.

"Don," Theo said, "meet Norrie, Francine's sister."

Don immediately rushed over to me and Theo returned to his customers.

"I can only stay for a few minutes," I said. "Francine's having me meet with our vineyard manager. This morning it was the tasting room manager and tomorrow the winemaker. Sort of a cross between speed dating and a crash course in Winery One-Oh-One."

"Yeah, we know. Francine and Jason told us. Listen, Theo and I are always here if you need anything. I mean that. We've bailed each other out on numerous occasions. That's what it's all about if we want our wineries to thrive."

"Thanks. To be honest, I really don't know what to expect. I figured the staff was going to coast along on its own, but now I'm not too sure. I met a horrid woman this morning who complained about the vineyard cannons and I found out some mega company wants to buy all of us out." I neglected to mention the bizarre encounter I witnessed in front of our winery door. "I just hope I'll be able to meet my screenwriting deadlines."

"You're a screenwriter? Francine didn't say that. Any movies I might've seen?"

"That depends if you like the Hallmark channel. I write for Canadian companies that produce romances. Maybe you've heard of some of them… *Kisses in the Snow, A Hug from the—*"

"Oh my gosh! You wrote *Kisses in the Snow*? I loved that movie. 'Hold out your hand and let the snowflakes melt into your heart. No summer's heat or winter's wind will ever take that away from us.'"

"You remembered those words? I don't even remember those words and I wrote it."

Don began to blush and he looked at Theo. "The movie was on TV the night we decided to tie the knot."

"Wow. I don't know what to say. I feel honored. Probably the next words you'll hear from me are 'Help! Something awful's happened at the winery.'"

"Eek. Let's hope not."

"Guess I'll be seeing you tomorrow night. That's really nice of you to invite us over for dinner."

"Tell me that after you've tried my cooking."

We both laughed. I said good-bye to Theo, who was still waiting on customers, and headed back up the hill. This time with company. Charlie appeared out of nowhere and followed me. When I got to the house, he bumped me and I immediately petted him. "So you're the smelly hound dog my sister took in." He bumped again. "We used to have a collie when I was a kid, but she was always brushed and seemed to stay clean."

The dog looked at me as if to say, "Good for her," and scratched at the kitchen door. Francine shuffled a pile of papers in the middle of the table and groaned. "Honestly, I'm trying to tie up all these odds and ends and hope I can make it by the end of the week. Did Jason get to talk to you about the banking?"

The banking. Two words that made my stomach twist.

"No. Not yet."

"The good news is, we don't have to go to the bank to add your name to all of the business accounts because it's already there. He'll need to go over everything with you, but don't worry, Lizzie handles the accounting and the billing. All you have to do is pay the monthly house bills for heating, electricity, that sort of stuff. I've got it all arranged. I'll give you my password into the online checking and you'll be all set. I've also pre-signed some checks in case of an emergency. I've got them locked in a file cabinet for you."

The more she talked, the more I saw my writing time fizzle. Then again, how difficult could it be to pay bills? I managed my own stuff. At least I didn't have to tackle the business. Apparently Lizzie did.

"The cash register lady handles the billing?"

"Lizzie is a retired CPA. She's widowed and her only daughter lives in California. Working in the winery gives her something to do. And that includes our taxes. Like I said, you don't have to worry."

I don't have to, but I probably will.

Just then there was a knock on the door and I heard a voice I recognized, even though it had been years.

"Come on in, John," Francine called out. "We're in the kitchen."

Charlie, who had just settled into a dog bed I hadn't noticed before, picked up his head and so did I. John Grishner looked the same as he did ten years ago, only his mustache was now completely gray and his hairline had receded a bit. He was just as sturdy and muscular as I remembered.

"Hey, Norrie, it's been a long time. Great to have you back."

I walked over and gave him a hug. "It's temporary, but yeah, I'm glad to be here."

"Can I fix you anything, John?" Francine asked. "We've got turkey and ham."

"I'm fine. I already had lunch, but thanks anyway. So, tell me," he said looking directly at me, "do you want the grand tour or the abbreviated version?"

"I want the CliffsNotes."

All of a sudden there was another knock on the door and Charlie lifted his head a second time.

"It's me, Peter."

"Come on in," Francine shouted. Then she turned to me. "Peter's the assistant vineyard manager. The one I told you about."

I opened my mouth to say something when the guy stepped into the kitchen. *Oh no. The gorgeous jerk from the truck.* My cheeks began to feel warm and I stood there wordless.

"Peter, meet Norrie, my sister," Francine said.

He held out his hand and gave me a wink. "Nice to see you again."

Chapter 4

"You two know each other?" my sister asked.

I cringed. "Uh, we sort of met earlier today. In the driveway."

"That's great," John added. "Hope you don't mind but I asked Peter to stop by and join us for the grand tour. He'll be taking over as manager once I retire, so it's important you get to know him."

I forced a smile and then bit the inside of my lip. *We'll see how this goes.*

John, Peter and I left the house and walked outside. It was a perfect early summer afternoon with a warm breeze and few clouds in the sky.

"If the rains can hold off," John said, "we may have our best grapes yet."

For the next hour, I followed them around the vineyards for a refresher course on growing grapes. John pointed out the weather-resistant vines, like Chardonnay and Cayuga, at the top of the ridge and the more sensitive ones on the bottom, where it's warmer due to the proximity of the lake.

My mind was on overdrive. Disease-resistant rootstock. Irrigation. Pruning. Fertilizing. Canopy management. Pest control. The process was never-ending. Each season meant work. And then there was the machinery. Machinery I never intended to go near.

John asked if I would mind having Peter continue the tour because there was some paperwork that required John's attention before he called it quits for the day.

"Uh, that's fine with me if Peter doesn't mind."

"Nothing I'd like to do more than explain how we plant and harvest with modern technology."

Bite me, I thought, but I didn't say a word.

"I don't want to bore you to death," he said, "so stop me if you already know this stuff."

He explained how a mechanical vine harvester was used for some of the grapes and why vineyard workers handpicked others. The real joy came when we went into the barn adjacent to the winery so he could point out the harvester.

I looked at the lumbering piece of metal and winced. "That must've cost a fortune."

"Farm equipment does. Most farms and wineries have more equipment loans than mortgages."

For an instant, I began to wonder about Francine and Jason's finances again.

Next, he pointed out machinery that looked as if George Lucas had designed it for the next *Star Wars* movie. Grape hoes. Leaf cutter rotary knives. Plows. Mowers. Sprayers. Mulchers. No wonder the guy had a degree in agriculture. It was the only way to understand this stuff.

"I think I'm good," I said. "The only piece of equipment I'll be using is an automobile."

"It's important to know all the aspects of running an operation like this so if you have any questions, ask."

I swiveled my head around and gave the harvester another look. "What happens if this stuff breaks down?" *Because I doubt Francine's checks will cover it.*

"Most of us know how to make repairs and get parts. In emergencies, other wineries help us out."

"Uh, one more thing." I don't know why it even popped into my head, but it did and I blurted it out. "What about injuries? I mean, how dangerous are these things?"

Peter stepped back and made some sort of *hmm* sound. "All farm equipment can cause injury or death. It's a risk the workers are aware of. We drill safety into all of our workers. And no one operates machinery unless they're trained."

"Okay, fine. I guess that's about it. I should be heading back up the hill. Thanks for the tour."

"I'm sorry if we got off to a bad start in the driveway. We're going to be seeing a lot of each other this year, and I don't want things to be uncomfortable. What do you say? Truce?"

He held out his hand once more and I shook it, but this time he held it longer and I thought I detected a slight squeeze. Then again, I had a tendency to imagine things like that. Especially when it came to reading men. I wasn't really good at it, even if I did write romance.

"We're good." I walked out of the barn and looked at the winery building. *That* nightmarish tour was scheduled for tomorrow. My brain was on overload and I couldn't possibly add one more thing. Then, out of nowhere, one word stuck with me—death. "All farm equipment can cause injury or death." Wonderful. And people say living in big cities can be hazardous.

I ambled up the hill and back to the house. While I was learning about leaf cutters and grape hoes, Francine had whipped up a strawberry and walnut chicken salad for dinner.

"How'd your tour go?" she asked.

"Fine. As long as I don't have to dig anything, plant anything or spray anything. By the way, the assistant manager seems a bit…bookish."

"Oh? Did he go on the tour, too?"

"No, John got me through the vineyards and Peter scared the crap out of me with the farm equipment. Hope you've got a heavy-duty insurance policy."

Francine laughed. "We do. Peter's a nice guy. He probably seemed bookish because he wanted to make sure he explained everything."

"He did. Believe me."

"Don't look so worried. Like I keep telling you, everyone here knows what to do. Hey, you might want to look up some of your old high school friends from Penn Yan."

"My three good high school friends are in Oregon, Colorado and California. They all wished me condolences when I told them I was spending a year back here."

Francine chuckled and brushed the hair off her brow. "I've decided to toss more baby spinach and kale into the salad."

"Need help?"

"No."

"Great because I've got some of my own work to do."

I went upstairs to my room, turned on the laptop and checked my e-mails. God no! There was an urgent message that was sent to me early this morning from the producer of the film company. I opened it immediately and held my breath.

"Norrie," it read, "We've cancelled Conrad Blyth's Amish love story series, which means the timeline's been moved up for *A Swim Under the Waterfall.* See attached deadline list and acknowledge. Call me if you have any problems. Renee."

A lump formed in my throat and I reread the message. *No problems whatsoever. I'll lock myself in this room and come out on the fourth of July.*

Francine and Jason wouldn't stop talking that night at dinner. He kept going on and on about how exciting it was to learn more about some kind of bug whose name I couldn't even pronounce. "You know what the odd thing is," he said, "I've been waiting so long for this opportunity to come through and all of a sudden—boom! If I didn't know any better, I would've thought someone pulled some strings but everything at the Experiment Station goes through a zillion channels. Guess it was just my time."

I chomped on a piece of date nut bread and nodded.

He looked at me and continued. "Yikes. Before I forget, the shotguns are locked in that old armoire in the den. A twenty-two, a thirty-thirty and a twelve gauge. Ammo and the key are in the desk. Francine said you know how to use them."

"Uh, sort of. My dad and I used to shoot soda cans by the woods, but that's the extent of it. And I've only used a single shot twenty-two. Why?"

"I'm sure you'll never have a need for them, but having some protection in the house is pretty standard for vineyard owners and farmers. I'll ask John or Peter to practice shooting with you sometime."

Oh joy.

Later that night I asked Francine again if everything was all right and she said yes. "It's a lot of stuff to absorb all at once so I can understand if you're a bit nervous. You'll be fine. Franz is expecting you at eight tomorrow morning. He'll give you the complete rundown on the winery."

"Aren't you coming?"

"Wish I could, but I need to do more last-minute shopping. Mainly toiletries and over-the-counter medicines we can't buy there. And I'm sneaking some toilet paper, too. Um, there's one more thing."

"What's that?"

"The West Side Women of the Wineries meets the first and third Thursdays at Billsburrow Hill Winery. Ten in the morning. That's right up the road, and the meeting usually lasts an hour. It's more of a social gathering than anything else, but it's a great way to find out what's going on behind the scenes."

"I remember. Mom used to say more mouth flapping went on at those meetings than anyplace else in the Finger Lakes."

"Some of the loudest mouths have retired, so it's not that bad. Only an hour."

I sighed and clasped my hands. "An hour. I've got a strict deadline coming up for one of my screenplays, and I can't miss it."

"I understand."

When I hit the pillow that night, I fell fast asleep. Unfortunately, I bolted awake and looked at the clock radio—three. I tried to close my eyes again, but all I could think about were guns, gruesome deaths caused by farm equipment and some miserable meeting I'd have to sit through. Not to mention my meeting with Franz, the winemaker, in five hours and the new deadline for the screenplay.

Since I couldn't sleep, the least I could do was work. I turned on the laptop and sat down at the sleek modern desk that faced the front window. Outside, nothing but darkness, a few stars and a crescent moon. I went back to where I had left off days ago with some dialogue. I wanted it sharp and snappy, in keeping with my characters' personalities. At one point I looked up and noticed the unmistakable beam from a flashlight coming from the edge of the woods past the vineyard.

Way too late for anyone to be traipsing around. I noted the time—three fifty-two. Whoever flashed that light quit a few minutes later and it was pitch black again. The next morning I mentioned it to Francine while we were at breakfast. Jason had already left for work and Charlie had taken off at the same time.

"Poachers," she said. "Damn it. It was probably poachers. We've had trouble with them before. I'll call the Sandersons, who own the woods behind ours, and let them know. They won't be too thrilled either. Usually it's much worse during deer season in November. Anyway, I'll report it to the sheriff's office, too."

I didn't think much of it since Francine didn't seem to be all that rattled when she left the kitchen, just annoyed. Sipping my coffee, I lingered at the table until it came time for me to go to the winery and meet Franz. I imagined my sister was in her room, presumably packing or maybe looking up antidotes for insect bites. I yelled out to her. "I'm off! See you later!"

"Have fun, Norrie. I may be gone most of the morning. Grab lunch at the bistro if you want. The food's great."

With that, I left the house and walked down the hill. Off to my right, a few vineyard workers were putting in a new drip irrigation system for the newest part of the vineyard. I think I remembered Cammy telling me they had planted more Riesling since it was so popular. I could see the black tubes on top of the burrows and hoped it wouldn't rain any time soon since the area was already muddy.

It was eight on the nose when I knocked on the door to the winery. Expecting to see an older gentleman, I was taken back when a good-looking black man, who appeared to be my age, opened the door.

I held out my hand and acted nonchalant. "Hi! You must be Franz. I've heard a lot about you."

The guy broke out laughing. "Wow. I've been mistaken for lots of people but not a short red-haired winemaker with horned-rimmed glasses. I'm Herbert, the intern from Cornell. I'm finishing my degree in viticulture and enology."

My God! If there isn't a degree for everything.

"I'm Norrie. Liberal arts major extraordinaire. Also screenwriter and Francine's sister. Franz is expecting me."

"A pleasure. Come on in. Franz is running wine samples through the lab and Alan, our technician, is checking analysis reports. Come on, I'll introduce you."

Herbert's description of Franz was right-on and, oddly enough, Alan had the same look and coloring, only he was much taller. Both of the men spoke nonstop about winemaking and their process.

I remembered certain areas in the winery were totally off limits to visitors due to the possibility of contamination, but the work lab wasn't one of them and neither was the steel barrel room. I got the grand tour of each as Franz went on and on about cold soaking and maceration time, hot vs. cool fermentation and something known as pump overs and punchdowns to stir the wine. I began to wish I was back in the barn looking at the vineyard equipment.

Then, out of nowhere, he paused and took a breath. "The risk from low oxygen and high carbon dioxide levels is always a concern. It can lead to death as I'm sure you're well aware."

I am now.

"I can't begin to tell you how many deaths were caused by workers climbing into the tanks and suffocating."

"I, uh, er…"

"We take the utmost precautions here, but please, under no circumstances, enter the winery without one of our technicians or me."

"No problem. None whatsoever."

I couldn't wait to get out of the winery fast enough. I thanked Franz and bolted up the hill to the tasting room. I couldn't believe it. In less than twenty-four hours I'd heard the death word twice and one thing became perfectly clear—I really was insane to agree to oversee Two Witches Winery for an entire year.

Chapter 5

Cammy waved me over as soon as I walked into the tasting room. "How's it going?"

"How's it going? How's it going? You really don't want to know. It's a nightmare."

I looked around and could see an older gentleman serving six women at one of the tasting room tables. It had to be Roger if I'd gotten my schedule right. From there, I glanced across the room to the cash register. An impeccably dressed gray-haired lady with wire-rimmed glasses and a colorful summer scarf scanned a credit card into the machine and handed it back to a middle-aged man along with a bottle of wine.

"Come on," Cammy said. "I'll introduce you to Lizzie and Roger. Then you can tell me what's going on."

"It's really very simple. I may be hanging out here more than I originally thought. This is the only place where the word death wasn't mentioned at least once."

I went on to tell her about my experience yesterday with Peter and my morning encounter with Franz and his crew. "Honestly, I felt as if I was in Dr. Frankenstein's lab. The only thing missing was the monster, but give it time."

"It can't be *that* bad."

"Oh, it was. Believe me, it was. Everyone's so...so...intense." I emphasized the word *intense.*

Cammy rubbed the back of her neck. "That's because what they do has to be precise and demanding. I'm not telling you anything you haven't heard before. Mistakes in the vineyard or the winery can cost this place a fortune. Now, don't get me wrong, we have to know what we're doing in the tasting room but our job is the fun one. We get to laugh and joke with the customers, get them to sample new wines and, most of all, go home with a bottle or if we're lucky, a case. We're entertainers as well as servers. Plus, we provide them with information about the business so we really have to know our stuff."

As if on cue, I overheard Roger telling the women about the fermentation process.

"I see what you mean. But at least no one's going to suffocate in here or get torn apart using a piece of heavy-duty equipment."

"You make a good point."

We walked over to the cash register and she introduced me to Lizzie, who immediately rushed over and gave me a hug. "Welcome. When Francine said her little sister was coming to manage the place this year, I couldn't wait to meet you. I'm at your disposal most anytime. I'll go over the accounts with you weekly and keep you updated on everything."

Lizzie was one of those people whose warmth was literally contagious. I found myself hugging her back. Something totally out of my realm. "You don't know how relieved I am to hear that."

Just then the group of six women approached the cash register, each one holding a bottle or two in their hands.

"I'd better let you get back to work," I said.

"Yep," came a voice from behind me. "I've already done my share."

"Norrie," Cammy said, "meet Roger."

"It's a pleasure to meet you," he said. "Are you going to be working in here, too?"

"Uh, maybe once in a while if I'm needed. I have a full-time job as a screenwriter, so I'll be spending most of my time with my laptop."

"A screenwriter? One of those fancy Hollywood ones?"

"More like up and coming Canadian romance releases." *Unless I get kicked to the curb like Conrad Blyth.*

"Bet my wife's seen some of your movies. I can't wait to tell her."

Suddenly two couples walked into the room, followed by three women. Cammy put her hand on my shoulder and whispered, "We'd better hail them over to taste the wine. Catch you later."

"Sure thing." I moseyed over to the bistro and introduced myself to Fred, who looked as if he was still in the seventh grade. No visible sign of facial hair but longish brown hair that he tucked behind his ears.

"Great to meet you. I got the word from Francine you'd be in. My wife and I run the bistro. We're both here on weekends but switch on and off during the week. Whatever you eat goes on a winery tab, so you don't pay for food. I suppose Francine explained all of that to you."

"Uh, sort of."

I ordered a bacon, tomato and avocado panini and washed it down with a raspberry iced tea.

"I could get used to this. Having someone make my meals. I'm not much of a cook. After I go through all of the casseroles my sister has in the freezer, it'll be One Eight Hundred Carry-Out."

Fred arched his back until his shoulder blades met. "I can always whip up something to go for you. Just give me the word."

When I left the tasting room building, my mood had improved considerably. That was before I ran into Elsbeth Waters again. This time in the parking lot.

"Oh good," she said. "You're right here. Saves me the time of walking into the building."

"Uh, how can I help you, Ms...Miss Waters?"

"It's Ms. and you can help me by keeping that miserable hound of yours on your own property. This morning I found him in front of my B & B shaking himself off and spreading nasty fleas all over the place. I shooed him off, of course, but he'll come back. Hounds do that, you know. They run all over the place. See to it he doesn't."

Before a single syllable could even form in my mouth, she turned away, walked to her car and slammed the door. There was something familiar about that encounter but I couldn't quite place it. Then it hit me—Almira Gulch. Straight out of *The Wizard of Oz.* At least Charlie didn't bite Elsbeth like Toto did Almira. I closed my eyes and tried to picture it. Then I burst out laughing.

A couple walked past me and I heard the guy say, "This must be a fun winery. They're laughing all the way into the parking lot."

I didn't bother to tell Francine or Jason about my latest encounter with their neighbor. I figured they had too much on their minds already. In less than three days they'd be in Costa Rica and Elsbeth Waters would be my problem. I tried not to think about it that night when we had dinner at Theo and Don's.

Theo was right. Don was quite the chef. I'd never had baked zucchini surprise and it was marvelous.

"What's the surprise in the recipe?" I asked. "It's fantastic."

Don and Theo looked at each other and laughed.

"Don't tell her it's cat hair from Isolde or she'll never eat anything here again," Don said. "As much as we shoo that cat out of the kitchen, she scurries back in."

I looked around but didn't see a cat in sight. "Isolde?"

"She's a long-haired Norwegian Forest cat we found last winter. Once we got her inside, she refused to leave. Right now she's sleeping on our bed. Anyway, cat hair is not the surprise in the recipe. I was only kidding. We use whatever we have on hand, but zucchini is always the staple. I soak it in egg and coat it in bread crumbs, along with eggplant or mushrooms. Or both. Then I bake it and toss whatever cheeses we have into the mix, along with my sauce. It's never the same twice. That's the surprise."

"Speaking of surprises," Theo said. "Your favorite persona non grata stopped by while you were cooking."

Don's eyes got wide. "Don't tell me. Not Elsbeth."

"The very harpy herself. This time she complained about our sign out front. Said the nautical look is akin to us offering bait and tackle instead of wine."

"I swear that woman is in everyone's business. One of these days she's going to go too far and I hate to think about what will happen next."

We moved on from discussing the Peaceful Pines's proprietress and talked instead about winery events, Jason's research project and movies we intended to see this summer. All in all, it was a really pleasant evening and when I went to bed, I slept through the night.

* * * *

Francine left a note for me on the kitchen table the next morning. It read:

I had to meet with John and Franz. There's cereal in the pantry and some English muffins in the freezer. Don't forget our meeting this morning. I'll be back in time to drive us over there. Oh, if Charlie begs for food, he's already been fed.
Love, F.

Charlie apparently didn't read the note because he whined and whimpered until I poured out a cup of kibble for him.

"I suppose you think I'm the new sucker around here," I said.

The dog rubbed against my leg and licked my hand before burying his face in the food dish. I spent the morning doing my work and began to feel as if I could settle into some sort of routine around here. Francine was back by nine fifteen and wasted no time getting us to that meeting.

"There are only five of us in the group and that includes me," she said. "You and I went to school with Steven Trobert. He was a year ahead of me. His folks still run Lake View Winery. I'm not sure if you ever met his mother, Catherine Trobert. Anyway, I heard Steven's a lawyer somewhere up in Maine. And Rosalee Marbleton keeps a tight grip on Terrace Wineries. Nothing gets past her. The other lady is new, although she's been in the winery business in Washington. I'll introduce you when we get there."

I remembered Billsburrow Hill Winery as being a small operation and nothing had changed, except for a sprucing up of the colonial building that housed their tasting room. It was under new management and Francine introduced me to its owner, Madeline Martinez, as soon as we arrived. Madeline was a brunette who looked to be in her late forties or maybe early fifties, with a short wedge haircut and slender figure.

"So pleased to meet you," she said. "Come on in and help yourself to scones and coffee. Or, if you'd prefer, we can always open a bottle of wine. It's a little past ten in the morning and perfectly legal to be selling and drinking in the county." As if to prove her point, she turned her head and acknowledged the two ladies who were serving customers in the tasting room. "Rosalee and Catherine are on the enclosed porch and Stephanie Ipswich should be here any second. She runs Gable Hill Winery. Bought it from the Hendersons six or seven years ago."

Madeline introduced me to the ladies just as Stephanie came into the room. Everyone chatted at once and I walked around shaking hands and nodding my head. I took a seat at the long rectangular table that overlooked their vineyard and watched as a steady stream of cars headed up the driveway.

"Well," Madeline said, "we might as well get started and get the Elsbeth matter over with."

I nudged Francine, who was seated next to me, and she whispered, "Elsbeth Waters has been such a pain in the butt for all of us we decided to allot the first five minutes of our meeting to talk about her so we can get it over with and discuss the other, more pressing matters. Otherwise, the conversation seems to revert back to Elsbeth."

"It never ends." Stephanie helped herself to a scone. "Last week she called and complained that our customers were trespassing on her property. We're on the same hill, for crying out loud. I can't help it if visitors who are viewing our vineyards go a few yards farther and wind up on their property. It's not as if they're camping out on the front lawn. All I can say is thank God for L'Oréal or my blond hair would be totally gray by now."

"That's nothing," Catherine said. "Can you believe that woman had the audacity to tell some of her guests, who had stopped by our winery, that they would be better off purchasing wine from California? Can you imagine? It's the wineries on this lake that keep her little B & B in business."

"The one I feel sorry for is that niece of hers. Mousy little thing. You'd never know she spent time in prison," Madeline said. "Of course, it was for insider trading, but still...Elsbeth's probably working that woman to the bone."

My eyes darted from speaker to speaker as everyone registered a complaint about that woman. It was mind-boggling. "Does anyone know anything about her? Like where she came from and all that?"

Stephanie wiped the crumbs from the side of her mouth and looked at me. "What I'm about to say is all secondhand information, mind you. Maybe even third-hand. Elsbeth's never been married. I heard she worked for one of the utility companies before her parents passed away and left everything to her. They owned a stationery and book store in one of those small towns near Syracuse. Sold it in the nick of time before anyone ever heard of e-books and Print-On-Demand."

"Where'd you say you heard this?" Madeline asked.

"The beauty parlor. Where else?"

Everyone gave a sigh of approval, as if the beauty parlor, wherever *that* was, was akin to a trusted government source.

"Uh, Elsbeth isn't dangerous, is she?" I asked. "I know she's miserable but she wouldn't...say...do any physical harm to our property or...us, for that matter, would she?"

They shook their heads in unison.

"Nah," Rosalee said. "Some people are big blowhards and she happens to be one of them. I listen to her complaints and go about doing the same things I've always done. The real worry is Vanna Enterprises. They've been putting the pressure on all of us to sell. Those developers, Lucas Stilton and his partner, have been a real nuisance. Did you know they've already gotten preliminary approval from the county to build a huge winery and hotel on this side of the lake? Not on my watch!"

"What?" Francine shouted. "How could they get approval without having a hearing?"

Rosalee shook her head, "It's a preliminary approval. They still have to go through the regular process, but it'll be easier. Especially since they've already purchased some vineyards."

"This is a nightmare," Madeline said. "We really need to bring it up to the wine trail and let them deal with it. We think Elsbeth is a problem, but she's Mother Teresa compared to them. Those guys play dirty and it's putting all of us on edge."

The next few minutes were spent talking about how worried everyone was about the real possibility of a mega-winery taking over this side of the lake. Then it moved on to a lighter topic—the late summer "Sip and Savor" event. The five wineries, in conjunction with the Grey Egret, whose former owner, Angela Martinelli, started the event, worked together to attract more visitors prior to the fall rush. "Sip and Savor" featured special food and wine pairings, whose recipes were printed out for the attendees. I figured Cammy was well aware of the program, but I'd make sure when I saw her the next time.

The meeting ran fifteen minutes overtime, but that wasn't too bad compared to what I had imagined. Everyone offered to help me out if I needed it and I thanked them. With Francine and Jason leaving for Costa Rica in roughly twenty-four hours, I started to feel nervous.

My hands shook on the way home so I sat on them while we were in the car. Francine didn't seem to notice. "That wasn't too bad, was it?"

"How often did you say they met?"

"Twice a month."

"I suppose I can muster through. The ladies really were nice."

Jason came home by noon and he and my sister spent the rest of the afternoon checking their luggage to make sure they had everything they needed and double checking with all of the winery managers to make sure there were no looming catastrophes in sight. Meanwhile, I buckled down with my laptop so I wouldn't be faced with any nasty surprises either.

We went out for pizza that night and everyone turned in to bed early. Their flight left at nine fifty-three AM from Greater Rochester International Airport to Toronto Pearson International Airport, where they'd have a short layover before making their connection to San José Juan Santamaria Airport in Costa Rica. I imagined it would be eight at night before they were comfortably settled in their hotel.

Jason explained they'd be meeting with other entomologists from the United States as well as Costa Rica before setting out on their research expedition. I asked if he knew the Spanish words for "Kill it! Kill it now!" but he didn't think that was very funny.

I got them to the airport without a hitch and got to acquaint myself with the Subaru. Not a whole lot different from my car, but the four-wheel drive would come in handy in the winter. I was able to walk them as far as the TSA checkpoint and give them each a hug.

Suddenly, out of nowhere, Francine said, "I don't want to scare you, but be sure to close and lock the downstairs windows at night. And the doors."

"You sound like Mom."

"It's inherited. Love you, Norrie. We'll e-mail you from the hotel so you'll know we arrived."

I waved good-bye and watched them as they showed their passports and tickets to security. Then I left the airport, stopping to grab a burger on my way home. It was one o'clock when I breezed into the kitchen and plopped down on the couch. I closed my eyes for a few minutes and when I opened them, it was three.

Charlie, who had let himself in the house via the doggie door, immediately came over and put his paws on my chest.

"Oh my gosh. I don't even remember if we fed you."

I filled another cup of kibble and wondered if I'd need to keep a list or a chart. Francine mentioned something about the vineyard workers feeding the dog as well, so I wasn't too worried.

That afternoon I visited with Cammy and Roger in the tasting room and met Sam, a part-time student at the local community college.

When I got back to the house, the silence was really noticeable. I turned on the radio and made myself a tuna sandwich. By then, the winery had closed for the day and I was on my own. I didn't want to lose the early evening breeze, so I left the windows open but put a yellow Post-it note by the stairs that read Windows so I'd remember to close them before going to bed.

When we were growing up, our windows were open all summer long and our door was never locked. Of course, there were four of us in the house. Now, with just Charlie and me, maybe it wasn't such a bad idea to take precautions after all. Lots of nutcases in upstate New York, as well as the city.

Chapter 6

"Miss Ellington! Miss Ellington! Quick! We have an emergency! Miss Ellington!"

The room was dark and I was sure I must've been dreaming. Then I heard the voices again. This time followed by someone pounding on the door. The clock radio said five thirty-seven and I turned on the lamp next to my bed. Charlie, who had slept in bed with me and on my feet, jumped off and charged down the stairs.

The shouting continued. "Wake up, Miss Ellington. It's an emergency!"

I didn't recognize the voices, but they were male and youngish. Instead of following the dog downstairs, I threw on my bathrobe, pulled the curtains and opened the front window. Outside, it was early dawn with scant light but clear enough for me to see two young guys in jeans and sweatshirts. They both looked muddy. It took me a second but I recognized them. They were our vineyard workers.

"What?" I yelled. "Don't tell me it has anything to do with a sewage backup."

That was the first thing that came to my mind because if it was a real emergency, like a fire, they would've called nine-one-one and the fire trucks would be here by now. Sewage backups weren't at all uncommon and I remembered seeing the Roto-Rooter truck in our driveway more than once when I was growing up.

"No sewage! We found a dead body in the new vineyard we're irrigating. Look, can you come downstairs and open the door?"

"Are you sure it's a dead body?"

"Yeah," came one of the voices. "We're sure."

I threw off my robe and got into jeans and a shirt, slowing down for a split second to tie my sneakers. Then I raced downstairs to let them in.

Charlie had already gone outside through the doggie door but scratched on the front door to be let back inside. He went straight for his food dish the second I opened the door to let the vineyard workers inside.

"Okay," I said. "Did you call nine-one-one?"

The guys shook their heads. Up close I could see they were young, early twenties maybe. Both of them well-built.

The one with the light hair said, "We don't have phones on us. John and Peter should be getting here pretty soon. We start earlier than they do."

I have no idea why, but I asked them again, "Are you absolutely sure it's a dead body? I mean, before I call anyone. Maybe someone's clothing blew off a clothesline and got tangled in the pipes. That could look like a body."

The guy with the darker hair stood absolutely still and took a breath. "It's a dead body all right. I walked over and touched the arm."

"Oh my God! Oh my God! I hope it's not someone we know. Okay, fine. I'm calling nine-one-one. Right now. On the phone. Nine-one-one. Stay calm. Everyone stay calm."

The dark-haired guy held up the palm of his hand and spoke slowly. "Um, we *are* calm. Sure you're all right?"

"I'm fine. I'm fine. Perfectly fine. A dead body in our vineyard not even twenty-four hours after my sister and brother-in-law leave the country. I'm as fine as it gets."

I picked up the phone and placed the call. It was getting lighter outside and I thought I heard a car pulling up the driveway.

"This is Norrie Ellington at Two Witches Winery on Two Witches Hill in Penn Yan. Our vineyard workers found a dead body. Here, let them tell you."

I held out the phone and the light-haired guy gave them more information, including his name, Robbie Jensen, and the other worker's name, Travis O'Neil. Then he hung up and looked at me. "The sheriff's office said they're on their way. Uh, maybe you want to comb your hair or something."

My hair! Terrific. I really was one of the witches.

"Stand here. Sit down. Wait outside. I'll be right back."

I flew upstairs, ran a comb through my hair and brushed my teeth. When I returned to the kitchen, they were gone. Charlie pawed my leg and whined. Dead body or not, I stopped and poured out some kibble for him before going outside. In the distance, I heard a siren.

Sure. Let's wake up the whole county and tell them there's a dead body at Two Witches Winery.

Robbie and Travis were on the porch staring at the vineyard. "Looks like John and Peter just got here," Robbie said. "I can see their trucks at the barn. Maybe we ought to go tell them."

"Yes, yes," I said. "Tell them. Great idea."

The guys took off running and I stood there, absolutely still, except for the fact I couldn't stop rubbing my hands together. Finally, I calmed down long enough to go inside and make another call. This one to Theo and Don at the Grey Egret.

The words spewed out of my mouth. "There's a dead body in our vineyard. I called the sheriff's office. A dead body."

"Pull yourself together, Norrie. We'll be right there." It was Theo's voice and it sounded reassuring.

"I'm on the porch."

"Okay. Stay there."

Next thing I knew, the sirens got louder and two trucks pulled up to the house—John's and Peter's. Robbie and Travis were with them. Red and blue lights flashed from down the hill.

John slammed the truck door and charged up the front steps with Peter at his heels. "Are you doing okay?"

My palms were getting raw from the nonstop rubbing. "Yeah, sure. I'm fine."

"Good. Looks like the sheriff's car is coming up the driveway. I told Robbie and Travis to start walking to the spot where they found the body. I'll get the deputy and meet them. Peter's going to stay here with you."

"Uh, I'll be fine. I called the owners of the Grey Egret and they're coming right over."

"I don't mind staying," Peter said. "I'll wait to see what the deputy wants us to do. Um, you don't happen to know whose body it is, do you?"

"Me? I was hoping it was a pile of clothes wrapped around a pipe. Geez, it better not be anyone we know."

John waved and walked toward the sheriff's car now parked in front of the house.

"Why would you think I'd know whose body it is?" I asked. "I don't even know if it's a man or woman."

Peter sat on one of the porch chairs and motioned for me to do the same. "Robbie and Travis were kind of tightlipped. I think they're both in shock. I thought maybe they might've said something to you."

"Nope. Nothing."

At that moment, I began to wish it had been a sewage emergency. Roto-Rooter would run a snake line through the pipe and it would be over with by noon. But a dead body? I tried to get the image out of my mind.

Theo and Don arrived a few minutes later. They parked their truck off to the side of the house and thundered up the front steps.

"Are you okay?" Don asked. "What happened?"

"The vineyard workers found a dead body in the new section where they're putting in the drip system. As soon as they discovered the person, they ran to the house and woke me up. I called nine-one-one for the sheriff's department and then you."

Peter gave them a nod and told them he didn't know anything either. "John and I arrived after the workers found the corpse. They're over there." He pointed to the new vineyard area on the right side of the house. "Now that you're here with Norrie, I probably should see what's happening." Then he turned to me. "I'll be back as soon as I find out what's going on."

He left the porch and all but ran to the new vineyard where the sheriff's deputy, along with John, Robbie and Travis, was standing. I could see their backs but nothing else.

"Why don't we go inside and brew some coffee?" Don said. It was more of a statement than a question. "You probably haven't had anything in your stomach and that's going to make you really lightheaded. Those guys are probably going to be a while. The deputy will have to call in for the coroner and a forensics team."

"Oh my God. It'll be a circus. They're not going to close us down, are they?"

Theo put his hand on my shoulder and gave it a squeeze. "Very doubtful. They'll cordon off the area and remove the body until their investigation is complete. Hey, for all we know, it might've been natural causes."

I bit down hard and caught a breath. "At the crack of dawn? That's when they found the body. I doubt anyone was walking around here in the middle of night and dropped dead from a heart attack or stroke."

Then I remembered that flashlight in the woods. "Uh, this may sound strange but I saw flashlight beams in the woods behind that vineyard the other night. It was about three in the morning. I told Francine and she thought it might've been poachers. Maybe it's a poacher who got shot or something."

"The sheriff's department will know soon enough," Theo said. "Come on, I'll make the coffee and Don will see what he can pull together for breakfast."

"Thanks. Uh, we've got a Keurig so nothing needs to be brewed. I'm not really hungry, but we have muffins and cereal if you guys want to eat something."

"We already did," Don said. "We're up before the roosters. At least have some coffee."

"Only if you do, too."

I looked out the front window. The men were still in the vineyard with their backs to me. Now, with Peter, there were five of them.

"This is awful," I said. "I don't know what I'm going to do."

Theo had popped in the K-cups and our coffees were ready in minutes. Francine had half and half in the fridge as well as milk. White and raw sugar packets were in a small tray on the kitchen table.

Half a cup later, I finally stopped rubbing my hands together.

Don paced between the kitchen and living room, pausing now and then to look out the window.

"More flashing lights coming up the driveway. Probably the forensics team. I don't think the county coroner's car has lights, but I could be wrong."

I bolted from my chair. "I've never seen a dead body and I don't want to see a dead body, especially one on my property. But I know how things work in this county and this is going to turn into some long-winded investigation. I need to get over there and see for myself so I know what I've witnessed. That way I won't be bamboozled by anyone else's observations."

My God. I've been writing screenplays way too long.

"Don, Theo, thank you so much. I'll call you or come over as soon as I can."

"Sure you'll be okay?" Theo asked.

"Probably not, but it won't really hit me until later. By then, I'll be ready for some wine."

"One more thing, in case you haven't thought about it. You really should call the tasting room manager and the winemaker to let them know. Or we can do it for you."

"My gosh, you're right. I'll do it as soon as I'm done looking at the... the...ugh, I can't even say it."

I gave them each a quick hug and walked directly to the new vineyard. For a second I had the feeling I was being followed and when I turned to look, Charlie was trotting behind me.

"Stay!" I said when I got to the vineyard. "Sit. Stay." I had no idea if the dog understood commands but thank goodness he didn't go charging off into the section where the body was located. At first, it looked like a clump of clothing, but when I got closer I could see it was a body all right. Facedown. The arms were outstretched slightly with palms up and the legs were, well, legs. Straight down. Not spread apart or anything bizarre. The vineyard guys were right. It was impossible to tell if it was a man or a woman.

The hair looked dark and hung down to the neck. Whoever it was, they were wearing tan pants (khakis maybe) and a navy-blue windbreaker. I didn't notice anything else near the body. No cell phone, bag or gun. If it was a poacher, maybe the other poacher took their gun.

"Miss Ellington. Norrie!" John shouted. "You didn't have to walk over here. We were on our way to the house. The coroner's right behind the sheriff's forensic team and they'll be removing the body and looking at evidence."

The deputy, who was frantically taking notes on his tablet, looked up. The deep furrows on his forehead and gray stubble told me he'd been around for a bit. "Is she the owner?"

"Co-owner," I answered. "Along with my sister and brother-in-law who are in Costa Rica."

"Hurumph." He rubbed his chin and groaned before continuing his notes. "They picked a convenient time for a vacation."

"Oh, they're not on vacation. He's an entomologist. They're on a study grant."

Just then, he was approached by another deputy and a middle-aged rotund man wearing a white shirt and black pants. I figured he had to be the coroner. The three of them conversed while John, Peter and the two vineyard workers stood there waiting. Finally the deputy spoke. "The coroner and the forensic team are going to examine the body at the site, then the coroner will take it to the county morgue for further study. The forensics guys need to stick around and get evidence from the scene."

The words popped out of my mouth as if they'd been rehearsed. "Do you know if it's a man or woman?"

The weathered-looking deputy sighed and shook his head. "At this juncture, no. And there's no sense in all of you standing around. This is a possible crime scene now. It'll need to be cordoned off before the body can be removed."

Theo and Don had been right. Cordon off the area. Remove the body. Now what?

The deputy continued as if he read my mind. "Our team will be questioning the employees at this winery as well as the one down the hill." He gave me one of those no-nonsense looks that every TV cop used. "And, of course, I'll need a few words with you, Miss?"

"Ellington. Norrie Ellington."

"Where can I find you?"

"At the house over there or the winery's tasting room."

"Fine. Don't leave the premises today. Understood?"

My God! I've used that phrase, too.

"It's a woman!" the coroner shouted.

I swiveled my head around to where the body was. "Appears to be in her early fifties. I'll know more when we get her on the table. Doesn't appear to have any identification on her."

I wanted to turn away but I couldn't. Like staring at a road accident with all of the twisted cars and broken glass. It must've been an automatic reaction or something. I took a few steps forward and eyeballed the forensic team as they turned the body on its back. Suddenly, I felt as if I was going to retch.

"I know her," I said. "It's Elsbeth Waters."

Chapter 7

The deputy eyeballed Elsbeth's lifeless body and then looked at me. "Might as well have that conversation right now. How do you know the deceased? Was she a relative? A friend?"

"She's the…I mean, *was* the owner of the Peaceful Pines B & B on the next hill. And no, she most certainly was not a friend."

I regretted uttering that last sentence the minute it came out of my mouth. Words like "most certainly was not" didn't sit too well when there was a chance the cause of death wasn't natural or accidental.

"What I'm trying to say is I didn't know her well. I only spoke with her on two occasions."

The deputy tapped the screen of his tablet. "What was the nature of those conversations?"

"Uh, once was when she came into our tasting room three days ago to leave a message for my sister and the other was the day before yesterday when I ran into her in our parking lot. She was concerned about our dog."

"Concerned how?"

I wasn't sure how to phrase it so it wouldn't sound accusatory. Finally I said, "Something about fleas."

"You wouldn't happen to know if she has any relatives in the area, would you?"

At last! A sentence I could answer without incriminating myself. "Yes. She does. A niece. I don't know her name but I believe she works at their bed and breakfast."

The sheriff kept writing. "If I think of anything else, I'll be in touch. Expect a call or visit later today to arrange for those interviews with your employees."

I nodded and watched as Elsbeth's body was placed on a gurney and loaded into the back of the van. There was dried blood on her chin and the shoulder of her jacket.

"I don't suppose you can tell me how she died?" I asked.

"That's why we have a county coroner, but if her clothing is any indication, you can cross off old age from your list. We'll let you know as soon as we hear anything. Got to notify that niece of hers."

The guy turned and walked away from me just as John and Peter approached.

John wiped his brow and shook the moisture from his hand. "Looks like the installation of the irrigation system will be on hold for the day. They can't possibly hold us up much longer gathering evidence. I told Robbie and Travis to get to work on the netting for the other section of Riesling vines. That vineyard is downhill and away from this area. You didn't need to speak to them again, did you?"

I had been so busy talking with the deputy, I hadn't noticed they left. "What? No."

John looked at Peter and let out a groan. "Of all things to happen. We're two months from harvest and we've got a new vineyard going in. How on earth did that woman's body wind up here? And please don't tell me she was taking a stroll."

Peter shrugged. "I'm as clueless as the next guy. Maybe once the coroner examines the body they'll figure it out." Then, to me, he asked, "You sure you're okay?"

"I suppose. At least it happened after Francine and Jason left. It could've prevented them from going and that would've ruined everything for my brother-in-law."

All of a sudden I heard someone shout, "Cordon off the whole damn acre if you have to."

John turned and made a mad dash for the vineyard. He was screaming so loud I thought his lungs would explode. "Not the whole area! Stop!"

Peter grabbed my wrist and gave it a slight squeeze. "I'd better go see what's going on. Last thing we need is to have an entire area roped off. We've got to get that new drip system in."

I watched as he hurried off. *Not only good looks but a decent butt, too. I'll have to remember that next time I develop a new character.* It was odd that neither John nor Peter seemed to show any emotion whatsoever regarding the gruesome discovery in their new vineyard. Then again, Elsbeth wasn't exactly the kind of person anyone would be mourning over. Especially vineyard workers.

Charlie followed me back to the house, drank some water and curled up in his dog bed. The clock on the microwave read 7:23 AM and I rushed for the phone. I had to get in touch with Franz before he arrived. Undoubtedly, he'd look up the hill and see not only the remaining sheriff's car but a slew of yellow tape indicative of a massacre and not a lone body.

He picked up on the second ring and said, "Hello. This is Franz." The same formal intonation as before in the winery.

"Franz, this is Norrie. I'm calling because the vineyard workers found a dead body in the new area where they're running the irrigation."

"Not one of our workers?"

"Oh no. I identified it. I mean, her. It was Elsbeth Waters from the B & B."

"I'm not acquainted with her but how did such a thing happen?"

"Uh, the sheriff's department is investigating. They're going to interview everyone on our staff."

"They can't come waltzing into our production area. It's a sterile lab."

"If they show up without notifying me first, tell them you'll meet with them in the tasting room kitchen. It's not sterile."

There was a short silence at his end.

"It's clean. Meets health department standards. Just not sterile. Will you please let Alan and Herbert know?"

"Of course. Of course. Naturally. I'm on my way in right now."

"Thanks."

I hung up and dialed Cammy next. Unlike Franz, it took five rings but luckily she picked up before voice-mail kicked in.

"Hey, this is Cammy."

"Cammy, hi. It's Norrie."

"Norrie? Is everything all right?"

"No. There's a dead body. A dead Elsbeth. In our vineyard. Well, at the morgue by now I should think. The vineyard guys found her. I wanted to let you know before you got in for work."

The composure I had shown with the deputy and Franz dissolved the second I got Cammy on the line. Maybe it was because I felt so familiar with her.

"Where are you now?" Cammy's voice sounded alarmed.

"At the house. In the kitchen."

"Good. Stay there. I'm on my way over."

"Wait! Not yet. Can you please call Glenda and Lizzie? Oh, and Roger and Fred? They should know even if they're not on the schedule today."

"I'll start with Sam and Roger. They *are* on the schedule."

"Okay. Good. No sense you driving to the house only to turn around to go back to the tasting room. I'll meet you there in an hour. How's that?"

"Good. Try to stay calm."

"I am calm."

"Sure you are."

When I hung up the phone, I looked around the kitchen. Theo and Don had cleaned everything and even wiped the counter with something that made it shine. I figured I'd better let them know what I found out.

I couldn't tell if Theo was alarmed or relieved when he got my call. "Norrie! Are you all right? Don wanted us to drive back up to your place but I told him you were probably besieged with questions from the sheriff. What did you find out? And more importantly, how are you doing?"

"I'm doing okay but it's kind of automatic. I saw the body. It was Elsbeth Waters. She was face down but when they moved her...there was dried blood on her chin and the shoulder of her jacket."

"My God! Hold on a second." There was a short pause and then, "Don! Don! It was Elsbeth. That's who."

Theo was back on the line with me and I could hear Don in the background, but I couldn't make out what he was saying. "That's horrible. Absolutely horrible. True, she was a despicable woman but still...dead in a vineyard. I don't understand. Do the sheriff's deputies think it was foul play?"

"There was only one grizzly deputy and he wouldn't say. They need the coroner's report and all that. Which reminds me, the deputy did say they are going to question the employees at Two Witches as well as the Grey Egret. Thought you should know."

"Sounds like normal procedure to me. Let's hope they'll be discreet. Last thing any of us needs is to frighten away the customers."

"One look up our hill at all that crime tape and they'll think a battle took place over here."

"Did they give you any indication of how long they'll have that area in your vineyard cordoned off?"

"Nope, but John was hoping it was only for today."

"I hate to say this, but those investigations can drag on. What do you say you pop over here after the wineries close? We can rig up something to eat and you won't have to be alone tonight."

"You sure that'll be all right with Don?"

"Are you kidding? It'll be fine. We'll see you later. Hang in there."

I thanked him and looked out the front window. The forensic crew was still in the vineyard, and I began to wonder how long they'd be taking samples of soil or whatever they thought they needed. Downhill, I saw

Alvin at the far end of his pen, facing the investigators. Unless he was in his little hut for the night, he was clearly the only reliable witness we had to whatever happened in the vineyard last night. Too bad he was a goat.

I poured myself a glass of juice and ate a few crackers. I wasn't sure if I could keep anything else down. Elsbeth's was the first dead body I'd ever seen, and hopefully the last. Although I'd been to a few funerals in the past decade, they were closed casket or the body had been cremated. I tried not to think about what I'd seen, but it was impossible.

First, the dried blood. Darkish brown. Then her face. Sallow and puffy. She wasn't wearing her glasses either. Maybe they'd been dropped and the forensic guys had found them. Unless she'd never had them on. I was fairly certain her body had been dumped on our property, but from where? The deputy refrained from using the word "homicide," but what else could it be? Even the most distraught person wasn't going to walk into a vineyard and commit suicide. Then again, I had no idea what had been going on in Elsbeth's mind, other than driving everyone crazy.

I ran my fingers through my hair. It felt heavy and lifeless. Damn. When was the last time I'd taken a shower? I couldn't even remember. Maybe I was in a state of semi-shock. I took the stairs two at a time when I thought about the West Side Women of the Wineries. Drat! I really needed to let them know, but the last thing I wanted to do was get trapped on the phone.

The sheriff didn't say anything but I knew I shouldn't be mentioning the name of the deceased until the next of kin was notified, but what the heck. That niece was right next door, in a manner of speaking, and they were headed over there. How long could it take to tell her that her aunt had met with an unfortunate circumstance? By now that mousy little girl was either bawling her eyes out or looking for the insurance policy.

I decided to call Madeline Martinez, inform her of what had transpired and ask if she would be kind enough to let the other ladies know that they no longer needed the five-minute Elsbeth Waters portion of their meetings. As things turned out, it was a quick call.

"Mrs. Martinez? Madeline? This is Norrie from Two Witches. Uh, I'm sorry to bother you, but I thought you should know Elsbeth Waters's body was found in our vineyard this morning."

I heard a gasp and what sounded like wheezing before she spoke. "Her body? Oh heavens! How on earth… I mean, what could have possibly… Oh never mind. Are you all right?"

"Yes, yes. I'm fine. I notified everyone on our staff as well as Theo and Don from the Grey Egret."

"Is there anything we can do?"

"Can you please call the other ladies from the winery group and let them know? I don't have details other than the fact two of our vineyard workers found her facedown in that new area where we were putting in irrigation drip lines."

"Certainly. Certainly, I'll call. What a shock. What on earth do you suppose happened?"

"I have no idea. The deputy sheriff's coming back to question all of us."

"Elsbeth Waters more than ruffled feathers around here. She made life miserable for all the wineries at this end of the lake. It wouldn't surprise me in the least if she acquired enemies along the way. Please let me know if we can help in any way."

"Thanks. I appreciate it."

I put down the phone, walked to my bedroom and tossed my clothes in a heap before taking a shower. I must've been really flustered because I couldn't remember if I had fed Charlie. I made a mental note to add some more kibble to his bowl.

Once out of the shower and dressed, I left the house and went straightaway to the tasting room. Cammy was already there and the aroma of coffee met me.

"You look awful" were the first words out of her mouth, followed by, "let me get you some coffee and a scone. We've got some leftovers from the bistro."

"Really? I look that bad?"

"Not your hair or clothing. Your coloring. You look drained. Of course, that's probably normal under the circumstances. Come on, eat something."

We sat in the kitchen and she placed a cranberry scone in front of me and a cup of coffee. Cammy didn't say a word until I'd finished half the scone.

"Yeesh. What a way to start your first day here. You're not going to tell your sister and brother-in-law are you?"

"Not right away. I haven't heard from them yet, but I imagine there's an e-mail waiting for me. I haven't checked. Wow. Usually I start my day scrolling e-mail and Facebook, not standing next to a muddy vineyard watching the coroner remove a corpse."

"That must've been horrible."

"Not horrible, as in those gruesome things on *Criminal Minds,* but horrible as in dead. Absolutely lifeless and dead. At least I was prepared for it after Robbie and Travis woke me. Imagine their reaction."

"So, Elsbeth, huh? I don't want to speak ill of the dead, but I doubt she'll be missed much."

"I kind of got that reaction from Madeline Martinez when I called her this morning. And Theo and Don from the Grey Egret, too."

"Did the deputy think it was a homicide?"

"He wouldn't say, but what else could it be? I figure I'll know more later today when he returns. He'll be questioning all of our employees. Did I tell you that before? I can't seem to remember anything."

"Take it easy. It's okay. I figured as much and ran off a timesheet for you with everyone's hours. Of course, that's just the tasting room employees. You'll have to check with John and Franz for their departments. Might as well meet here. The kitchen is separate from the tasting room and bistro. When they come to question employees, we'll usher them in there. If anyone asks me why there's a sheriff's car in our parking lot, I'll tell them it's a routine visit."

"Not very routine if they look up the hill and see the yellow crime tape."

"From here it just looks like tape. Vineyards get taped off all the time for planting. I doubt anyone will even notice."

"I hope you're right."

Just then we heard a voice from the other room. "Hey! Anyone working today? And what's with the crime tape on the top of the hill?"

Chapter 8

"Sam," Cammy said. "Didn't you get my message? I left you a voice mail and I sent you a text."

A young, stocky guy with reddish hair and slight reddish-brown stubble walked into the kitchen. "Sorry. I must've been in the shower and then I raced off to work."

He paused for a second and looked at me. "Sam Kasten. You must be Francine's sister. You look like her."

"Really? Yeah, I'm Norrie. Nice to meet you."

We shook hands and he helped himself to a cup of coffee. "So, what's going on?"

Cammy looked at me and I gave her a slight nod before I spoke. "This morning, the vineyard workers found a dead body in the new area. It was a neighbor. Elsbeth Waters. The sheriff's office is investigating and they'll be questioning all of our employees."

My response was beginning to sound automatic. Rehearsed and detached. Maybe that was a good thing.

"Cripes!" Sam said. "That's pretty insane, huh? Any idea who wanted to do away with the old witch?"

"We don't know if she was killed. It might've been something else."

Sam cocked his head and took a sip of coffee. "Uh-huh. Protocol and all that. The deputy probably told you that they won't know anything until the coroner's through, huh? Was it Gary? Older guy with the personality of a backwoodsman?"

My eyes widened. "Maybe. Do you know him?"

"If it's him, his nickname is Grizzly Gary. He's been around forever."

"Is he a decent investigator? I mean, we can't have this death hanging over our winery all summer. It'll be awful."

Cammy made a slight groan. "This is Yates County. Small towns and wide-open spaces. Not many suspicious deaths here. In fact, I can't think of the last time there was one. Now, Geneva, on the other hand, keeps their police department working all the time. But that's a big city. It's different."

I took my last bite of the scone and washed it down with the coffee. "What you're saying is this investigation could drag on and on. Is that so?"

They both answered. Almost in unison. "Oh yeah."

"Well," Sam said, "I'll get the tasting room all set. Roger should be here any second. I'll fill him in."

Then he turned to me. "Don't worry about it. The investigation, that is. I doubt they'll get in our way. And again, it was nice meeting you."

"Likewise."

The second he left the room, I leaned my elbows across the table to where Cammy was seated and whispered, "This winery can't afford to wait while that sheriff's department diddles around with its investigation."

"What are you saying?"

"I think I'm going to do some sleuthing on my own."

"Seriously?"

"I've written lots of screenplays. Mainly romance but sometimes mystery-romance. I know how investigations work. Lots of questioning. Picking up clues. Checking on people's backgrounds…"

"I hate to break it to you, but isn't that what the sheriff's office is going to do?"

"Oh, sure. But if what Sam says is true, maybe it wouldn't hurt if we got in on the act. After all, it *is* our winery and last thing we need is for some dark cloud to be hanging over it. I can hear it now, 'Were the grapes in this wine near a corpse?'"

"You said *we*. What do you mean by *we*?"

"Uh, yeah. That's the other thing. I've got a really tight deadline for the film company, so I'm going to need some help. I was thinking maybe you, Lizzie and Glenda can sort of pitch in."

"Pitch in how?"

"Relax. Nothing you're not already doing. I need you to listen carefully to the conversations the customers have while they're tasting wine or paying for it. If anything sounds as if it might have to do with the Peaceful Pines or Elsbeth, jot it down. That simple. I don't want it to go all hog-wild so it would only be you, Lizzie and Glenda, okay?"

"All right. I can broach it with them when I see them. Lizzie will be in later and I'll catch Glenda on Tuesday when I'm back in."

"Great. Meanwhile, I'd better get back to the house. If a deputy stops in here, call me."

"Absolutely."

I trudged back up the hill but not before stopping to check on Alvin. Someone had put new hay in his pen and filled a bucket with grain. His water bowls were full and he was busily chomping on some grass when I walked over to him.

"Too bad you can't talk, big guy." I gave him a pat on his head. Then, out of nowhere, he spat on my face. Icky green stuff that I wiped off with my hands.

"Hey! This craps stains," I said. "Not to mention how gross it is."

The goat bent down and resumed chomping. I looked up the hill and sighed. *Yep. The only one with a bird's-eye view to murder spits like a llama.*

The forensic crew was still in the vineyard, but John and Peter had left. I took a deep breath, used a tissue I had in my pocket to wipe the rest of that sticky, yucky goat spit off my face and then walked directly over to them. I was partially out of breath when I got there.

"Excuse me. I'm Norrie Ellington, the owner. Well, one of the owners. I was here earlier this morning when the, uh, discovery was made. I was wondering, do you know how much longer you're going to be? Or how long this area's going to be off-limits?"

I hadn't gotten a good look at the men this morning so I was surprised when they swung their heads around and one of them was a woman. About my age with a ponytail tucked under her collar. I could've kicked myself for thinking in stereotypes.

"Not too much longer with the preliminaries. Mostly taking photos at this point. All of the hard evidence, soil and the like, was removed."

Her partner nodded and continued snapping photos with his phone.

"Do you own those woods?" She pointed past the vineyard.

"Yeah, up to a certain point, then the Sandersons own them. I think we go a mile in. Oh. The Sandersons own the land, but there's no house. They live in town. In Penn Yan. Do you think that's how the victim got here? From the woods?"

"We're really not at liberty to say," the guy answered. "You should direct all of your questions to the deputy in charge of the case."

"The one from this morning?"

"Uh-huh," the woman said. "That's the one. Deputy Hickman."

She turned away and took another look at the woods. I knew the Sandersons relied on those woods for their maple syrup production in early spring. We let them tap our maple trees, too, in exchange for syrup and candies. There were narrow logging roads all over the place. Francine and I used to cross-country ski in those woods and tromp through them when we were kids. I hadn't been back there in over a decade, and I doubted she'd been there either. Our woods were off limits to hunters but, like the poachers, that didn't mean they obeyed the No Trespassing signs.

I took a step back and stretched. "I'm not a detective, but what the heck, I can see rut marks coming out of the vineyard. Like from a wheelbarrow. Real easy to plop a body in a wheelbarrow and dump it facedown."

The woman didn't take the bait. "Like I said. You'd better speak with the lead deputy."

"Okay. Fine. I'll do that."

I meandered back to the house to find Charlie asleep on the front porch. His ears perked up and he raced down the steps as soon as he heard the crunch of loose driveway stone underneath my feet. The road was paved up to the winery, but not the house.

"Looks like it's going to be name, rank and serial number, boy. That's all they're willing to give."

With that, I went inside the house and poured myself a glass of juice before grabbing my laptop. It was barely noon and I figured I might as well get some of my work done before the inevitable interrogation from Grizzly Gary. Oh my gosh. I needed the days and work hours for the winemaker's crew and the vineyard guys.

Scattered. That's what I was. Scattered. Sure, waking up to someone announcing there's a dead body a few yards away would do that to anyone. I could always blame my lack of focus on delayed reaction or something but I didn't feel as if I was in shock. I just felt, well...weird. I grabbed the phone and got hold of Herbert in the winery lab.

He expressed how sorry he was and proceeded to give me everyone's days and hours. Then I called John on the cell number Francine had left. The vineyard workers were rarely in the barn, and the mobile phone was my best bet.

"You wouldn't happen to know if they're still up there?" he asked. "I checked about an hour and a half ago and they hadn't budged."

"Yeah. I just came from there. It won't be too much longer, but I think that tape's going to stay put for a while."

"Crap" was his only response before giving me the hours and days for his workers.

"If the deputy sheriff lets me in on when he's coming back to speak with everyone, I'll give you a heads-up. If not, well, deal with it, I guess."

"It'll be fine. Sorry to be so grouchy. It's just we can't afford a slowdown. Um, any word from your sister or brother-in-law?"

Francine. Jason. I had completely forgotten to check my e-mails.

"Maybe. I'm getting around to opening my e-mails now."

"I wouldn't mention this if I were you. Not that I'm telling you what to do, but—"

"I know. Cammy in the tasting room had the same reaction. No reason to get my sister in a panic over something neither she nor Jason can do anything about. And I'd feel miserable if they had to cancel their bug expedition or whatever the heck you call it."

"Okay, then. Thanks for calling."

So much for my screenplay. I opened my laptop and spent the next hour answering e-mails. Including Francine's. They arrived without a hitch and met up with the field advisor. She said they were inundated with preparations for their trek to Talamanca Mountain Range and Cerro Chirripó, where they'd be tracking down the elusive insect whose name was too difficult to spell in any language. Communications were going to be next to impossible and they'd be e-mailing or calling me whenever and wherever they could. Whew! She wouldn't be watching the local news out of Rochester.

I e-mailed back and told her everything was running smoothly. Technically, I didn't lie. The winemaker was doing his thing and the vineyard manager had lots of vines to keep his crew busy, even if one itty bitty area was roped off. As far as the tasting room went, it was a matter of keeping the customers happy and promoting the wine, not the grisly discovery.

My muscles began to relax and I didn't feel as if I was going to hurl up anything I ate. Then, something dawned on me. My parents were in Myrtle Beach, along with half the retiree population from Geneva and Penn Yan. They'd be bound to hear the news. Only worse. Exaggerated. I couldn't risk it. I took a deep breath and picked up the phone.

Fortunately, it was my dad who answered. My mom would've been hysterical, insisting they book the first flight back. I explained the entire sequence of events, including all of the support I got from the neighbors.

My dad's voice was amazingly calm. "First of all, we don't know if it's a homicide or not, but even if it turns out to be murder, it most likely wasn't random and wasn't committed in the middle of our vineyards. Let the sheriff's department conduct its investigation and cooperate. But listen, Norrie, stay out of their way. You don't need to get yourself embroiled in all of this, understand?"

I said "uh-huh" but I had no intention of sitting back. The call ended with me agreeing to keep them posted and my dad telling me not to be surprised if I get a call later from Mom.

My iPhone read 1:43 and suddenly I was famished. I nuked two eggs with cheese and made myself a piece of toast. Charlie must've been close by because he raced inside from his doggie door and stood directly in front of me.

"I suppose a little egg on top your kibble won't hurt," I muttered.

The dog devoured it and went back outside. Good timing because the phone rang at that precise instant. It was someone from Channel 13 WHAM out of Rochester, asking if they could send a crew to interview the owner and workers who discovered the body. Word traveled fast. The last thing this winery needed was a sensationalized sideshow. I told them we were under a strict directive from the county sheriff's department to not say a word. If they wanted information, they'd have to go through the lead deputy.

"Can we at least send a photographer to snap a picture of the vineyard where the body was found?" the woman at the other end of the phone asked.

"Uh, er, I think you'd better check with the Yates County Sheriff's Department. I wouldn't want us to do anything to jeopardize their investigation."

My hands were sweating by the time the call ended and it wasn't from the humidity. I poured myself another glass of juice and went into the den to tackle my own workload. About an hour later, I got another call. This one from the deputy himself.

"Miss Ellington? Deputy Hickman here. We met earlier today. I'm calling to let you know we'll be sending two deputies out to your winery this afternoon to begin questioning the employees. Should I direct them to your house?"

"No. To the tasting room. It's the large building that looks like a lodge. There's a kitchen in there that's separate from the rest of the area. You can talk to people there."

"I'll need a list of all your employees and anyone else associated with the winery."

"Sure. Fine. What time will they be here?"

"Twenty minutes or so."

That Costa Rican rainforest is beginning to look pretty darn good.

"Deputy Hickman," I said. "Do you know a cause of death yet?" *Because that body's been with the coroner since morning.*

"Blunt force trauma to the back of her head. We notified the niece."

"To the head? Uh, I saw blood on her chin and shoulder."

"Minor lacerations. Could've come from her attacker but not the cause of death. Someone must've hit the victim with a heavy object. We'll know more when the toxicology report comes in. It's fair to say, at this point, it was a suspicious death."

"Suspicious as in murdered?"

"We'll leave it at suspicious."

"Oh, one more thing. One of the Rochester news channels called me for an interview."

"Figured as much. Surprised the other stations haven't called. Don't say anything to any of them. All that lip flapping mucks up an investigation. Direct them to our office."

"I already did."

"Thank you for your time, I—"

"Wait! One more question. How did the niece take the news?"

"I'm not sure I understand what you're getting at."

"When you told her…was she hysterical? Crying? Sobbing? Or was she stoic? Calm and pensive?"

"All of the above," he said, and hung up.

The twenty-minute warning that the deputies were on their way had now dwindled to ten. I placed a quick call to Cammy, followed by one to Franz at the winery, with Alan picking up the line, and one to John's voice mail. So much for my screenplay. I rinsed off the dishes, made sure I looked presentable and walked downhill to the tasting room.

Chapter 9

The questioning went as well as could be expected, according to Cammy, who did her own unofficial debriefings while I kept trying to reach John or Peter. Finally, Peter answered and explained they were outside fixing some equipment and didn't hear their phones.

"I think they'll be interrogating our employees forever," I said. "It's not as if everyone works the same days and hours. We've got part-timers in the tasting room and I'm not sure about all of your workers."

"Don't worry. It'll get taken care of. Hellish day, huh?"

"More like the day that will never end."

But it did end. With the last of the tasting room customers walking to their cars with bottles in their hands. A few of them paused to visit with Alvin and I prayed he didn't spit on them. I hung around the tasting room that afternoon, mainly because I wanted to make sure everything went okay with the questioning but, truthfully, I was too wired and twitchy to write any kind of script.

At least I didn't have to concern myself about dinner. Don made us an incredible mushroom and feta cheese omelet with a side salad of tossed greens, crotons and walnuts. It beat the hell out of peanut butter and jelly.

"I guess your winery will be next." I washed down the last of my omelet. "I'm so sorry. I hope those deputies don't get too long-winded with their questioning."

"Nothing to be sorry about," Theo said. "Elsbeth's body could've been dumped anywhere. Lucky we didn't find her on our front porch." Then he paused. "They do think she was dumped, don't they?"

"The deputy was kind of noncommittal but yeah, that's the impression I got. And the niece. I asked him about the niece. You know, she could be a suspect. Domestic violence and all that."

Theo wiped a few crouton crumbs from his mouth. "What about the niece?"

"That's just it. The deputy seemed perplexed about her. According to him, the woman went through more emotions than a daytime soap opera star. Cried. Stoic. Sobbed. Calm. You name it."

Theo and Don were silent. For a few seconds anyway.

Then Don spoke. "People are known to go through all kinds of emotions when tragedy strikes, but usually not at once. Think she was giving a performance?"

"I'm about to find out."

That's when I shared my little plan with them about the sleuthing I intended to do.

"Be careful, Norrie," Don said. "And don't leave yourself alone with anyone you suspect. Especially the niece. It's no secret she spent time in prison. Maybe she was in cahoots with a violent cellmate."

Theo let out a groan. "For crying out loud, the niece served a short sentence for insider trading, not bludgeoning people to death."

I let out a quick laugh. "Still, it's a good place to start. But I'll wait a day or so. Maybe I'll talk with the women from that winery group of Francine's. See what they know. Oh, before I forget, she and Jason are fine. I got an e-mail. They're on their way to a rainforest in some mountain range."

"That's good news," Don said and Theo nodded. "Jason was ecstatic when that grant came through." Don stood up from the table and looked at the wall clock. "Hey, it's time for the news. Let's see if Elsbeth's untimely demise is on the air. Leave the dishes. We'll get them later."

The three of us plopped down in the living room and Don turned on the TV. A commercial for laxatives seemed to go on forever. Finally, it was back to Channel 13 with the anchor announcing they had a series of breaking news. "A string of burglaries in Brighton, a water main break in Fairport and a grim discovery at one of our local wineries are all on the line-up this evening. We begin with Brighton."

We listened halfheartedly to the first two stories then perked up when Two Witches Winery was mentioned.

"Oh no," I said. "They named the winery. Why did they name the winery? This stinks."

The anchor had the same information we already had, so there really wasn't anything new to glean from the story. Except one little tidbit. They were able to find out the approximate time of death–about seven or eight hours prior to the discovery of her body. That meant the heavy object must have collided with her head between nine and ten the night before. Like hell it happened in our vineyard. It was pitch black out there at that time of night.

It would be darn near impossible to locate a big rock or a heavy chunk of wood in the dark. Sure, the winery buildings all had motion sensor devices for their doors and windows, but not the vineyard, or the house, for that matter. And there was no full moon. Or partial moon. Only a sliver.

"She was dumped," I announced. "Someone had to have been pretty familiar with the logging roads in the woods behind the vineyard. It's the only way they could've gotten the body there. Those dirt roads open up to two adjoining roads—Billsburrow and Rock Stream. Whoever did that wouldn't have been stupid enough to drive straight up our road. They wouldn't risk being seen or heard. But on a backroad…anything's possible."

"That flashlight you thought was a poacher the other night…" Don said. "Maybe it wasn't a poacher and maybe whoever it was, came there more than one night."

"I used to know those woods pretty well," I said. "What I should do is—"

"Call the deputy sheriff and tell him. They'll probably be scoping out the woods anyway," Theo said. "I wouldn't take a chance going in there if I were you."

"I wouldn't go alone. I'd take Charlie with me. He's in and out of those woods all the time, except during hunting season when they keep him in a fenced-in area."

"Charlie's a hound. Not much protection. Look, if you insist on traipsing through the woods, one of us will go with you, won't we, Don?"

"Huh? What?"

"I'm serious, Norrie," Theo said. "For all you know, whoever killed Elsbeth might still be wandering around the woods. You know what they say about criminals going back to the scene of the crime."

"I don't think the woods are the scene. More like the trade route."

This time Don spoke up. "Scene, trade route, whatever. Don't go alone. Promise?"

I let out a long sigh. "You're worse than Francine."

My head was spinning when it hit the pillow that night. I was so tired I barely noticed Charlie's weight as he made himself comfortable on my legs. I was pretty certain Francine didn't allow him in their bed, but Francine wasn't alone in the house with a murderer on the loose.

* * * *

The next morning, I poured a cup of kibble for the dog and forced myself to concentrate on cranking out that screenplay before I ate breakfast. My stomach grumbled for three hours but I ignored it. The only reward I allowed myself was a cup of coffee. At a little past ten, I rinsed off, threw on some clean clothes and walked to the tasting room. My culinary skills were no match for Fred's paninis.

Glenda rushed over to me the second I walked in the door. The red lipstick and hoop earrings were the same, but her hair looked different and I found myself unable to stop staring at her. "Um, new hairdo?"

"Do you like it? I think the mauve and purple highlights add some gaiety to the summer season. Don't you?"

"Well, sure. Very nice. Very summery."

Sam was serving a handful of customers, along with Roger. He waved when he saw Glenda and me talking.

"It's been pretty steady since I got here," Glenda said. "My group left a few minutes ago. Cammy called last night and told me your plan. I'm all in. And I mean, *all* in. I've got a Ouija board at home we can use to conjure up Elsbeth. Of course, that wicked old bat will probably ignore us, even in the other realm."

Is she serious? "That's not exactly what I had in mind. More like listening to the conversations around here from our customers to see if they drop any clues."

"Oh, *that.* Sure, we can do that, but let's not be too hasty in brushing off the idea of a séance. You do realize the dead are more likely to communicate when they first cross over, right?"

I did at least two mental eye rolls. "I'll keep that in mind." *Did we know Glenda was so weird when we hired her?* "Right now, let's concentrate on the living, okay?"

"If that's what you'd like. Cammy said the sheriff's department will be sending deputies to question us." She grabbed my wrist and held it. "Don't worry. I won't let them in on our plan."

"It's not really much of a plan, but good. No need for them to know."

"Have you spoken to Lizzie yet? Because she already has a plan. Oh look! Here she comes now. She went into the kitchen to get something to drink."

Before I could respond, Lizzie put her glass of juice by the cash register and waved me over. At that precise instant, the door opened and two couples walked in.

"That's my cue," Glenda said. "I'll chat with you later. And keep an open mind. Restless spirits tend to be very communicative." She walked to her spot at the tasting room table and I made a beeline for the cash register.

"Good morning," Lizzie said. "I was hoping I'd see you. Got the word from Cammy last night. Not to worry. Do you know I've read all the Nancy Drew books and the official handbook? I can even tap out Morse Code with my heels. That is, if I wear them."

Oh my God! First the séance, now this. Who on earth did we hire? "That's uh, wonderful. It'll be a great help."

"I thought so, too. Tell me, how do you propose to start the sleuthing?"

I told her the same thing as Glenda–simple snooping and listening in the tasting room.

"You'll need a better plan than that. It doesn't take a genius to figure out Elsbeth had enemies. We simply need to know who despised her enough to kill her. Or…who was after something. Her money…her property. Maybe that niece of hers. I'd start there if I were you."

"Actually, I was planning on visiting the niece but I thought I should wait a while to let her get over the initial shock."

"No, no. That's too long. If she's guilty, it'll give her time to come up with an alibi. Go now while the body's still warm. So to speak."

I hated to say it, but Lizzie had a point. If that niece killed her aunt, she might be more likely to let it slip while conversing with a pleasant, nonthreatening neighbor than the grizzly old deputy.

"You may be right. Meantime, keep your ears open."

"Always," Lizzie said.

I left the tasting room area and went straight to the bistro. A few customers were ordering sandwiches but the second Fred saw me, he said, "Same sandwich as before?" and I nodded vigorously. Less than ten minutes later, I was savoring the blend of bacon and avocado and washing it down with iced tea.

Other than the fact Elsbeth's niece served time for insider trading, I knew very little about her. Including her name. I couldn't even do a simple Google search. Instead, I had Fred wrap up two giant cranberry scones and a chocolate croissant. I hesitated about bringing a bottle of wine to the niece for fear she might be a teetotaler or a recent inductee to AA.

Keeping a wide berth from Alvin, I went back to the house, got in my car and drove the short distance to Peaceful Pines Bed and Breakfast. The white and blue cottage reminded me of something out of a fairy tale. There was a white picket fence, lots of annuals and daylilies and, of course, pine trees that framed the recently painted building.

Two cars were parked out in front, both with out-of-state plates. Within seconds, a twenty-something couple emerged from the house and walked to the car with the Pennsylvania plates.

"Hi!" the woman said, brushing the blond bangs from her eyes. "Are you visiting the Finger Lakes, too?"

"No. I'm a neighbor. From Two Witches Winery on the next hill over. If you're doing wine tasting, please stop by. Oh, and don't get too close to the big goat in front. He's friendly but has some bad habits."

"Sounds like fun," she said. "We'll do that. Won't we, Seth?"

The guy grunted and the blonde continued, "My boyfriend and I are here until Tuesday. We got in really late Friday night. We reserved the room online and pre-paid so they held our reservation."

Late Friday night. After dark. And well after the proprietress' body had been removed from our vineyard. I caught a quick breath and smiled. "Who was working here that night?"

"Just the couple who own the place. Or manage it. We're not sure. Like I said, we did everything online. They were nice enough to leave apples, cheese and breads for us in our room, and breakfast the following morning was wonderful—lemon-filled French toast with blueberry sauce. Today was amazing, too. Maple-flavored bacon and eggs. Those two really have their act together."

Those two? What two? And she said couple. What couple? I thought it was Elsbeth and that niece of hers.

"Are they both inside now?"

The blonde shook her head. "Only the young woman. Yvonne. She's a terrific cook."

"Yes, I've heard that. I really don't know her. In fact, I came by to say hello. I grew up here but I've been away for a few years."

"Come on, Cheyanne," the guy said. "The wineries will close by the time you get a move on."

"I'm sorry if I've kept you. Enjoy the wineries. It's a great day to be out and about."

I felt as if I was blubbering and, truth be known, I was. I desperately wanted to get a description of "the other half of the couple," but it was too late. Cheyanne and her grumpy other half got in their car and sped off. I stood in front of the house for a few minutes trying to decide on my approach. Finally, I gave up and walked in, fresh pastries in my hand.

"Hello!" I shouted. "Good morning!" I stepped inside a cozy living room, complete with a stone hearth, floral couches and lots of tourist guides on the coffee table. A small bouquet of white mini-carnations and purple asters was the centerpiece. The vase, wrapped in raffia, gave me the impression it was a gift, and not something the B & B had purchased. And, given the timing, not a sympathy arrangement.

I detected the faint aroma from the morning breakfast. A slender, petite woman walked into the room and paused for a moment to adjust her glasses. Dark rectangle frames. Her wavy chestnut hair was pulled back in a loose ponytail, giving her the appearance of the stereotypical spinster. Hanging from her neck was a small heart-shaped pendant with the letters PY in the center. *I love Penn Yan.* Every wine trail gift shop sold them. Only the insert in her design allowed the letters to move. Any gimmick to sell stuff to tourists.

"Hi! We're filled up until Tuesday," she said. "But you might check some of the hotels in Geneva. It's only ten or eleven miles up the road."

"I'm not looking for lodging. I'm Norrie Ellington, your neighbor from Two Witches Winery. You must be Elsbeth's niece. I came by to tell you how sorry I am about your loss."

I handed her the scones and croissant.

"Thank you. I'm Yvonne. Yvonne Waters Finlay. It was a shock. An awful shock. All I'm doing is going through the motions because we have guest reservations lined up all through the fall. I can't up and leave. Not that I have any other place to go. I've been living with my aunt for over a year now."

"I see."

Yvonne put the pastries on the coffee table. "Oh, this is so rude of me. I'm not thinking straight. Have a seat, won't you? Can I get you anything? Coffee? Tea?"

"No thanks. I ate a little while ago. I'm fine. So, it's only you here?"

"That's right. Even though I've been here a year, I haven't had time to make many acquaintances. With the shopping, cooking and cleaning, I don't have much spare time. People don't realize how much work it is to run a B & B."

"I imagine your aunt did quite a bit, too."

"Mainly the finances and arranging the routine maintenance and yard work. We've got—I mean, *I've got,* a guy from Armstrong Road who does the mowing and winter plowing."

Damn! How am I ever going to find out who the other person is? I can't blurt it out like a belch.

"Hmm, I understand. It must've been terribly difficult for you last night. Getting the news and all from the sheriff's deputy and then having to be here all alone."

"Oh, I wasn't alone."

Finally.

"I had guests staying in all three of our rooms. Two were here and another couple arrived yesterday."

"So, uh, you and guests…"

"Uh-huh. At least I wasn't alone in an empty house. I knew there were other people in their rooms."

Just then the phone rang and she excused herself to walk into the kitchen. I moseyed about the living room, looking for anything that could be used as the murder weapon, but all I noticed were small knickknacks and brochures. Not very likely someone was going to clock Elsbeth in the head with a Hummel figure. A black baseball cap with a red helmet logo hung on a hat rack near the door, along with a floral sun visor. They probably belonged to one of her guests.

In the hallway past the living room, I spied a large laundry basket filled to the top. Ugh. I hated doing my own linens, let alone someone else's. I turned away when something nagged at me. I looked at the basket again. On top of the sheets was a rumpled red bandana. Just like the ones John, Peter and the vineyard workers had in their pockets when I first saw them. With the sweat and dirt, carrying a bandana was commonplace for winery workers. I sank down on the couch and waited for Yvonne to return.

In the background, I heard her say, "Two o'clock would be fine," and then the thud of the receiver being returned to its cradle.

Yvonne came back to the living room and I stood. "Well, I really should be going. I wanted to give you my condolences. Please feel free to visit us anytime or call me if you need anything." *Like a good lawyer.*

"Thanks, that's very nice of you. It was the sheriff's department on the line. They're sending over another deputy for a few more questions. This is never going to end. I've got to make burial arrangements, meet with her attorney and get death certificates for the banks and social security. I swear, dying is a royal pain."

And so is murder.

Chapter 10

I took a few steps toward her and reached out to shake her hand. "Again, it was nice meeting you. I hope the sheriff's department can offer you some closure on your aunt's death."

"You can say it. She was murdered. I know about the blunt force trauma to the head. What I don't understand is how her body got into your vineyard. It *was* your vineyard, wasn't it? Two Witches? Honestly, my mind isn't absorbing much of anything."

"Yes. Our vineyard workers discovered your aunt around sunrise when they came to work yesterday. Do you have any idea what could've happened?"

"Certainly nothing here. Last I saw of my aunt was at dinner around six. After I washed and put away the dishes, I went back to my room to watch TV. Around nine, I took a shower and went to bed. I also took an Imitrex because I had a horrible migraine. The medicine knocked me right out. I didn't hear any noises from our guests and I assumed my aunt was fast asleep when I got up the next day to make breakfast. I thought it was odd she wasn't there for her usual tea and bran muffin, but sometimes she slept late and I wasn't about to disturb her."

Yvonne sounded almost too docile and accommodating. A regular Cinderella without the fairy godmother.

"When did you notice she was gone?" I asked.

"Around ten. After our guests had eaten. I called out to her and when she didn't answer, I knocked on her door. Then I opened it. The bed was made up and she was nowhere in sight. That's when I went into the garage to see if her car was there and it wasn't. I figured maybe she had gone out on a very early errand or had some sort of appointment she didn't tell me about."

"Does the sheriff's department know about her car?"

"Yes. I gave them the make, model and license number. They're on the lookout. It's the only transportation I have. I thought it funny I never heard the car backing out of the garage in the morning. I guess that's because everything happened while I was sleeping. Tomorrow, I plan to call Enterprise and rent a vehicle. I don't have a choice. Like I said, I've got lots of legal matters to deal with."

She brushed some wisps of hair from the side of her face and I noticed something interesting—small pierced holes for earrings. At least three. Why was she trying to look like Little Miss Sunshine when her real persona was more Madonna? *Maybe our mousey little girl is a rat in disguise.*

"Um, you mentioned blunt force trauma. Do you have any idea who could've done such a thing?"

"Not a clue. My aunt didn't endear herself to many people around here. Or her own relatives, for that matter. Of course they've all passed away, including my mother, her younger sister. When Aunt Elsbeth offered me the invitation to come live with her and work at the B & B, it came at a time when I needed a new start. She considered it an obligation, but it was forced labor if you ask me."

Hmm, Cinderella with a real grudge. "Will you continue to run Peaceful Pines?"

"That's a good question. My aunt had an offer from a major wine company looking to buy property on this side of the lake, but she declined. Our property runs to the middle of the hill where that other winery is, Gable Hill. We've got good drainage and slopes for vineyards. And our soil is topnotch. The well's decent, too. I might take them up on it."

I cringed and bit my lip. "Don't do anything hasty. Please. I know the loss of your aunt is a sudden shock, but give yourself some time." *And me, too.* "You can always hire help to run your business and the tourist industry is strong year-round."

Yvonne didn't say anything and I knew it was time for me to make my exit. "Well, I hope things work out. Have a good day."

"You as well."

As I started down the hill, I thought about Elsbeth's car. Drat! I should've taken a better look when I ran into her in the parking lot. I remembered her slamming the door but not much else. It was too late to ask Yvonne what kind it was. Maybe Cammy would know. If the car was in the garage, the sheriff's department would have a good reason to point a finger at Yvonne for her aunt's murder. Of course, that still didn't leave the niece off the hook as far as I was concerned.

It was quite feasible Yvonne, with or without an accomplice, could've murdered her aunt, carried the body to the car, dumped it in our vineyard via the logging road in the woods and returned to the B & B. Then again, there were guests at the Peaceful Pines. Wouldn't they have noticed? I was beginning to think maybe Glenda had the right idea all along. Conjure up the old witch and ask her.

At least I left the place with a key piece of information—Yvonne's last name—Finlay. It must be the mother's married name and when Yvonne was born, she acquired the mother's maiden name as well. A trend that was becoming more and more common. *Yeesh. I'd be Norrie Wellington Ellington!*

I drove straight back to the house and immediately plunked the name into a Google search. Lots of profiles, image results and LinkedIn information appeared on the screen. I kept scrolling until an article caught my eye. It was from a Syracuse newspaper and it read: *Local College Grad, Yvonne Finlay, Sentenced for Embezzlement.*

Insider trading, my foot. I went on to read that Yvonne Finlay was sentenced for six months in county jail and two years' probation for something called "siphoning." While working for a department store, Yvonne pocketed money from cash sales at the register. She didn't enter the transactions on the computer and instead kept the moolah for herself. Until she got caught. They always did. No wonder a clean start with her aunt sounded good. Even if it meant child labor.

There was really nothing to link Yvonne to her aunt's death, except my imagination, but I'd only begun my sleuthing. Unfortunately, Grizzly Gary wanted to put a stop to it before it even got underway. He called me late that afternoon as I was reviewing my screenplay notes on the kitchen table.

"Am I speaking with Miss Norrie Ellington? This is Deputy Hickman."

"Yes. Hello."

"Miss Ellington, it is my understanding, after a visit I paid today with the niece of the deceased, that you've been pestering her for information regarding her aunt's death."

"I…I what? No I didn't." *Okay, maybe a little and it wasn't pestering. She offered up that information like a car salesman with a business card.*

"Regardless of your recollection, I am directing you to steer clear of this investigation. Do you understand? You are *not* a detective. Our department is highly qualified to handle this matter."

"I was only paying a condolence visit. Besides, how am I supposed to know with whom I may or may not speak?"

"Speak all you like but do not discuss Elsbeth Waters's suspicious death with anyone."

Yeah. Like that's going to happen.

"Miss Ellington, am I making myself clear?"

"Yes. No talk about death. I mean, suspicious death. Elsbeth's suspicious death."

"Fine. Now that we have an understanding, I'll let you get on with your evening."

When I hung up the phone, I was more adamant than ever to find out who killed that woman. I opened a new file on my laptop and listed the names of those people I knew who had a possible motive.

Francine would've gone ballistic. All but one of the names on that list were the ladies from the West Side Women of the Wineries. And while I seriously doubted any one of them could be the culprit, it was a good starting point for my sleuthing. I had to find out if Elsbeth had done anything, other than flap her mouth, to threaten them in any way.

I had scratched Theo and Don off my list simply because…well, they were Theo and Don. Friends of ours. Other than a general annoyance they faced from Elsbeth, there really was no strong motive for murder. The last name was Lucas Stilton, the developer from Vanna Enterprises. Yvonne told me her aunt refused an offer and I assumed it came from him. Maybe he needed to get her out of the way.

Francine had placed Lucas's business card in a kitchen drawer somewhere. She mentioned it when the subject of that mega-winery was first broached. I got up and started rummaging through the drawers. Good to know my sister and brother-in-law had more kitchen gadgetry than IKEA. Drawer after drawer I found dishcloths, trivets, all sorts of jar and can openers, misplaced silverware and small piles of mailing address stickers.

Finally, after what seemed like an inordinate amount of time, I located the card. It was rubber-banded with a few other cards–Pampered Chef, Walden's Garage, The China Garden and Bristol's Nail Salon. As I ran my fingers over the edge of the card, I wondered how I was going to approach this. As Deputy Hickman pointed out, "you are *not* a detective."

It was Sunday and it was doubtful anyone would be answering the phones at Vanna Enterprises. I decided to call them first thing in the morning and set up an appointment with Lucas Stilton. After all, I wouldn't be discussing death, only winery business.

I was about to get back to my screenplay when a nagging thought came out of nowhere. What did I really know about any of our employees? Francine and Jason hired them. They were the ones who did the background checks and all that. Maybe there was something they missed. Maybe the real killer was on our payroll.

At that moment, I felt a nudge on my leg and looked down to see Charlie. Yikes! When was the last time that dog ate? I jumped up, poured out some kibble, changed his water and sat back down.

Unless things had changed since our folks ran the winery, the employee records were kept in a locked file in the tasting room office and Francine made certain I had all the keys. I waited until seven, when I was positive everyone had gone home for the day, and then I coaxed Charlie into following me to the tasting room building. He could just as easily curl up on the floor of the office as our kitchen.

Sunset was at least an hour and a half away when I turned off the alarm system, unlocked the front tasting room doors and locked them behind me. I reset the system to "Stay" mode, which meant I could move around the place without fear of walking into one of the motion-sensor lasers. Next, I walked into the office. Other than a few framed photos of the wine trail that hung on the walls and two ridiculously silly paperweight birds Francine bought when we were in high school, the room looked rather nondescript. I picked up one of the birds and laughed. It was a long-billed Dowitcher. Long-billed being an understatement. That bill could impale someone. The only reason she bought them was because of the word "witch."

The silence in the building was creepy and I was glad Charlie ambled along. I threw a small rug on the floor for the dog and told him he was a good boy.

If I was certain of one thing, it was the fact Francine would have hard files of employee records even if Two Witches maintained computerized documents. Yep, the minute I slid the small key into the file cabinet, I patted myself on the back for knowing she would never deviate from the way our dad conducted the business.

Alphabetized file folders in assorted colors were arranged in two sections—current and past employees. I decided to use my own system and start with function instead of alphabet. I pulled up the winemaker first. Franz Johannas had been employed for over four years. I read his references and looked over his education and work experience before declaring there was nothing that could remotely link him to Elsbeth Waters.

I did the same for the other two members of his crew, Alan and Herbert. Alan was a graduate of Washington State University with an undergrad degree in horticulture and agronomy and a graduate degree in viticulture and enology. (What else?) Herbert had already told me he was an intern at Cornell and had gotten his Masters of Science degree there as well. Unless there was something about Elsbeth I didn't know, I couldn't possibly fathom a relationship, not even a passing one.

It was on to the tasting room employees and not a single red flag waved. All clear in Cammy's department. I tackled the vineyard workers last. Most of the crew were high school grads whose families owned farms at one time or another. And almost all of them were part-time workers attending community college. I imagined their files would be relegated to "past employees" by next summer.

That brought me to the remaining two files—John's and Peter's. I already knew about Peter's college education because Francine had made a point of drumming it into my head. And not because she wanted me to think they'd made a good hire by offering him the position of assistant vineyard manager. Oh no. It was never that easy with my sister. I truly believed, in the back of her mind, she was hoping he and I would hit it off. Sorry, the guy wasn't my type.

I perused the rest of his file and, other than noting he was a past president of the Tully Junior-Senior High School chapter of FFA, Future Farmers of America, nothing stood out. Same deal for John Grishner, who had been with our family for as long as I could remember.

"Guess that's it, Charlie boy," I said. "Time to head home."

The dog arched his back then stretched for what seemed like forever until he got up from the rug. I made sure to put all the files in order, lock the cabinet and turn off the lights in the office. It had already gotten dark outside, but the small safety light above the front entrance to the building gave off enough illumination for me to lock the place and turn the alarm system on again.

It was almost nine and I realized I hadn't eaten anything since that bacon and avocado panini.

"Come on, boy. What do you say I cook us up some eggs?"

The dog's ears perked up as if the word "egg" was part of his vocabulary. The glow from the tasting room porch lights made it easier for me to find my way up the driveway. In the distance, I saw the faint light coming from our kitchen. I had made it a point to leave the lights on when I left and it was a good thing. There was practically no moonlight and the few specks of illumination in the distance, although lovely for a postcard of the lake, offered no help whatsoever in terms of visibility.

Charlie and I were only a few yards from the house when all of a sudden he bolted for the woods. Now what? A raccoon? Deer? *Damn it. It better not be a deer. There are fines in this county for dogs that chase deer.*

"Charlie!" I yelled. "Charlie! Get back here! Come!" Other than a soft rustling sound in the distance, I didn't hear a thing. I yelled again, but the words caught in my mouth the second I saw the beam of a flashlight in the woods. I knew Francine and Jason kept the dog inside at night and now I understood why. If there were poachers in there, they might mistake that Plott Hound for game and shoot him. I took a deep breath and screamed at the top of my lungs. "Charlie! Get back here now! We mean it."

I put extra emphasis on the word "we." I knew I could call on Theo and Don to help me out, but honestly, what could they do that I couldn't? Moreover, I didn't want to take advantage of their friendship. Instead, I ran to my car, started it up, turned on my high beams and drove it to the edge of the woods. My heart was beating a mile a minute and I held my breath. No sign of a flashlight beam, but no sign of Charlie, either.

If anything happened to that dog, I'd never forgive myself. I rolled down the window and shouted for him again. Then I waited. The good news was I didn't hear any guns go off so that meant no one shot him. *Not yet.* I tried not to think about it, but that only made things worse. I called again and listened for any possible sounds. This time I got lucky. At first I thought it was my imagination, but I swore I heard a soft crunching sound. Charlie?

My hands were shaking and I was too scared to get out of the car. I made sure the doors were locked and I kept the engine running. The clock on the dashboard read 9:44, but I had no idea what time it was when the dog first ran into the woods. The crunching sound got louder and I held my breath, telling myself over and over again that a car could outrun a human any day of the week.

My eyes were fixed on the high beams and I held still. Two glowing orbs stared back at me and I froze. Whatever it was, it was approaching quickly. I revved the engine and started to make a three–point turn when I took another look. It was Charlie. At that moment, my senses returned and I remembered that dog and cat eyes reacted differently to light than humans.

I leaned over and opened the passenger door. "Come on! Get in. You scared the crap out of me."

Charlie jumped up on the seat and I immediately detected a rancid smell of something that had quite possibly been dead for a while. I reached over to pet the dog and felt sticky moisture on his fur. Then the odor blasted at me with a vengeance. Skunk! The dog had an encounter with a skunk. We were only yards from the house so I drove back as quickly as I could, got him out of there and dragged him to the garden hose.

"Stay!" I commanded as I raced into the house. I knew tomato juice removed skunk odor from dogs, but I didn't remember seeing any in the house. Then I remembered reading somewhere that Scope mouthwash did the same thing. I charged upstairs to the bathroom, snatched my only bottle from the medicine cabinet, grabbed a few towels and raced outside.

Charlie hadn't budged. In fact, he was grooming himself without a care in the world. I immediately turned on the hose, splashed the mouthwash and got to work. By the time he was clean enough to be let in the house, it was almost eleven.

"So much for eggs, buddy." I poured some kibble for him and filled a bowl of cereal for myself. Then it dawned on me. My car must stink to high heaven. I left the dog inside, took the remainder of the mouthwash and proceeded to wipe down the passenger seat and anything remotely near it. At that rate, I wasn't sure I'd have any clean towels left for my own shower.

Finally, when the car stopped smelling like a city dump, I gathered all the towels in my hand, including the ones that had dropped on the floor of the car and went back inside the house.

Charlie was sleeping soundly in the kitchen as I loaded the pile of noxious laundry into the washer. Two light blue towels, one pink, one off-white, two beige and—the other towel wasn't a towel at all. It was a scarf. One of those fringed summery scarves I wouldn't be caught dead in. But someone else was. Well, not with the scarf on her, but it was hers all right. She was wearing it the first day I met her.

The dog had found Elsbeth Waters's plum-colored scarf in our woods.

Chapter 11

Wonderful. The only piece of tangible evidence proving Elsbeth's body had been in our woods now had my fingerprints on it. I felt the shimmery material and wondered if those forensic guys in the sheriff's department could really pull prints off silk or polyester or whatever this was. It didn't matter. I wasn't going to conceal what the dog had found. And what did that deputy expect me to do anyway? I had no idea it was even in the car until I found it with the towels.

I called Deputy Hickman the next morning and told him what the dog had literally dragged in. He jumped all over me before I had a chance to explain, making me wonder if I had made the right decision by calling him in the first place.

"It wasn't as if I went traipsing all over the woods looking for evidence," I said. "The dog discovered it. I thought you'd be pleased."

"The dog might've destroyed a crime scene, for all we know. You, your employees and your four-legged entourage need to remain clear of the woods and that patch of vineyard until we complete our investigation."

Four-legged entourage? What does he think? Alvin's going to march through there? And another thing, if he thinks I'm keeping Charlie tied up, he's bonkers.

"Okay. Fine. Did you want to send someone over here to pick up the scarf?"

"I'll be there in about an hour. Will you be at the house?"

It was almost lunchtime and I needed something more substantial than cereal.

"I'll be in the tasting room building."

"Very well. Thank you."

Next, I called Vanna Enterprises, hoping to make an appointment with Lucas Stilton. All I got was their answering service and I decided not to leave a message. I'd try back later.

Glenda was serving customers and Lizzie was ringing up a sale when I walked into the tasting room. I waved at both of them and headed straight for the bistro.

"Good morning," Fred said. "What would you like?"

I ordered a tuna and dill wrap with black olives, onion, lettuce and tomato.

"What? No bacon? That's almost sacrilegious."

I laughed. "I draw the line when it comes to mixing fish and meat. Unless they're separated by a costly price tag, as in Surf and Turf."

"I'll remember that. Say, Peter was looking for you earlier this morning. Thought you might be in here."

I shrugged. "He could've called me at the house. Did it sound important?"

"If you mean was he pacing or tapping like he usually does when something's going wrong, then no."

"Good. I'll catch him later. "

I figured John wanted to know if I had heard anything from the sheriff's department about the release date for our vineyard and decided to send Peter on that quest. Knowing my sister's penchant for matchmaking, it wouldn't surprise me in the least if she'd told John about her thoughts regarding a possible fix-up. I would've thought she'd have given that up after a series of near disasters when we were in high school.

I was halfway through my tuna wrap when Grizzly Gary took a seat next to me in the bistro. I heard his boots on the tile floor and knew, without looking up, it was him.

"I've got the, uh, evidence with me. Hold on."

The deputy didn't say a word as I fumbled through one of Francine's canvas totes to find the small plastic bag where I had put the scarf.

"Here you go. I'm positive it's Elsbeth's. I saw her wearing it, or one that looked identical to it, when I met her last week. Before she—"

"You said your dog found this in the woods?"

"That's right. Last night. He ran in there after something. A skunk, actually, and came out with the scarf."

The deputy caught a slight whiff from the bag and recoiled. "I'll see if the niece can identify it further before I turn it over to our lab. And please keep this information to yourself."

"I guess that means your team hasn't searched the woods yet," I said.

"Our investigators follow a strict procedure for conducting outdoor searches. They don't go sniffing about like hound dogs in any willy-nilly direction."

"But wouldn't a hound dog make sense? I mean, they're always following a scent to locate lost hikers or contraband, that sort of thing. Not that I'm offering up my dog, mind you. I'm just saying…"

"This isn't a search and rescue, nor is it a drug bust. It's a homicide and we know what we're doing."

"Good. Always good to hear."

I gave him one of my cutesy fake smiles and he nodded in return. I knew that was the best I was going to get. I moseyed back to the tasting room, only this time three men were at Glenda's table tasting wine and Lizzie's counter was free and clear.

I was certain the men would be purchasing wine, so I hurried over to Lizzie before she got busy. "Hi! I wanted you to know I met the niece."

She motioned me closer and whispered, "How'd it go? I felt horrible about what I said yesterday. About you questioning her. I must've gotten carried away and didn't think it through. You didn't approach her alone, did you? That woman's got a record, you know."

"It was fine. I went into the B & B. In broad daylight. She didn't strike me as a killer, but I found out what she was really arrested for—siphoning money. Not that she told me. I got her last name and then looked it up."

"Siphoning money? That's despicable. She must've worked for a large company or agency. By the time they go over the accounting and the records, it's too late. I heard of a case once where some doctor's bookkeeper opened a bank account under the name of Nancy J. Bell. She wrote out checks for herself under N.J. Bell and the doctor assumed it was for the telephone company—New Jersey Bell. Of course that was years ago before they all merged and started to do Internet transactions."

"That's very interesting, but—"

"Tell me. What was the niece like? What did you notice? What clues can we write down in our notebook?"

"Our notebook?"

Lizzie turned her head in both directions before bending down to pull out a small notebook from under the counter. "I always have lots of notebooks on hand. Whenever I hear something questionable regarding Elsbeth's demise, I plan to write it down. I'll be happy to add your findings as well."

She really does take this Nancy Drew stuff seriously.

"Nothing definitive, but I have a hunch the niece is hiding something. When I did that Google search to find out about her, none of the images matched up. Not that it matters, because she is who she is, and we know she committed a white-collar crime. Still, I get the feeling the way she looks now is a cover-up."

"Do you think she's a murderess as well?"

"I didn't get that impression, but it's not like someone is walking around with a giant scarlet A plastered across their chest."

"Who do you plan to interview next?"

"I was hoping to get an audience with Lucas Stilton from Vanna Enterprises, that mega-winery company. They're trying to buy all of us out. And not too politely either, from what my sister told me."

"See whose arms they've already twisted. That's what Nancy would do."

"I was planning on meeting with the ladies from the Women of the Wineries group. You know, pay each of them a visit on the pretense of getting better acquainted."

"Excellent idea. Take copious notes. You don't happen to have good shorthand skills, do you?"

Shorthand? I thought that went out with World War II.

"Sorry, no. But I have an iPad."

"I suppose that will have to do."

The three men who were at Glenda's table walked over to the cash register and I stepped aside to let them through.

"Catch you later, Lizzie." I tromped over to Glenda. "Hi there! I know you'll be getting busy so Lizzie can fill you in. I met the niece."

"That's it?"

"She didn't confess, if that's what you mean."

"Did she act all spooked, as if her aunt's tortured soul was haunting her?"

"Not in the least."

Glenda looked genuinely disappointed. "The aunt's soul must still be on our property. We really owe it to ourselves to summon her up before she moves on."

Let her move on. What am I saying? The moving truck's been packed and she bolted out of town when that blunt object knocked her in the head. "I'm still in the note-gathering phase."

"Don't tell me—Lizzie's rubbed off on you."

"I suppose."

"That's all right. We'll do things your way and keep our ears open."

"Fine. Fine."

Just then, the door swung open and two middle-aged women walked in.

"The rest of our bridge club will be here any second," one of them said. "There'll be six of us in all. Is that okay?"

"It sure is!" Glenda replied.

"I should get going," I told her. "I'll see you tomorrow."

"Remember, souls only stick around for a short time."

Thank God!

I tried Vanna Enterprises again but got the same answering machine. They either filtered their calls or the receptionist had one heck of a busy schedule. I decided perhaps an impromptu visit might be the best approach and proceeded to look up their address. It was located in Penfield, a wealthy suburb of Rochester, with easy access to the airport. I rationalized that if I turned up a big zero by finding the place closed, I could always console myself at the Eastview Mall, one of Metro-Rochester's biggest shopping centers.

So as not to worry about it for the remainder of the day, I filled up Charlie's food dish and changed his water before swapping my jeans for tailored slacks and my shirt for a rayon top that could pass for silk. The fifty-minute drive to Penfield was uneventful. A few county roads and the New York State Thruway.

Vanna Enterprises was housed in an upscale office complex between an investment company and a real estate office. A red Audi and a blue BMW were the only cars parked directly in front. I added my Toyota to the lineup and proceeded to their door. No mall shopping for me. Vanna was indeed open for business, although I didn't see any clients in their posh reception area. I did, however, notice their receptionist immediately. The flash from her crystal necklace all but blinded me.

"Good afternoon." Her contoured hair, a mix of light and dark blond tones, gave me the impression she spent a heck of a lot of time in a salon. "How can I help you?"

"I'm following up on a matter that Mr. Stilton broached with our winery a few weeks ago."

She tapped the keyboard and stared at the computer monitor on her desk. "Did you have an appointment? If so, the date must be wrong. I do hope it's not an error on our part."

"Um, no. I don't have an appointment. Not an official one. Please give him my name. Norrie Ellington. I'm certain he'll want to meet with me."

"I'm afraid that's impossible, Miss Ellington. Mr. Stilton is out of town for a few days but his partner, Declan Roth, is in. Perhaps you'd be willing to speak with him. I'll see if he's available. Please make yourself comfortable. There's bottled water on the credenza as well as coffee."

I took a deep breath, nodded and grabbed the seat closest to the credenza. My hands were shaking slightly and a strange panic was beginning to set in.

I hadn't rehearsed what I was going to say once I got past the receptionist. The last time I had a feeling like this was when I had a role in my high school's production of *Auntie Mame* and had to be cued three times before I remembered my lines. Suddenly I thought of Lizzie and Nancy Drew. The panic began to subside and I was able to swallow some bottled water without choking. That was the moment Declan Roth stepped out of his office and walked toward me.

He was an older gentleman, late forties perhaps or early fifties. Impeccably dressed in dark blue pants with a light blue shirt and geometric tie. His dark brown hair had slight hints of gray but it made him look even more distinguished.

"Miss Ellington? Declan Roth. A pleasure to meet you. Follow me. We can chat in my office."

He held the door open to a fairly large workspace that looked professional in every sense of the word. Large wooden desk with two computer screens and assorted paper files adjacent to a long counter that housed maps and architectural drawings. Paintings that depicted vineyards and clusters of grapes were tastefully hung on the walls.

"Can I get you anything?" He pointed to a chair in front of his desk.

"The bottled water's fine, thanks."

I sat down and he followed suit, only instead of sitting behind his desk, he pulled an armchair over and sat across from me.

"You'll have to forgive me, I'm not familiar with the matter you discussed with my partner, but I think I may have a general sense. You said your name is Ellington, right? Two Witches Winery in Penn Yan?"

"That's me. Uh, not one of the witches."

He laughed and, in that second, he didn't strike me as the villainous wretch everyone had made him and his partner out to be. Then again, looks and behaviors could be deceiving. "Does this matter have anything to do with the sale of your winery? Because if it does, we can make you a very appealing offer."

Okay. Nothing like going for the jugular.

"Mr. Roth, I've just assumed the responsibilities for Two Witches and I'm not exactly sure what your company is proposing. It was actually my sister who had the original conversation with your partner a while back. She's out of the country with no immediate plans to return. So, tell me. What is it exactly that your company is planning to achieve?"

He stood and, for a moment, I thought he was going to escort me out of the office. "Come on over and take a look."

He walked to the counter and motioned for me to join him. "I'm sure you're familiar with the Finger Lakes giants in the winery industry, past and present—Taylor, Bully Hill, Constellation Wines..."

I nodded and he kept going. "None of them are located on Seneca Lake. What we propose is to build a mega-winery that would encompass all three of the hills between Penn Yan and Geneva. We'd hire the best of the best in the industry and create a brand that would be as well-known as Disney."

Disney? Did I hear him right?

I swallowed what little moisture was in my mouth and looked directly at him. "Mr. Roth, Seneca Lake has numerous wineries. Granted, no mega giants, but there are some substantial ones, as well as burgeoning ones. By building an enormous structure or complex or whatever you'd call it, it would destroy the very fabric of the region. We'd lose all those little wineries and their unique personalities. Not to mention, the wines."

"That's not our plan at all. Take a look at this map and these architectural drawings."

He showed me an enormous map of the lake that took up a good portion of the counter. Next to it was an even larger rendering of some buildings and a few structures I couldn't quite figure out.

"Here." He pointed to our hill. "Let me explain. We're not proposing eliminating every single small winery. Quite the opposite, in fact. We want to take them under our wing, that's all. They can still maintain their own style. Tourists love all that cozy ambiance."

"I'm not sure I understand."

"Okay. Think of it this way. Picture a huge shopping mall like Mall of America or even Eastview Mall here in Rochester. Our mega-winery would be the anchor store. It would attract people from all over the world. That's why the location is paramount. So close to the Thruway and the Greater Rochester International Airport. We plan to develop our winery on those hills. The vineyards are already firmly established. It would simply mean a massive rebuild of the winery labs and support structures. Our brand would, in essence, be a new brand and the little wineries that now dot those three hills would—"

"Be gone once and for all?"

"You sound so maudlin. Those businesses would be compensated well or they could come under our umbrella. They'd keep their structures, but it would be our mega-winery brand that they sell. If they really wanted to maintain their winery business, they could always rebuild on another lake or lower down the lake, say, near Watkins Glen."

The thought of rebuilding Two Witches was about as appealing to me as jumping into the lake itself. "It's not that easy finding a quality winemaker and vineyard managers who know how to handle all facets of planting and harvesting grapes. It's a specialized industry."

"We, of all people, understand that. But you, yourself, have to admit that the tourists are always seeking out entertainment. Here, let me explain what our development company has in mind."

With that, he unrolled a large coil of paper and took some paperweights from his desk to hold it down. "These structures to the left are the winery labs, the tasting rooms and gift shops, the barns and the eateries. From bistro to fine dining."

"We already have classy restaurants on the lake."

"Restaurants, yes, but resorts, no. True, there are some hotels but not what Vanna Enterprises has in store. Do you see this complex?"

He pointed to a series of buildings and what looked like some sort of lake. "Have you ever heard of Atlantis in the Bahamas?" Before I could say anything, he went on. "We plan to build a resort that would rival even Atlantis. Gourmet restaurants, spas, a lazy river and entertainment. Music, theater, you name it."

I think they already built this and it's called Las Vegas. "The Bahamas are warm. We get winter here."

"Winters with a spectacular indoor water complex and—"

At that moment, the receptionist knocked on his door, opened it and spoke. "I'm sorry to interrupt you, Mr. Roth, but the dealership just called. They've finished detailing your Mercedes and you can pick it up tonight or tomorrow. Their collision department also managed to buff out those small scratches on the side of the vehicle. Your service rep said to tell you that you might want to consider purchasing a Mercedes-Benz G-Class AMG or even a GL-Class SUV if you intend to do off-roading. They can make you a very tempting deal."

"I have no intention of trading in a brand-new coupe. Please call them and tell them to expect me this evening. I can't wait to drop off the loaner."

The receptionist said "Okay" and walked out of the room.

"I, uh, really should be going. I think I've taken up enough of your time. I get the idea, Mr. Roth, I really do, but I don't think money is going to sway any of those wineries on our hills."

The minute I said that, I regretted it. What if he took that as a dare? Francine told me about some of the issues the little wineries were having. Still, Declan Roth didn't strike me as the kind of person who would put a dead animal in a mailbox or a closed sign by the road. He was far too classy and possibly dangerous. If anything, he'd be scoping out legal reasons to put a chokehold on each of us.

"Don't be too hasty, Miss Ellington. Give it some genuine thought. Maybe we could get together, say, for lunch sometime next week? I'd like to continue our conversation. Right now I've got a shiny new black coupe waiting for me."

Oh my God! The shiny new black coupe. Just like the one I'd seen in front of the winery when those men were arguing. It was a no-brainer in my book. Declan Roth had to be one of them.

Chapter 12

Famished, I stopped at nearby Bruegger's Bagels for their broccoli soup and a turkey sandwich. I was certain it had to be Declan Roth who argued with one of our winemakers the second day I was here. As I stirred the thick soup, something clicked—the term "off-roading."

Declan had his car detailed, a process that went far beyond the usual washing and polishing. Kind of like the difference between something a restoration company did to a house as opposed to a cleaning service. I put two and two together and shuddered. If Declan Roth was the one who killed Elsbeth, because she wouldn't sell him her B & B, he had to get rid of the body.

It was quite feasible, in my mind, that he drove her corpse through our woods and dumped her in our vineyard. That would account for his car getting scratched a bit and the interior in desperate need of a thorough cleansing.

Can detailing remove blood stains? DNA?

With Elsbeth gone, Vanna Enterprises could certainly put the pressure on Yvonne. I couldn't very well point the finger at Declan and insist the sheriff's department seize his car for evidence because all I had was a theory. Not to mention a sheriff's deputy who wanted me as far away from this case as I could get.

I bit into my bagel and tried not to think about it. I had other pressing matters to attend to, like my screenplay, and I kept brushing those aside in order to play amateur sleuth. Then again, the thought of a murderer so close to our winery left me no choice. I decided to organize my days so I could do both. I'd get up early and work on the screenplay and then attend to winery stuff and my unofficial investigation later in the day.

That night I had the worst sleep imaginable. Even Charlie got off the bed in favor of the floor because all I did was toss around. I dreamed Renee, the producer, kept moving up my deadline and when I objected, she cackled, "You'll be tossed to the curb like Conrad Blyth."

I tried to envision peaceful scenes that would lure me into a restful sleep but every time I did that, the images changed to the vineyard and I saw Elsbeth's body lying there. By morning, I couldn't wait to get out of bed.

True to my word, I sat at my laptop drinking coffee and sketching out the screenplay until noon. I prayed my script analyst wouldn't tear it to shreds once it reached his hands. No way was I going to wind up like poor Conrad. For some inexplicable reason, I looked at Francine's wall calendar when I got up to stretch and noticed she had written *winery meeting* for the day after tomorrow. Hell! It didn't take a genius to figure out I'd have to conduct it. After all, I *was* managing the place, wasn't I?

I grabbed a quick shower and hightailed it down to the tasting room. It was Tuesday and that meant Cammy would be in. I really needed to get her take on things because, number one, she struck me as being reasonable and pragmatic as opposed to her coworkers and, number two, she was far more approachable than those crews in the winery lab and vineyards.

"Hey! Good morning," I called out as soon as I stepped inside. "Or should I say good afternoon?" Lizzie was at her usual spot at the cash register and Glenda was with customers. Cammy was restocking bottles and I walked over to her.

"You got a present," she said. "I put it in the kitchen. Didn't know if you wanted to leave it in the tasting room or take it back to the house. It got delivered here. I thought you might be in sooner."

"A present?"

"Yeah. Someone sent you flowers."

"Huh?" I charged into the kitchen and stared at the bouquet. I didn't have to read the card to figure out who sent them. The mini-white carnations and purple asters were a match to the arrangement at the Peaceful Pines. Right up to the raffia on the glass vase.

"Oh no!" I shouted, loud enough to be heard in the tasting room.

"Did you break the vase?" Cammy yelled out.

I ushered her into the kitchen and tried to keep my voice low. "I'm going to be the next one who's about to be murdered."

"What? What are you talking about?"

"These flowers. I haven't even read the card but I know they're from Declan Roth, Lucas Stilton's partner from Vanna Enterprises. I saw the exact same arrangement at Elsbeth's B & B the other day. He must have sent them to her, too, before he killed her."

"Whoa. Slow down. I'm not following any of this."

I was talking a mile a minute and making absolutely no sense. To make matters worse, my stomach sounded like Mt. Vesuvius before it wiped out half the coast of Italy.

"Uh, maybe I should get something to eat, first."

"Yeah," Cammy said. "That's a good idea. Get a sandwich and then we'll talk."

I took the little card from the bouquet with me and opened it after I had given Fred my order for a Reuben. Suddenly I was back in my ninth grade algebra class with my foot tapping the floor and my fingers clicking the table, praying I wouldn't get called on. Too late. The bouquet with my name on it was staring me in the face. I took a breath and read the contents of the small envelope. It said:

Atlantis can be your dream, too. Let's talk about it later this week.
Declan Roth.

I honestly didn't remember eating the Reuben but I was sure it was delicious. So far, all of Fred's creations turned out to be mouthwatering. Cammy was finishing up with three ladies and I stood patiently near her table, waving the little card at her and mouthing, "I was right." Finally the women walked over to the wine racks to select their purchases and I grabbed Cammy by the arm.

"Here. Read this."

She furrowed her brow and read it. Then she read it again. "Holy cow, Norrie. This doesn't sound like someone who wants to kill you. More like someone who has the hots for you."

"Ew! No! He's at least fifteen years older than I am. No way! What he has is some sort of wackadoodle vision that he shares with his partner about turning our small patch of the Finger Lakes into the next source of global entertainment, using the wine industry as a lure. And I'm an obstacle. Just like Elsbeth was."

"Are you sure you're not blowing this out of proportion? After all, we're talking a floral arrangement, not a horse's head at the foot of your bed."

"I can't prove anything, but I'll tell you what I think."

I then proceeded to explain about the car detailing and what I had seen in front of our own winery lab. "Let's face it. I'm stuck. All I have is a theory. Oh, and a motive. I have that. All I'm missing are the facts. Elsbeth's niece said the last she'd seen of her aunt was around six at dinnertime. Then they went their separate ways in the house, with the TVs turned on, and the niece never knew Elsbeth was missing until the following day. She thought her aunt had left early the next morning to run errands because the car wasn't in the garage. Seems that's part of the mystery, too."

"Not anymore. Didn't you catch the news last night?"

"What? No. I was so exhausted when I got back from Penfield, all I did was answer my e-mails and crawl into bed. Why? What was on the news?"

"The Ontario County Sheriff's Department located Elsbeth's car in the Geneva Walmart Supercenter on Routes 5 & 20. They notified their counterpart in Yates County and the car was taken to a forensic lab for testing."

"I doubt they'll find much. Either Declan and Lucas wiped it clean for prints or they were never in that car to begin with. For all we know, they might've arranged for Elsbeth to meet one or both of them at Walmart. It's such a bustling store, no one would notice. Then she got in one of their cars. Declan's to be precise. Oh my gosh. Wouldn't the Walmart security cameras have this information?"

"Funny you should mention it. So did the news anchors. Apparently, that particular camera was out of order. Seems it got busted earlier in the day with a bb gun."

"That's convenient."

"That's Geneva. Always something."

Another group of customers approached Cammy's table and I told her I'd catch up later. Glenda looked swamped, with at least eight people, but Lizzie motioned me over to her spot.

"Well?" she asked. "What did you find out from the Sisters of the Holy Winery?"

For a minute, I thought there was a wine-producing convent I hadn't heard about. Then I realized she meant Catherine, Rosalee, Madeline and Stephanie.

"I haven't gotten in touch with them yet. I drove to Penfield instead to meet with those developers from Vanna Enterprises."

"I wouldn't waste too much time if I were you. Those women are bound to know something and my gut tells me those developers are bound to lie."

"You could be right, Lizzie. I'll keep that in mind."

I waved good-bye to the tasting room ladies and headed to the house. Alvin made some sort of guttural noise and I actually turned around, walked back and petted him. This time no spit. Someone had cleaned his pen and put down fresh hay. Francine was right. The vineyard employees made sure the animals were taken care of. I made a mental note to tell John I'd be feeding Charlie from now on so not to have his staff give the dog more food. That hound was already milking me for every last bit of kibble.

When I got back to the house, my first intention was to call one of those wineries and invite myself over to speak with their proprietress, but as soon as I picked up Francine's list of names, I realized something. If Declan and Lucas were the real perpetrators and not Yvonne, then what would stop them from putting the pressure on her? Aargh. Yvonne was already considering a possible offer. Wasn't that what I heard her say?

My finger couldn't tap her number fast enough on my cell phone. She picked up on the second ring and I started right in. "Hello. Yvonne? This is Norrie from the other day. Hope you're okay. Listen, there's something you should know." *What? That I have absolutely no proof those developers killed your aunt.* "You may be in danger. Don't say anything to Declan Roth or Lucas Stilton from Vanna Enterprises for a few days. And whatever you do, don't meet them anywhere."

"What are you talking about? What do you mean?"

"They may have had something to do with your aunt's death."

"I just got off the phone with Deputy Hickman and he didn't say anything of the sort. He told me my aunt's car would be unavailable for at least a week. Maybe longer if they find something. One way or another, I have to get a rental. What's going on?"

I didn't want to go into too many details because I was concerned she'd call that deputy back and then he'd traipse over here to read me the riot act again. Instead, I kept it short with lots of innuendo. After all, if I could do that with screenplay dialogue, I'd certainly be able to pull it off with Yvonne.

"Oh my word," she said. "That's troubling. Keep me posted, will you?"

"Absolutely."

I let out a slow breath and tapped the red end-call button. Next, I looked up Catherine Trobert's number at Lake View Winery and dialed. Hers was the first name on Francine's list.

Her voice sounded warm and welcoming when she picked up the phone. "Norrie, how are you? Is everything going smoothly? I mean, as well as it can since the you know...since Elsbeth's—"

"Unfortunate ending in our Riesling vineyard? Yeah, we're doing okay, Mrs. Trobert."

"Please. Call me Catherine. You're one of us now. A bona fide member of the West Side Women of the Wineries."

"Well, sure. Thanks. I was actually hoping you might have some time to spare this week. I'm trying to piece together all the possible information I can on Elsbeth Waters. It might give me a better idea of how she wound up where she did."

"I'm not sure I can be much help but I'd love to chat with you. What are you doing right now? I made some sunshine iced tea and I've got a good hour or so to spare before I get dinner on for tonight. What do you say? Can you stop over?"

"Yes. Sounds great. Give me a few minutes and I'll be on my way."

I quickly brushed my hair and pulled it back into a ponytail. The jeans and lightweight top I had on were fine for vineyard visiting. I felt as if I shouldn't go there emptyhanded but it wasn't as if I had time to bake cookies. Even the readymade, put-them-in-the-oven kind. Then I remembered the pantry and a whole shelf of strawberry jam Francine had made. The season started in early June and she had told me she was done with her jellies and jams two weeks later. Martha Stewart had nothing on my sister. I grabbed the nearest jar and bolted out the door.

Catherine Trobert was sitting on the porch of her forest-green Victorian house and waved to me the minute I got out of my car. "Come on over and make yourself comfortable. It's a perfect afternoon. We won't be saying that in a few weeks when the heat kicks in."

She poured me a glass of iced tea and I handed her the jelly.

"Goodness. You didn't have to do that, but thanks so much. One of Francine's?"

"Uh-huh. Domesticity isn't exactly my strong suit."

"Oh, I don't think that matters much in today's world. Men seem to be equal partners now. Speaking of which, I told Steven you were back in Penn Yan and he sends his regards. He'll be here Labor Day Weekend to help us kick off the fall rush. He's a junior partner in a law firm in Augusta. So busy with work, he's still single. I imagine the same goes for you."

Boy. I didn't see that coming. "Uh, yeah. Work. My writing career doesn't give me a whole lot of spare time. Not if I want to succeed in this business. Even though I'm technically watching the winery for Francine and Jason, I've still got deadlines and all."

Catherine nodded and smiled. "You really should get together with Steven when he visits. I'm sure you both have lots of catching up to do."

Catching up? He was two years ahead of me in school and the only thing I saw of him was the back of his head on the school bus, and that stopped the minute he got his driver's license.

"Sure. No problem. Maybe by then the sheriff's department will have solved Elsbeth's murder." *Whew. Finally managed to get to the real reason I'm here.* "I know she sort of pushed everyone to their breaking point at the wineries but would someone have had a motive for killing her that wasn't, say, as obvious as being the irritating witch she was?"

Catherine shrugged and refilled my iced tea. "The niece, maybe. Very strange woman. Almost as if she's acting the part. Very timid and withdrawn. Then again, living with that harpy may have caused the niece to suffer a complete breakdown and murder the aunt in a fit of fury."

"I didn't get that impression. I visited the B & B and the niece seemed, well, pretty grounded. And if she did kill her aunt and dump the body, wouldn't she have driven the car back? They only had one car."

"True. True. Well, I'm certain none of the winery women had anything to do with it. I've known these ladies for years. Except Stephanie Ipswich. She's fairly new. Hmm, and she owns the bottom part of Gable Hill, right below the spot where Peaceful Pines is located. You know, come to think of it, I recall Stephanie once saying how they'd like to buy up the entire hill and expand their winery. They made an offer to Elsbeth about a year ago, but it was rejected." She paused for a moment and stared off in the distance. "All that wonderful sloping land...perfect for vineyards. Elsbeth could've still kept the B & B, but she'd have no part of it. Said the last thing she needed was all that noise, not to mention the haze and dust from the spraying. You don't suppose Stephanie had anything to do with it? She seems like such a lovely lady. And a mother, as well, with two young boys."

It's always the ones we least expect.

Catherine took a long sip of her tea. "Stephanie wasn't the only one who wanted the land. Vanna Enterprises is circling all of us like a shark. I hope it turns out they were responsible and not Stephanie. Dear Lord. To think, if it *was* Stephanie, I've been cavorting with a murderess."

"I wouldn't exactly call monthly winery meetings *cavorting.* But you're right. Gable Hill Winery did have a motive."

"Norrie, you're not going to say anything to the sheriff's deputies, are you?"

"Heck no! I've been told, in no uncertain terms, to mind my own business. But it *is* my business. Elsbeth wound up dead in what might be next year's vintage."

"I'm sure the case will get solved. In the meantime, if I were you, I'd be extra cautious. You know, keep your doors and windows locked. And if you need anything, don't be a stranger. I'll let Steven know you're looking forward to seeing him in a few months."

What? How did that happen? "Uh, yes. Well, I should get going. It was really nice talking with you."

"When you hear from Francine, send our regards. That experiment station doesn't offer many grants like that. Jason is one lucky entomologist."

Chapter 13

Humph. It was probably nothing but that was the second time I heard something like that. About Jason getting the grant. Maybe someone pulled some strings but not because they were dying to learn more about rare bugs. Maybe they wanted Jason and my sister out of the way. I tried to push that thought from my mind because I had enough to deal with. Still, it wouldn't hurt to poke around and see what I could find out. The trouble was, I had no idea where to poke.

In addition to Yvonne and Declan, I added Stephanie to my list of possible killers and called her as soon as I got back to the house.

"You must've been reading my mind," she said, "because I've been meaning to invite you over here. Especially after that awful shock you had. How about stopping by Friday morning for coffee and muffins? Any time after nine works for me. The boys will be at school and my husband will have barricaded himself in the winery by then. It's one of the few times I can catch my breath. Whatever idiot said it was easier to raise twins than having children spaced apart in years needs to have his or her head examined. Two first graders are beyond exhausting. Anyway, can you make it?"

I really wanted to stick to my original plan of working on the screenplay in the mornings and snooping about later in the day, but I wasn't about to blow my chances with Stephanie.

"How about nine-thirty?"

"Perfect. I'll see you then."

I made myself some French toast for dinner and tossed a few pieces into Charlie's kibble. It was gone before I even put the first forkful in my mouth. I caught a bit of the evening news and all but had a coronary when they showed a picture of our vineyard. Yellow tape and all.

Damn it! When are they going to remove that crime tape?

Nothing new for the sheriff's department to share with the public. I did some quick channel surfing and that same, or similar, photo of the broken irrigation pipe in the Riesling section flashed on the screen again. At least it wasn't anything gory that would bring out the kook and nutcases.

Boy, was I wrong.

The next morning, the parking lot to our tasting room was filled to capacity by nine-forty-five and the doors didn't open until ten. I couldn't believe my eyes when I stared out the window. I pushed the File Save button on my laptop, left my protagonist sweating over her decision to quit her job and all but ran down to the tasting room.

"Stay!" I commanded Charlie. I snaked my way past a long line of tourists and muttered things like, "I work here" or "I'm opening up the place." Only one person told me not to cut in line. I blew past them.

"Cammy! Cammy!" My voice exploded as I unlocked the door and latched it behind me. "What's going on?"

Cammy and Roger both came rushing over. Lizzie manned her position at the cash register as if it was the Alamo.

"The news. That's what," Roger said. "I got an earful from the crowd on my way in. They all want to see where the dead body was found."

For a moment, I thought I didn't hear him correctly and I stood there, speechless, with my mouth wide open.

"He's right," Cammy said. "What a bunch of ghouls. We've got to do something before they take it upon themselves to go trampling all over the place. We give tours but only on the weekends in June. We don't start the daily tours until Fourth of July weekend. What do we tell them? I've got to let them in. We open in two minutes."

"Okay. Fine. Not a problem. I remember how to give tours. When they come in for a tasting, have them sign up with Lizzie. I'll take groups of ten. Tell them, for insurance purposes, we cannot have them go off on their own. Oh, and call down to the winery and the barn. Let Franz and John know what's going on. Use their cell phones if they don't answer."

I hadn't given a winery tour in over ten years, and I wasn't that good at it back then. Especially the winemaking part of the deal. After all, these were savvy wine tasters and no one wanted to hear, "Something happens in these tanks." Then a thought came to me—I'm the boss. I said it out loud but under my breath so no one heard me. *I'm the boss.*

I reached into my pocket for my phone and dialed Peter's cell number. Thank goodness I'd listened to Francine's advice and added all the important numbers to my contacts list.

"Peter," I said before the guy could catch a breath. "We've got an issue. I need you to step in and help out with the winery tours. Now. Before the zillion tourists who are in our tasting room turn into the next zombie apocalypse."

It took me a minute or two but once I'd explained, Peter agreed to *head it off at the pass*. His words, not mine. Then I called Franz and he agreed to have Herbert explain the fermentation process but only in front of the winery lab. Fine with me.

As horrendous as the scenario was at ten in the morning, we had it well under control by noon. It seemed most of the visitors were more interested in the crime scene than a winery, but we still sold a record number of bottles before the day ended.

"We can't possibly do this again tomorrow. *I* can't possibly do this again tomorrow. I can barely stand on my feet," I wailed to Cammy once she had locked the tasting room doors for the day. "Who usually does the tours for us?"

"College students. We've already got them lined up."

"Great. Can you call them and get them started tomorrow?"

"No problem."

"Oh my God. Tomorrow. The winery meeting. I'm supposed to conduct the winery meeting. What time do we meet?"

Cammy put her hand on my shoulder and gave me a pat. "Relax, will you? We meet at eleven in the kitchen. The meeting only lasts an hour unless Franz goes off on some ridiculous tangent. Don't worry about it. All you have to do is ask each manager for an update. Once that's over with, you ask for any concerns or suggestions and review the upcoming calendar with them. By the way, if they have a concern, ask them for their solution. That's what your sister did. That simple."

Yeah, simple for her. Not me. When I left the winery, I trudged back to the house and spent the next hour and a half reviewing Robert's Rules of Order. Just in case. Then I made myself a grilled cheese and tomato sandwich and returned to my screenplay. By then, my mind was a complete dribble. I closed the laptop and spent the next two hours watching the TV and dozing on and off, with Charlie curled up next to me.

The nap must've done me some good because I woke refreshed and ready to get back to work. Last thing I needed was to become the next Conrad Blyth. It was well after midnight when I finally called it quits and crept into bed. That was when something dawned on me—Elsbeth's cell phone and purse. Where were they? They weren't next to her body in the vineyard. And Yvonne didn't make any mention of them. Were they in the car found at Walmart?

I was positive Deputy Hickman wasn't about to share that information with me, but I desperately needed to find out. Maybe I'd find another way...

My stomach was in knots the next morning and I had to shove my thoughts about Elsbeth to the far reaches of my consciousness. It was Thursday. Winery meeting day. I racked my brain, trying to remember the last time I had conducted a meeting and realized, with no uncertainty, never! I had never conducted a meeting. Even back in high school. I was in all sorts of clubs but never the president. Aargh. I hoped Francine and Jason stepped on those damn bugs!

To make matters worse, and to add to my growing sense of frustration with everything, Peter phoned at a little past ten to ask if everything was okay and if I needed anything. He sounded condescending, but maybe it was my imagination. I thanked him for pitching in yesterday. Cammy had already informed him, as well as Herbert, that the same tour guides we used last year from Hobart and William Smith Colleges in Geneva were back at the winery and raring to go. At least that nightmare was over with.

The kitchen table was strewn with my notes for the meeting. Everything appeared organized. Why, then, did I feel as if I was about to throw up? I grabbed the phone and dialed Don and Theo. Mainly because I needed reassurance.

"Cut yourself some slack, Norrie," Theo said. "It's only a winery meeting. Stay on task and, whatever you do, don't let anyone pull you into a different direction. If they bring up something and you're not sure, just say 'That's very interesting. I'll give it some thought and get back to you.'"

"Thanks. I really appreciate it. Listen, there's something else. I need to talk with you and Don about the investigation. I've got a few thoughts rolling around in my mind."

"Any time. Just give a holler. By the way, what were you selling up there yesterday? The traffic up the hill was nonstop and we did a record business for the day."

I told him the real reason the tourists were out in full force and he groaned. "Ugh. That's really morbid. They wanted to see where Elsbeth's body was found? Downright creepy, if you ask me."

"Oh, it gets worse. One of the people asked if the toxins in her body could contaminate the soil and render it useless for planting."

"You have *got* to be kidding me."

"I explained that, according to the preliminary coroner's report, it was blunt force trauma, not poisoning that killed her. Honestly, I felt as if I was conducting a murder scene tour and not a winery visit. Thank goodness Peter and Herbert did their part. I'm really worried that if those deputies don't figure out something soon, we'll be besieged with a lot of nonsense."

"As long as you're besieged with customers, don't worry about it."

When I stepped inside the tasting room building for the winery meeting, I felt better. Until I saw Deputy Hickman waiting for me. It was ten twenty-five and I had thirty-five minutes to prepare myself for that production.

"Good Morning, Miss Ellington. I won't keep you long. I stopped by to let you know your vineyard area is free and clear. Our forensic team is finished processing it and they sent someone to take down the yellow tape a few minutes ago. Same goes for the wooded area behind your house. The ground was soft, so we were able to extract some tire prints. The lab is working on matching them to particular vehicles."

"Tire prints you said? So there was more than one kind?"

"Those woods of yours had lots of dried prints. A regular KOA campground. And who knows how long they could've been there. First thing the lab did was check to see if they matched Elsbeth's car, but they didn't."

"I guess that means whoever dumped her, didn't use her car and then drive it to Walmart. And before you say anything, it was on the news. About Walmart. So Elsbeth's car was never in the woods."

"No, it wasn't. The perpetrator must've driven his or her own vehicle through those woods. The scarf was definitely Elsbeth's, but how it wound up in the woods is anyone's guess. Unless that dog of yours found it elsewhere."

"I don't think so. He came out of the woods with it. What about her cell phone and purse? Did you find them? Because they weren't with her body in our vineyard. Were they in the car?"

"We're not at liberty to disclose that information at this time."

"Look, don't take this wrong. I'm not telling you how to do your job, but whenever there's a cell phone involved in a crime on TV, they always call it or triangulate the location."

"Thank you, Miss Ellington, for keeping me abreast of how Hollywood writers conduct their investigations. In the meantime, we'll follow our own procedures. Oh. One more thing. I'll need a list of the vehicles your employees own. Make. Model. Year."

"You can't be serious. You think just because a body was found in our vineyard one of us had something to do with it?"

"I am. Very serious. Please e-mail that information to me by the end of the day. As of four p.m. yesterday, Elsbeth Waters's death was officially ruled a homicide."

"Yeah. I kind of figured as much when you originally mentioned blunt force trauma to the head."

He glared at me. "The woman could have fallen and hit herself. That's why we have a coroner. To make those determinations."

He handed me a Yates County Sheriff's Department business card and reminded me to leave the investigation to the professionals.

"What was that all about?" Cammy asked as soon as the deputy left the building.

"It's officially a murder. As if we didn't know. Anyway, that forensic crew found tire prints in the woods. Big surprise there. And now their lab needs a list of all our vehicles. You know. To see if any of those prints might match a particular tire type."

"Oh, brother. Listen, whatever you do, don't start the meeting with that. You'll never get past square one. Save it for the very end and pass around a sheet of paper for us to fill out. My car's that cutesy little 2014 Buick Encore. I bought it used last year and, believe me, the woods are the last place I'd drive it."

"This is such a waste of time. The car they really should be checking is— Oh my gosh. I'm surprised I didn't think of this before. I'm going to write down the make and model of Declan Roth's car. I'll just say it belongs to the winery as one of our vehicles."

"That's a stretch, you know. A truck, maybe. That's believable. Lots of wineries own their own trucks, but didn't you say he had a Mercedes?"

"Yes. A coupe."

"Oh, what the heck! Go for it anyway. That deputy's just going to take the list and pass it over to the lab. And if they do question you, tell them the car is used for fancy winery events."

"If that car turns out to be a match, *then* I'll tell him the truth. That I think Declan Roth might be involved. I can't say anything now because I'm not supposed to be sleuthing."

Just then, Glenda rushed over to us and I could see the customers she had at her table were now selecting wines for purchase. At least that was a good start to the day.

"Hi, Norrie! I was hoping I'd catch you before you took off for that meeting. I really think we need to conduct a complete smudging of the tasting room. We can't take any chances."

"A smudging? What on earth's a smudging?"

Glenda took a deep breath and enunciated every word. "It's a ritualistic cleansing of a building to eliminate any negative energy. And believe me,

Elsbeth spewed plenty of that whenever she came in here. Now, her restless spirit will never give us any peace."

"Uh, okay. A cleansing. Like washing down everything? Because that's not a bad idea. I mean, we clean and all, but a good deep cleaning never hurt anything."

Glenda crinkled her nose and shook her head. "Not that kind of cleaning. It involves burning special herbs, like sage, and chanting. When the smoke floats about the room, it removes any of the restless spirits."

"It will also set off our smoke detectors." *And stink up this place.*

Cammy's eyes looked like saucers as she stared at Glenda. "Norrie's right. I'm not so sure this is a great idea."

Glenda was unmoved. "We can't have negative energy in here. Especially Elsbeth's. I happen to have smudge sticks at home that I made from sage and lavender, but if you're really concerned about the smoke, I suppose we can use white sage incense sticks. I can order them online if you'd like."

Suddenly I remembered what Theo told me and repeated it. "That's very interesting. I'll give it some thought and get back to you."

Cammy bit her lip and turned toward Lizzie. "You've got the watch, Lizzie. Norrie and I have that meeting." Then, to Glenda. "Hold down the fort. See you later."

Before Glenda could respond, Cammy and I went into the kitchen and waited for John and Franz to arrive. My stomach felt as if it had gone ten rounds with Muhammad Ali.

Chapter 14

"I hope you don't mind"—John tossed a frayed notebook onto the table—"but Peter's on his way. Since he'll be taking over for me next summer, I figured now would be a good time to have him attend our meetings and, little by little, shoulder more of the responsibilities."

Wonderful. As if I don't have enough stress. "Uh, sure. Makes sense to me."

Cammy took out five bottles of spring water from the fridge and placed them on the table while we waited for Franz and Peter.

"Any news on the investigation?" John asked. "I saw the sheriff's car pulling out of our driveway."

Just then Franz walked in and took a seat. "Sorry. I meant to get here sooner but it's always one little holdup after another."

"You're fine," I said. "It's eleven on the nose."

With that, Peter walked in and said something similar about being late. He took the seat next to John and nodded at everyone. All eyes were on me and it was show time. *I hate you, Francine, and all those stupid bugs, too.*

"Thanks, everyone, for coming." *What the heck's wrong with me? Like they have a choice?* "I know everyone's time is valuable, so we'll begin the usual way with your reports and then move on to concerns, suggestions and upcoming events."

"Might I suggest we begin with the elephant in the room?" Peter asked. "John and I saw the sheriff's car leaving a few minutes ago."

I took a breath and curled my toes so I'd have something else to think about, and swore I wouldn't get sidetracked or trapped. "I promise we'll talk about that but right now we need to begin with our regularly scheduled format. Cammy, can you please give us an update on the tasting room?"

Wasting no time, Cammy reviewed the number of tasters we'd had in the last month and our sales, wine by wine. The blends were way out in front, probably because they were the least expensive, but we'd had a substantial number of sales from all of our wines.

"The prior year was a fantastic vintage," she said. "We're hoping we'll be in the same boat next summer and fall."

As if on cue, Franz gave his report. The wine was in the aging process and, according to the samples the winemakers took periodically, all was going well. Bottling would happen next, but that was a while off.

I thanked Franz and turned to John. "I know we've had some changes here with the introduction of the Veltliner and some new Riesling vineyards. Like Cammy, I'm hopeful this fall's yield will mean a good vintage for us."

"Keeping our fingers crossed Mother Nature feels the same way. You do realize that the newer Riesling vineyards won't really produce any viable grapes for another year or so. It takes that long for the grapes to have a decent flavor so even if the clusters look good, the taste won't be. The vines have to mature."

"But we're okay as far as quantity goes, right? I mean, we have mature vineyards and varieties that have been with us for years."

John clasped his hands together. "Absolutely. And worst-case scenario, we can always purchase grapes from the big vineyards in Hammonsport. But honestly, it won't come to that."

Peter sat motionless as John spoke. I wondered if perhaps I should include him in the conversation, so I asked if he had anything else to share about their progress.

"I think John's got it covered. I was concerned we wouldn't be able to get back into our new Riesling vineyard and replace the drip system, but on my way over to this meeting, I saw the yellow tape had been removed."

If ever there was an introduction to the next part of the meeting, Peter made it. I was about to launch into the deputy's request for the make and model of each employee's car when I realized I still had to ask about concerns and suggestions. Not to mention the calendar of events. Thankfully, Cammy stepped in.

"The tasting room has a few suggestions for better traffic flow in the fall, but we can go over them with you at another time. Nothing major."

Franz cleared his throat and held out a brochure for me to take. "We need to discuss which wine competitions to enter. The deadlines are fast approaching."

"Can you make your suggestions to me by Monday and we'll figure it out?"

"Certainly."

That left John and Peter. They looked at each other and groaned at the same time.

"If you must know," John said, "we've got all sorts of wackadoodles out there who are ignoring our signs to keep out of the vineyards. I've never seen anything like it. They're snapping selfies and searching for 'the dead body drop-off' according to one lunatic."

I cringed. "Aargh. What suggestions do you have? Does *anyone* have, for that matter?"

We batted around a few ideas, including hiring more tour guides who would essentially be vineyard monitors, but opted instead for roping off the entrances to the rows of vineyards.

"It'll be a pain in the butt," John said, "but ultimately, it'll be worth it."

Peter suggested posting "please protect our vines" signs and I said, "Good idea but maybe something like, 'Watch for hazardous snakes' might be more effective."

The calendar of events, including the "Sip and Savor," was reviewed in a matter of minutes. Before I knew it, it was time for the elephant. Not mine. Deputy Hickman's.

"I suppose you're all wondering what I've heard about the investigation Especially since one of the sheriff's deputies left a few minutes before our meeting started. Not much, really. Except for one thing. Well, maybe two. The case is now officially a homicide. They have reason to believe someone drove Elsbeth's body to our vineyard through our woods. They've taken tire impressions and asked me to get the make and model of each employee's vehicle. So, I'm passing around this sheet. No big deal."

"I'm outraged," Franz said, "that they would point a finger at one of us. Well, they won't find my Volvo's tires in those woods. I'm no Daniel Boone."

John and Peter grumbled under their breath and jotted down the information. I already had Cammy's.

"I'll also need you to get the same information from the people on your crews—vineyard workers, Alan and Herbert in the winery and the entire tasting room and bistro employees. Here's the form for each department."

"Did he say what evidence he found?" Peter asked.

"No," I lied. And not because Grizzly Gary directed me to "keep that information to myself." I didn't want to get the reputation of a tell-it-all. "The sheriff's department isn't sharing a whole lot of information with us."

More grumbles. I thanked everyone for coming and stayed seated while they left. I didn't want any of them to notice the giant perspiration spot on my rear end from the combination of nerves and heat.

"See, that wasn't so bad," Cammy said when the rest left.

"Oh yeah, it was. Francine owes me big time. By the way, no matter how much Glenda whines, we can't hold a smudging ceremony or purification or whatever she calls it."

"No kidding. Wine tasting is a sensitive business. The least little odors can ruin it. Look, Glenda's a good soul and she'll do as you say, but she'll be persistent. I'm thinking maybe we can offer up that séance sometime and get it over with."

"Okay. Okay. As long as it's after hours. And outdoors."

All sorts of bizarre ceremonial smells accompanied by wailing, keening or both immediately sprang to mind and I shuddered. When I walked into the tasting room, Lizzie motioned me over. "You got a phone call from Declan Roth. He wants you to call him back. He left the number."

I took the slip of paper and tucked it in my pocket. My next stop was to grab a sandwich at the bistro. Whatever Declan wanted, and I was sure it was that lunch date, could wait.

One chicken chipotle salad later, I returned the call. I was back at the house checking for any new e-mails. I figured I'd get Declan's call over with before I continued with my screenplay.

"Hi, Norrie. Thanks for getting back to me so soon. I won't keep you. I wondered if you'd be free sometime next week for lunch. I'd really relish going over Vanna Enterprises's plan for the Finger Lakes. I'm hoping I might sway you into seeing things differently. We can select a restaurant near your winery so you won't have to drive into the Rochester area."

My first instinct was to say no. Politely, of course, but emphatically. Then I had second thoughts. Declan Roth was my number one suspect for knocking off Elsbeth Waters. Like it or not, I needed to pursue that theory.

"All right. I'm not quite sure of my schedule, so how about if I give you a call the beginning of the week?"

"I'll look forward to it. As much as to our lunch date."

Yeesh. Why did he have to use the word "date"? "By the way, the flowers you sent were lovely. It was very thoughtful of you."

"Glad you liked them. I look forward to seeing you again."

"Me too. Good-bye."

"Me too?" Why the hell did I say that?

Detectives were really good at pulling information out of people without having their suspects realize what was happening. I had no idea how I was going to get Declan Roth to admit to his role in Elsbeth's suspicious death. At least I'd bought myself some time.

With that looming screenplay deadline getting closer and closer, I all but chained myself to the kitchen and my laptop. Thankfully, the only interruptions I had were from Charlie. Once, around five to demand food, and an hour later when I swore he brought a decaying corpse into the house. Luckily, and I use that term loosely, he had rolled in something obnoxious but left it wherever it was. I was able to wipe him off with some wet paper towels I dosed with Dawn. I figured if that stuff was good for wildlife, it wouldn't hurt the dog.

At seven-thirty, I called it quits and dug up one of Francine's casseroles for dinner. Some kind of pasta and veggies. I flipped on the TV and, at that exact moment, the phone rang. It was one of those rare moments when I prayed it was a telemarketer.

"Norrie? Hope we didn't disturb you. How's it going?"

"Oh, thank goodness it's you, Theo. I was beginning to get jumpy wondering what might happen next."

"Yeah, that's understandable. Listen, tomorrow's Friday and Don and I are going to grab a bite to eat at Port of Call around seven. Want to join us? You can't stay cooped up in the house all the time."

The aroma from Charlie's latest encounter with God-knows-what still lingered in the room. Maybe eating out would be preferable.

"Sure. Sounds great. Where's Port of Call? I've never heard of it."

"It's a new restaurant about five miles up the lake near Geneva. It's got a fabulous deck for alfresco dining and the food's wonderful. The usual stuff like steaks and seafood, but it's their appetizer menu that keeps us coming back. It changes weekly. Don is smitten with their deck and refuses to eat indoors in the summer."

"I'll meet you over there. Unless Deputy Hickman returns with more tidings of good cheer."

"What do you mean?"

I told him about the tire tracks and how the sheriff's department wanted a list of our employees' cars.

"Don't sweat it. It's all procedural stuff. They stopped by here, too, asking us to provide the same information."

"I sort of embellished our list. I'll tell you about it tomorrow night."

"This I've *got* to hear."

"Thanks for the invite. Catch you later."

Funny, but our employees seemed more bent out of shape with that request than Theo or Don. I doubted it meant anything other than annoyance, but when I went to sleep, I found myself thinking about each and every worker we had at Two Witches and wondering if Elsbeth's killer was one of them.

* * * *

If I was sitting in the kitchen of a murderess the next morning, it certainly didn't seem that way. Not with the yellow and red gingham curtains that matched the farm-themed wallpaper in Stephanie Ipswich's dining area. Then again, what was I expecting? *American Gothic?* I took in the cutesy decorations and fixated on the piglet salt and pepper shakers on the table. The refrigerator showcased what I presumed to be her boys' artwork—finger paintings, cutouts of zoo animals and drawings of beach scenes.

"This is my last Friday morning of sanity for the next two months. The final day of school is this coming Wednesday. I feel like throwing myself over a bridge. Preferably one in the Caribbean." Stephanie poured me a cup of coffee and motioned for me to help myself to one of her giant chocolate chip or cranberry muffins. Stephanie's long blond hair hung loosely about her shoulders, and she reminded me of a younger version of Christie Brinkley. Even her voice was chipper. "I'm really glad you could stop over. I wanted to connect with you. This must be a nightmare. And to think I was alone in my house when all of it took place."

"Oh?"

"My husband was at his sister's in Watkins Glen. Her son is the same age as our boys and it was his birthday, so they invited us for an overnight. I wasn't feeling well, so I stayed here. Anyway, like I was saying, it must've been a horrible nightmare for you."

I brushed some hair from my forehead and took a quick sip of coffee. "It's creepy, that's for sure. But not terrible. I mean, it's not as if anyone at Two Witches was really close to Elsbeth."

Stephanie shook her head. "I don't know how anyone could've been. She was a miserable wretch of a human being. And I'm being polite. Of course, I probably have more reason to dislike her than anyone in our women's winery group."

Oh my gosh. I can't believe she's telling me this. "Uh, what do you mean?"

"When my husband and I left the West Coast to start a winery business in the Finger Lakes, we expected to expand. That's the thing with wineries. Or all businesses, really. If you're not growing, you're dying. Anyway, we were poised to buy the property that we already own, which we did, as well as the Tyler property on top of the hill. A few days before our scheduled closing on the Tyler place, we got a call from our bank informing us the property had been sold out from under us to Elsbeth Waters. A cash deal."

"Oh my gosh. Can they do that? Er, um, I guess they did. But how? You had a contract."

"Unfortunately, there was a contingency clause that stated if someone made a cash offer, our agreement would be rendered null and void. We never, ever, expected someone to cough up half a million dollars for a rundown house and the accompanying acreage. Our attorney approached Elsbeth to see if she would be willing to sell us a portion of that acreage so we could establish vineyards for our winery. Needless to say, she refused."

"That's terrible."

"Elsbeth Waters knew all along we were vying for that property, and she literally stole it from us. Of course, that didn't stop us from continuing to approach her from time to time on the off chance she'd have a change of heart, but that never happened. Well, enough about Gable Hill Winery. How are you doing? Are you settled?"

"Oh, yeah. I'm fine. I really like our tasting room staff and I know Franz is a topnotch winemaker. Too bad John's leaving in a year. Of course, that will be Francine and Jason's problem when they get back."

"I thought they had an assistant vineyard manager poised to take over."

"Oh, they do. But between you and me, I think he's somewhat of a jerk. Overly sure of himself and all that."

"Good looking?"

"A ten out of ten."

"Ugh. They're the worst kind."

We both laughed and Stephanie poured me another cup of coffee. "Elsbeth Waters may have hurt us financially, but I think there was something really fishy going on between her and Madeline Martinez."

"Fishy how?"

"On more than one occasion, when I took Billsburrow Hill to get to Route 14 and Tops Market, I saw Elsbeth's car in her driveway. Not the winery. The driveway on the left, to the house. Now what would Elsbeth be doing there?"

"Complaining?"

"I don't think so. Her complaints were like microwave popcorn. Three minutes or she'd self-destruct. I'd see her car on my way up the hill and at least forty or fifty minutes later on my return trek. Something was going on, but I never got up the nerve to ask Madeline. Now, it would seem like an accusation."

For you, maybe, but not me, if I can figure out how. "I see what you mean. By the way, what can you tell me about Declan Roth from Vanna Enterprises? He wants to meet with me."

"Declan Roth? He must be the other partner. I've only met Lucas Stilton and it was bone chilling."

"He's that horrible?"

"Oh no. Nothing like that. He's good looking, eloquent and extremely polite."

"I'm lost."

"I'm not sure how to phrase this so I'll just spit it out. When I met him, it felt as if he was undressing me with his eyes. He never laid a hand on me, never said anything off-color or the least bit inappropriate, but there *was* something. A feeling I had that he was looking at me stark-raving naked."

"Oh my God!"

"He stopped by our winery to introduce himself and tell me about Vanna Enterprises. When he left, I felt as if I needed a cigarette and I don't even smoke." Stephanie stopped for a moment, looking at me. "Are you okay? You look as if you've seen a ghost."

"I hope that, if I do meet with Declan Roth, he doesn't bring his partner along."

"If you *do* meet with him, meet in a public place, preferably with a friend. Those men can be very manipulative, and they'll do anything to fulfill their agenda for that mega-winery. Don't let them unnerve you."

"Thanks for the warning. Too bad it's summer. It sounds as if I should be layering up in ski gear."

I thanked Stephanie for her hospitality and headed home. If I was lucky, I'd be able to get in a few hours of writing before my brain turned to mush. Then I could always pester the tasting room staff.

Chapter 15

Port of Call was absolutely packed when I got there a few minutes after seven. I elbowed my way through their long indoor bar and maze of bistro tables until I reached the deck. Theo wasn't kidding when he said the place was popular. Seneca Lake had a number of restaurants with boat docks when I was growing up, but they were mainly rustic in nature and their top culinary delight was usually a burger. Things had certainly changed.

I was staring at a chalkboard menu at the entrance to the deck and I was flabbergasted at the appetizer column. Lobster salad on kale, toasted asiago cheese straws, brioche rounds with goat cheese, shrimp canapes, nachos with Kobe beef and cheese and firecracker rolls with assorted fillings. The soups blew me away, too. Four different kinds of clam chowder and one spicy seafood chowder.

"Norrie! We're over here!" Don shouted from across the deck. I don't know how he and Theo managed it, but they were able to get us a table at the far end with a fabulous view of the lake.

"Wow. Looks like all the tourists decided to convene here, huh?"

"It's always packed," Don said. "Especially in the summer and fall. Then, when it's winter, we've got the whole place to ourselves. Did you check out their gigantic fireplace?"

"No, I skirted through the bar trying not to knock into anyone."

"Hope you don't mind but we ordered a sampling of appetizers. They should be here any minute."

He waved a waitress over to take my drink order and then leaned back.

"Geez," I said, "it feels as if I haven't talked to either of you in ages and it's only been a few days but so much has happened."

Don sat bolt upright in his chair and scanned the deck. "It looks like mainly tourists here, but you never know. Ever since Elsbeth's murder, I've had this unsettling feeling that I'm being watched."

"I can pretty much guarantee you're not," Theo said. "It's that wild imagination of yours, that's all. Anyway, let's let Norrie bring us up to date."

Francine and Jason had told me that Theo and Don could definitely be trusted. The four of them had been close friends for over five years and knew how to keep each other's confidences.

"I'll give you the abbreviated version," I said. "Not in any particular order. Declan Roth, one of those unscrupulous developers, sent me flowers. Wants to have lunch with me this coming week. I met with Stephanie Ipswich. Elsbeth gave her the royal screw job and bought the Tyler place out from under her. I chatted with Catherine Trobert. She wants to fix me up with her son. Yuck. And I found out Madeline Martinez was playing hostess to Elsbeth on more than one occasion. Oh, and did I say I talked with the niece? Seems nice enough but I'm sure she's hiding something."

Theo took my wrist and gave it a slight squeeze. "Whoa, slow down. How did you meet Declan Roth to begin with?"

"Forget Declan Roth," Don said, "I want to know more about Madeline and Elsbeth."

Just then our waitress appeared with my soda and a tray of steaming appetizers. All conversation ceased as we stared at the feast in front of us.

"Can I get you something from our main menu?" she asked. "Or maybe a soup."

"I'll have a bowl of your Cajun clam chowder," I said.

"Make that two," Don added.

Theo opted for a shrimp Caesar salad and the waitress nodded before she took off.

For the next fifteen minutes, between bites of firecracker rolls and stuffed mushrooms, I went on and on about Glenda's idea to smudge the tasting room and my latest conversation with Deputy Hickman. Theo and Don were kept apprised of every single thing. Except one. My theory to catch the killer.

"I've got to admit," Don said, "that was pretty darn clever of you to list a Mercedes as one of the winery vehicles."

I all but gleamed. "Yeah. I'm banking on the fact the tire prints will be a match with the kind of tires those cars have."

Theo scrunched his nose and shook his head. "I hate to break it to both of you but, like any other car, that Mercedes coupe could have the same kind of tire—Michelin, Continental, Hankook…"

Don gave his partner a funny look. "How do you know so much about tires?"

"Because I'm the one who always gets stuck at the garage for repairs."

"Hey, don't look so dejected, Norrie," Theo said. "The sheriff's department wouldn't be interested in tire tracks if they didn't think it was a good start. But they could've saved themselves some time if they asked all of us to write down what kind of tires are on our cars."

Don let out a laugh. "Hell. I don't even know that."

Theo groaned. "The name's usually on the side, above the rim. And you've given me a terrific idea. I'm going to snoop around the parking lots and see just what kind of tires everyone's got on their vehicles."

I couldn't believe it but we had scarfed up the appetizers and were now devouring our soups, or in Theo's case, his salad.

"I don't really feel like ordering a full meal at this point," Don said, "but I sure could go for their fried clam strips."

"My God. I can't believe I'm saying this," I said, "but me, too."

"Fine. When the waitress comes back we'll put in an order. You in, Theo?"

"Oh hell yes."

By the time we had eaten the last morsel of our meal, I felt confident enough to let Don and Theo in on my plan to trap Declan Roth. True, I had skimpy evidence, only a shared floral arrangement with Elsbeth and my assumption his was the car that drove through our woods with her body, but still…I was certain he and his partner were the ones responsible for the murder.

"Are you nuts?" Theo said. "I can't believe you'd even consider doing such a thing. It's beyond dangerous. It's, it's—"

"Insane?" Don's voice went one decibel louder. "You could lose everything. Listen, it's one thing to go snooping around gathering information, but it's another to put your winery at risk."

"I wouldn't exactly be putting it at risk. I'd be giving the impression I was willing to put it at risk. I wouldn't actually go through with it."

Don kept shaking his head. "It's still dangerous. Besides, how do you know it wasn't someone else who killed Elsbeth? Maybe you should give the county sheriff's department some time to complete their investigation."

"Come on. They didn't even think about asking us for the brand of our tires. I don't really have a whole lot of confidence in them."

"I see your point, but I still think you should wait. At least about this. But nothing says you shouldn't be looking into the other possibilities. In fact, Theo and I will poke around, too."

"Huh?" Theo looked as if Don had suggested they join the Foreign Legion, if that sort of thing still existed.

Don must have noticed the expression on Theo's face, too. "What I'm saying is, we'll use our contacts to ask questions, look for connections, that's all."

"Oh," Theo said. "For a minute you had me scared. You mean, do the usual busybody stuff you're famous for."

"Very funny. Hey, before I forget, I'll have our vineyard manager give John a call to see if he needs any help roping off your vineyards. I'm sure we can spare a few guys. I couldn't imagine what was going on the other day with all those cars."

"Thanks. I really appreciate it. Is it my imagination or are people getting weirder each day? Like everyone's fascination with crime scenes and dead bodies. I mean, I could understand if it was near Halloween, but it's the end of June."

"People have a morbid sense of curiosity," Theo said. "Too bad they don't respect boundaries. At least they didn't wreak havoc on your vineyards traipsing about."

"Thankfully, no."

It was a quarter to nine and the sun was setting. Had we been on the east side of the lake, we would've been dazzled by it. As it was, the sky turned different hues of pinks, mauves, yellows and blues before calling it quits.

"Before we head out," Don said, "I have to commend you. You've had one hell of a time since you got here and you're still in one piece. I thought maybe Glenda's smudging idea would put you over the edge, but from what you told us, you handled it well."

"Actually, Theo handled it well. I used one of his lines and it worked. The tasting room staff at Two Witches is, well, unique. Lizzie's a regular Nancy Drew buff, Glenda is a throwback to the nineteen-sixties and who knows what's with Roger and Sam. At least Cammy seems normal."

Theo and Don exchanged glances and I bit my lower lip. "What? What do you know that you aren't telling me?"

"Have you had a chance to talk at any length with Roger?" Theo asked.

Please don't tell me he's got some bizarre habit like yodeling at dawn. "Only the usual formalities. Why?"

"Whatever you do, do not, and I repeat, do not get him started on the French and Indian War. He'll never shut up. He did his dissertation on it long before either of us was born and it's a passion of his."

"I don't think you have to worry. It's not as if I'm going to bring that up." *Because History wasn't one of my strong suits.*

"You don't have to bring it up. He'll find a way to link it to anything you say. I'm right, aren't I, Don?"

Don nodded and shuddered as Theo went on. "Our combined tasting room staffs were at a symposium at Cornell a few years ago and someone mentioned wineries in the Ohio River Valley. Next thing we knew, Roger shouted out, 'Were you aware the French and Indian War began over the issue of whether or not the Ohio River Valley belonged to the French or the British?' Before any of us could catch a breath, Roger relived battles, troop strategies and God knows what else. None of us could think straight for the remainder of the day."

"I'll be sure to avoid the subject."

Suddenly Don leaned into the table and whispered, "Speaking of avoidance, look who just walked in. Don't stare. Act nonchalant."

I saw a strikingly handsome man in his late forties or maybe even early fifties walk toward a table at the other end of the deck. It was getting darker and, in spite of the candle-lit sconces on our tables, I couldn't make out who was seated there.

"Who am I looking at?"

"The other half of Vanna Enterprises," Don said. "Lucas Stilton."

In a flash I remembered everything Stephanie had told me about him and my face warmed thinking about it. Other than meandering over to the other side of the deck for no reason, there was nothing I could do to find out who he was seeing.

"He's probably putting the screws to some poor unsuspecting winery owner," Theo said.

The three of us sat almost motionless, with the exception of occasionally nursing our drinks.

"I wish there was a way to find out," I said. And then, as if providence was on my side, a waiter lit the torch behind that table and I caught a glimpse of someone standing up to shake Lucas's hand. It was a woman with short brown hair and a white shrug sweater over a sundress. No one else appeared to be at the table.

"I've got a bird's eye view," I said. "He's meeting a woman. A brunette."

"That narrows it down," Don said before Theo shushed him. "What? I'm as curious as Norrie."

We continued to sit for a few more minutes and I was reminded of James Stewart, Grace Kelly and Thelma Ritter in *Rear Window*. All we lacked was the binoculars.

"Well, this isn't getting us anywhere," I said, "because— Oh my gosh. He's getting up to leave. Quick. Act natural. Laugh or something."

Don and Theo made small talk as I kept my eyes glued to Lucas. He was only feet away from our table as he exited the deck and presumably, the restaurant.

I tried to keep my voice low. "What do you suppose that was all about?"

Theo whispered back. "Not what, *who*. Someone else is joining the woman at the table."

All we could make out was a man's silhouette. Shorter than Lucas and a wee bit stockier. The three of us tried to get a better look when we stood to leave but it was impossible. The man had his back to us and the woman's face was in the shadows. Damn it. Why couldn't she lean into that candle sconce like they did in all my screenplays?

Then my mind raced into gear. I'd seen that hairdo before. It was a wedge cut and if I wasn't mistaken, Madeline Martinez wore the same style.

Chapter 16

"Are you one hundred percent sure it was Madeline?" Theo asked when we got to our cars.

"I wouldn't swear to it in a court of law but honestly, it sure did look like her—slender brunette with a wedge haircut. That's not a style everyone can pull off. I don't know about you guys, but my suspicion meter is going up. Especially after what Stephanie told me."

Don turned around and glanced at the restaurant. "I could always go back inside and pretend I forgot something."

Theo shook his head. "What? What could you have possibly forgotten? Besides, it might look too obvious."

"Theo's right," I said. "Since I'm the newbie around here, the ladies seem pretty amenable to having me over for coffee. I'll get Madeline to do the same and go from there."

"As long as you don't do the other thing you mentioned. You know. That plan of yours to trap Declan Roth. Promise us you'll let it ride for a while."

I could sense the sincerity in Don's voice. "All right. I'm not making any promises except this one—if I decide to go through with it, I'll let you know ahead of time. Okay?"

"I suppose," he said.

"Uh, before we call it a night, I have a question for you. Francine mentioned someone playing not so nice pranks on the wineries and I wondered if that was still going on. I haven't noticed anything but that doesn't mean it's not happening elsewhere."

Don and Theo looked at each other before Theo spoke. "Not in a while. It was really crazy a few months ago, but things seemed to have died down. To be honest, I'd rather put up with those idiotic shenanigans than having a dead body appear in one of our vineyards."

"Ditto for me."

We said good night and agreed to go out again soon. Don mentioned a really neat restaurant on Keuka Lake that served the best Jamaican jerk chicken and I told him I was in. When I got home, Charlie was curled up in his usual spot in the kitchen. The moment he saw me, he bumped me and walked to the pantry door where his food was stored.

"You've got my number, don't you, buddy?"

His eyes got wide as he waited for me to pour some kibble in his bowl. That done, I headed upstairs to my comfy queen-size bed. Unfortunately, no matter how hard I tried, I couldn't get to sleep. Usually when that happened I'd find something really boring to read and next thing I'd know, I was out like a light. I went downstairs into the den to see if Francine or Jason had anything that would fit the bill.

The two of them had stashed lots of novels on the bookshelves, but they all looked too interesting for what I wanted. I needed something that shouted "boredom personified." Jason's desk was in the far corner and I decided to see if he had anything that might suffice. Lots of reference books on insects but they seemed so creepy I knew I'd only succeed in keeping myself up all night. I'd attribute every itch, twitch or sensation that came my way to some bloodsucking insect that was lurking underneath the sheets. Nope, no entomology books for me.

I was about to call it quits when I noticed a copy of the *Cornell Agricultural Experiment Station's Annual Report*. It screamed "deadly." An initial perusal verified my assumption. I was about to walk off with it in tow when I saw another smaller booklet. It was entitled *Applying for Federal Capacity Funds*. Who needed Ambien when lots of financial figures and gobbledygook could render the same result?

Charlie was already nestled with his head on my pillow and I had to shove him off to the other side of the bed so I could get in. The dim light from the small lamp on my nightstand was fine for reading all about funding cycles, research and extension priorities, guidelines for applicants and eligibility requirements. Dear God. If I were Jason, I would've poked my eyes out with a fork.

Next, I picked up the annual report. Apparently there were layers and layers of donors. Corporations. Societies. Foundations. Individuals. Couples. I read through the list, hoping my eyes would blur over and I'd fall asleep. Some names were actually familiar like Leona Helmsley and Bill and Melinda Gates. Charlie snored and I was glad at least one of us was getting some sleep. I kept reading. Then, without warning, a name bounced out at me under the "individual male" designation—Lucas Stilton.

It had to be him. How many Lucas Stiltons were there? The footnote on the bottom of the page indicated readers could learn more by going to the university's philanthropic website. I all but shoved the dog off the bed in my rush to run downstairs and boot up the laptop. An hour and a half later, after exhausting every possible search imaginable, I had the answer I needed. Well, one of them.

The generous donor, aka Lucas, had specified where his money was to go. In no uncertain terms, it was directed to the Experiment Station's entomology department and specifically to the research of new insect strains in Costa Rica. It didn't take a rocket scientist to put two and two together. When someone donated that kind of money, they were either extremely altruistic or they wanted something in return. In Lucas's case, I was certain it was the latter. I was willing to bet money Lucas Stilton arranged for Jason Keane to land that stupid grant so he'd be out of the country for a year. Enough time for Lucas and Declan to put the pressure on me.

It was no secret I had an undividable half interest in Two Witches Winery, along with my sister and brother-in-law, who shared the other half between them. In their absence, all financial and other decisions regarding the winery, its operation and wine distribution would go to me. Lucas and his partner must've known that all along. Thanks to social media, no one's life could remain hidden.

I shut down the computer and trudged back upstairs. If all Vanna Enterprises wanted to do was coax me into selling them the winery, then why would they go to all of this trouble to get Francine and Jason out of the way? At least it was a temporary fix for them. Not like Elsbeth. More than ever, I needed to go through with my plan. But now, given the extent of what I had learned, I had to be absolutely, positively certain I could pull it off. Maybe Theo and Don were right. Maybe I needed to wait a few more days to see if the sheriff's department could link Declan's car to the murder.

In the meantime, I could concentrate on Madeline and whatever she was hiding when it came to Elsbeth. When I opened the door to my bedroom, Charlie was still sleeping but I nearly gagged on the smell. Cammy was right. The dog did pass gas. I went back downstairs and, oddly enough, fell asleep right away on the couch.

I awakened to sloppy, smelly dog kisses on my face and stumbled into the kitchen to feed the hound. Then it was my turn for food. I was about to pour myself some cereal when I realized I was out of milk. Not only that, but out of eggs, too. I splashed some water on my face, brushed my teeth, fixed my hair and changed into jeans and a top before getting into the car and driving to Wegmans.

The aroma of freshly baked breads and pastries hit my nostrils the second I walked into the supermarket. The heck with cereal. I made a beeline to their bakery, took the nearest bistro chair and ordered a large coffee with a giant chocolate muffin. Bite after bite, I was in ecstasy. So absorbed I didn't hear the woman's voice calling my name. Not at first anyway.

"Norrie? Is that you? I thought it was."

"Mrs. Marbleton, hi!"

"Oh, call me Rosalee. Everyone else does."

She took the chair next to mine and placed a large almond croissant on the table. "I'll be right back. They're still making my latte."

It was tough enough getting used to calling Mrs. Trobert Catherine, but Rosalee Marbleton was old enough to be my grandmother. And she looked the part, too. Short gray hair styled to perfection, wire-rimmed glasses and more than her share of love handles. She was the quintessential grandmotherly type.

"It's nice running into you," I said. "I haven't really been out and about too much." *Other than the occasional trip to Vanna Enterprises in Penfield or dinner on the lake.*

"That's certainly understandable. Forgive me for not calling you after hearing about that grim discovery in your vineyard. It's unforgivable. Not Elsbeth's death. Me. It wasn't right. I should've called. The truth of the matter is, I didn't quite know what to say. I didn't want to sound like one of those busybodies looking for gossip and I'm afraid that's what you would have thought. Anyway, please accept my apologies."

"You have nothing to apologize for. Honest."

Rosalee smiled and patted my hand. "That's very sweet of you. I hope Elsbeth's murder hasn't discouraged visitors from your winery."

"Quite the opposite. If they could create a bus tour, it would be a sellout."

"Honestly, I'll never understand people. This region offers splendid vineyards and award-winning wines and what does the public want? To see where someone found a dead body."

"I know. Gruesome, huh?"

"If you ask my opinion, I think it was the niece who killed her. Have you ever met that girl? Very strange. Even by today's standards. Elsbeth must've pushed her over the edge with all that work at the B & B. I think the poor girl simply snapped and gave the old aunt a slug with the nearest heavy object."

"How did you—Oh, that's right. The news."

"The TV commentators said it was blunt force trauma to the head and yesterday's paper called it a murder. Did the deputies share any titillating tidbits with you?"

Titillating tidbits? Dear Lord. "Uh, no. I'm getting the mushroom treatment."

"The what?"

"They keep me in the dark and feed me B.S."

Rosalee laughed. "So you don't have any idea what the murder weapon was?"

"None whatsoever. But I do have an idea of the time of death— somewhere between nine and ten the night before."

"What station were you listening to? WHAM didn't mention time of death."

"Um, I'm not sure. Channel 12 I think."

I couldn't believe I was babbling so freely with Rosalee. For all I knew, she could've been the one who made Elsbeth see stars. Although I seriously doubted it.

"Nine and ten, eh? Real easy for the niece to do the deed, especially if Elsbeth was already in the car. Did anyone think of that? A whack to the head and that was that! All the niece needed to do was dump the body. Domestic violence is a leading cause of death in the United States. Were you aware of that?"

"Uh, no."

Rosalee took a bite out of her croissant and washed it down with a sip of her latte. Maybe she had a point. About them being in the car. Then again, the logistics didn't make sense. I leaned my chin on the palm of my hand and looked directly at her. "If Elsbeth was behind the wheel, they would've crashed or, at the very least, veered off the road into a ditch. These hills have deep gullies on the sides."

"Maybe the niece was driving."

"Still a little difficult, don't you think, for someone to be driving and then reaching over to clock the person in the passenger seat?"

"What if there was an accomplice? Someone in the backseat who did the nasty deed?"

"Who? From what I've been told, Elsbeth kept to herself. Yvonne, too. That's the niece's name. And yeah, you're right. I did meet her and she was rather standoffish. But that might be explainable under the circumstances. It was right after her aunt's body was discovered."

"I still think it's the niece. Maybe by the time I get back from Alaska the murder will be solved. My flight to Seattle is tomorrow. That's why

I came in here. To pick up my prescriptions at the pharmacy and some odds and ends."

"Alaska? You're flying to Alaska?"

The way Rosalee said it took me totally off guard. All I could do was stare at her while she went on and on.

"Can you believe it? I'm still pinching myself. All my life I've wanted to visit the Glaciers and Denali National Park. And now it's finally happening. The vacation of a lifetime and to think, I won it!"

"You won it? Holy cow! What contest? Or was it the lottery?"

"This is so embarrassing, really, but for the life of me, I can't even remember entering that sweepstakes contest. Of course, I've entered so many over the years but this is the first time I won anything."

The last thing I felt like doing was to burst that happy little bubble of Rosalee's but the only word that came to my mind was scam. What if it *was* a scam and she fell for it? Did she pay money upfront and will she get to the airport only to learn her ticket was bogus? I bit my lip and cringed. "Are you sure the sweepstake's legitimate?"

"Absolutely. The company—some name with a bunch of initials—went through the local travel agent here in Geneva. My granddaughter, who lives in Ithaca, is joining me for a three-week cruise and an interior tour of Alaska's major attractions. Everything's been totally paid for, including the gratuities. I feel as if I'm in a dream."

"How did you find out?" I asked.

"From the local travel agent. She called to tell me that I'd won this sweepstakes and needed some information so she could make the arrangements. The company works directly through the travel agencies."

"So you handled it on the phone?"

"No. I drove directly to the agency and sat down face-to-face with Bonnie Frisk, the agent. She was the same one who booked a flight for my husband and me two years ago so we could visit his family in Cleveland. I'm glad we went because he passed away a few months later."

"I'm sorry. About your loss."

"Thank you. Listen, I know what you must be thinking but don't. I didn't fall for one of those scams. In fact, I had my attorney check the whole thing out."

"Oh my gosh. I'm really happy for you. But over three weeks? That's a long time to be gone from your business."

"Not three weeks, more like four and a half. I made temporary arrangements for my sister, Marilyn Ansley, who lives in Penn Yan, to oversee the operation. The most she'll have to do is pay any unexpected bills and take care of the corgis. It'll give her something to do other than gossip with her friends at the senior center. As far as winery operations go, I can trust my managers to make sure things are running smoothly. Besides, Marilyn owns the vineyard's land. About time she did something."

"The land?"

"That's right. My parents' trust left Marilyn the land and me the winery. At that time it was only a small building, no bigger than a garage. Marilyn didn't want any part of the business but I had just gotten married and my husband, who was a farmer, thought running a winery would be perfect for us. As things turned out, he was right. We put a lot of sweat equity into the place. Marilyn better not screw it up. She'll be in charge of all the decisions for the month."

Gee, where have I heard that before? I took another sip of my coffee and debated buying another cup but at that moment Rosalee stood and excused herself.

"I'd love to stay and chat with you, dear, but I've got so many things to do today. I'll send you a postcard from Denali. Or someplace in Alaska. We'll be off the beaten trail for part of the excursion. Anyway, I'll be back in time for the "Sip and Savor." Send my regards to your sister when you hear from her. Tsk. Tsk. Costa Rica. Exotic bugs. Not my idea of a pleasant trip. Well, to each his own."

"Nice seeing you Mrs. Marbleton. Have a good time."

"It's Rosalee. And I will! I most certainly will!"

I watched as Rosalee Marbleton strode toward the pharmacy. An odd feeling came over me and, for a brief second, I shivered. I couldn't prove anything but it seemed more than coincidental she "won" that trip to Alaska. Same way Jason secured his study grant at the last minute? If Vanna Enterprises was behind all of this, I froze at the thought of what they might do next. Theo and Don wanted me to wait and be cautious but maybe that was what got Elsbeth killed. Maybe she knew too much.

Then there was Yvonne. Was she the scheming little wench who killed her aunt or an unwitting victim herself? The more I thought about it, the more it began to sound like one of my screenplays. I stood, tossed my empty coffee cup in the trash and proceeded down the aisle to buy milk and eggs.

Chapter 17

The entire situation seemed more than coincidental. First, Elsbeth out of the way for good, then Francine and Jason in a Costa Rican rainforest for a year and now Rosalee Marbelton "off the beaten path" somewhere in Alaska. It was way too contrived for my liking. It felt as if all of us in these little wineries were links in a chain and Vanna Enterprises was going to find the weakest ones and take advantage. That awful line from *The Godfather* played over and over again in my head as I drove home. *Make you an offer you can't refuse.*

Yvonne was all but ready to throw in the towel when I spoke with her right after the incident. She told me there had been an offer from a winery to buy the B & B and I knew it had to be Vanna Enterprises. In fact, I warned her to steer clear of them until I had a chance to talk with her again. Now she had to be told the truth—that Lucas and Declan most likely were the ones responsible for her aunt's murder—even though the sheriff's department hadn't reached that conclusion yet. Vanna Enterprises needed the property and knew Elsbeth was so obtuse and stubborn, she'd never sell it. Even if they offered her a generous deal. Yvonne, on the other hand, would be darn pliable.

If I didn't have milk and eggs in my car, I would've driven straight over to Peaceful Pines to tell Yvonne what I'd learned about Jason's grant and Rosalee's unexpected vacation. Instead, I went home, intending to phone her the second I got in the door. Too bad I was sidetracked on my way up the driveway.

On the left, Peter, Robbie and Travis were fast at work installing mesh barriers in front of the vineyard rows. Up ahead of them, in another part of the vineyard, I saw a few more workers. Peter waved me over and I rolled my window down.

"Hi. How's it going? I didn't expect to see you working on Saturday."

Peter took a few steps forward. In the early morning sun, with light beads of sweat on his brow, he really looked smoking hot. I tried not to think about it because the last thing I needed was to complicate my life.

"My schedule's flexible," he said. "Besides, we're almost done with this project. Not bad for starting it two days ago. John's way up the hill by the Riesling and the Grey Egret sent over a few men early this morning. That's them, in the Chardonnay section. All of us have been busting our chops."

"Wow. Guess it paid off. Thanks." *And thank you, Theo and Don.* "Will the barriers work?"

"If nothing else, it'll make the tourists think twice before entering the rows. Say, any news about the investigation? Did the sheriff's department find any more clues?"

I shrugged. "Not since our meeting the day before and if they did, I seriously doubt they'd share that information with me. As far as they're concerned, we're all suspects."

"You'll let us know if you hear anything, won't you?"

"Sure. Have a good day."

By the time I'd put the milk and eggs away and picked up the phone for the Peaceful Pines, I got their answering machine. It was Yvonne's voice and I left her a message to call me. I was about to open my laptop and pick up where I left off on my screenplay when the landline rang.

"Hello. Am I speaking to Jason Keane's sister-in-law? This is Godfrey Klein. I work in the same department as Jason."

"Oh my God! Has something happened?"

My mind flooded over with horrific images that would rival Dante's *Inferno.*

"Everything's fine. Spectacular, really. The team has already spotted the Culex aegypti and the Culex albopictus, but, of course, you probably know that last one by its common name."

"Uh, er, um…"

"Anyway, we were able to hook up on a satellite transmission but only for a few minutes. They wanted you to know they are fine."

"And that's it?"

"Well, they did provide us with information for the Global Invasive Species Database if you're interested, but I'd have to clear that first with my department head."

"No. That's not necessary." *Not in this lifetime. Not in any lifetime.*

I was about to thank him and hang up when I had a chilling thought. *What if someone told them about Elsbeth?*

"Um, Mr. Klein, Godfrey, when your department spoke with Jason, did they happen to tell him anything about, say, local events?"

"Goodness, no. It was a research call. We have to abide by certain parameters and that includes limiting the conversation to our findings."

The tension in my neck began to release and I took a deep breath. "That's wonderful. Wonderful. Nothing worse than government waste."

"How true. Anyway, I thought you'd like to know about their status."

"I did. I do. I appreciate it. If you reach them again, please let me know."

"Certainly. We expect to have monthly communiques."

"Okay, then. Thanks for calling. Have a nice day."

My heart was still pounding nonstop when I got off the phone, but I knew one thing—Francine and Jason were still in the dark when it came to the dead body in our vineyard. I poured myself a huge glass of iced tea and booted up my laptop. As much as I hated to admit it, Francine's kitchen table wasn't a bad place to work. The only sounds were birds and the occasional motorboat on the lake, unlike the ongoing cacophony outside my apartment. Endless honking of horns, the rumbling of traffic and, oh yes, expletives that came out of nowhere, usually accompanied by doors slamming.

At a little past one, I saved my file and made myself a toasted bagel with cream cheese. Charlie must've smelled it from somewhere outside because he bolted through his doggie door, looked at me and whined. I gave him a decent-size chunk and chastised myself for not following Francine's explicit feeding directions for him.

Satiated, I reopened my laptop and was about to get started again when the phone rang. "Norrie? This is Yvonne. I got your message. I was busy making up the rooms and running the wash."

"Yvonne, it's really important I talk to you. You haven't signed any agreements yet with any companies for your B & B, have you?"

"I wish I could. I'd pack up and leave right now. Have you ever watched *Beachfront Bargain Hunt* on HGTV? I want to relocate to Baja California. And I would, too, if I could ever get out from under here. But finalizing my aunt's estate is taking forever. Thank God the will didn't go into probate. And then there's her burial to deal with. The county didn't release the body to the funeral home until yesterday."

"You're having a funeral for her?"

"No. I'm saving myself the time and embarrassment. And money. No one would come. I'm having her cremated and I'll hold a small service for her in her hometown near Syracuse."

"Sounds like a very sensible idea. Listen, about the sale of your property... I can't prove it, but I really think those developers from Vanna Enterprises are responsible for your aunt's murder. Lucas Stilton and Declan Roth. They wanted Elsbeth out of the way so they could pressure you."

"Is that what the sheriff's department thinks, too? Because, as of this morning, they were still questioning me. That's why I had such a late start around the place today. Luckily I baked a frittata last night. It saved me time this morning when I had to prepare breakfast. Geez, if I could just hand these people a coupon for McDonald's, I'd do so."

"I don't blame you. I hate cooking. What did the deputies want?"

"Believe it or not, they came with a search warrant. They think my aunt's purse and cell phone are here. Duh. If I killed her, and I most certainly was not the one who did, I wouldn't be stupid enough to leave such telling evidence behind."

"I take it they didn't find anything."

"Nothing incriminating. Or useful, as far as their investigation goes. If you think it's those other guys, did you tell that to the sheriff's department?"

"I plan to. At some point. Not just yet. Anyway, don't turn over anything to them. No matter what kind of offer they make. Okay?"

"Like I said, the legal process is the hold up. Not me."

I couldn't get a yes or no from Yvonne, but I didn't blame her. Not really. She was thinking about what was best for her and if it meant some bargain hut in Mexico then so be it. The only option I had at this point was to go full steam ahead with my plan. Easy enough, except for one thing—I was the kind of person who had this insatiable need to have my ideas validated. Unfortunately, the two people whom I hoped would see the logic to my plan thought I would be taking a terrible, if not downright stupid, risk.

Maybe Cammy would see it differently. She struck me as being sensible and stable. The second I got off the phone with Yvonne, I called the tasting room and left a message for Cammy, asking if she'd please stay late for a few minutes so we could talk. That being done, I immersed myself in *A Swim Under the Waterfall*. Renee would be hounding me for the synopsis and, unlike those orderly, sequential writers who planned things out first, I worked by the seat of my pants. I wrote the screenplay and then did the synopsis. Come to think of it, I was that way in school, too. I had to write my papers first and then turn in the outlines.

It was Glenda's day off, so I was safe as far as séances, ritual cleansings and smoke-filled smudgings were concerned. Too bad I had forgotten about Lizzie. Or Roger, for that matter. It was a little past four and I was starving.

"Psst! Psst! Norrie! What have you found out so far from those winery women?" Lizzie called.

I looked around to make sure no one was in earshot. Cammy, Roger and Sam all had customers at their tasting tables and everyone was caught up in their own chatter.

"Uh, not as much as I'd like. Rosalee Marbleton thinks the niece did it, Catherine Trobert wants to fix me up with her son and Stephanie Ipswich thinks there was something fishy going on between Madeline Martinez and Elsbeth."

"What do you think?"

"I don't know. I haven't talked with Madeline."

"Hmm, I'd have to go back to my notes, but Nancy Drew was able to extract all sorts of information from suspects."

Nancy Drew is a fictional character! "I don't think that's necessary."

"What about the murder weapon? Did you look around their houses to see if anything was missing? Like a poker from a fireplace or a coal bin that didn't have a shovel."

"I didn't notice any coal bins or fireplaces."

Lizzie adjusted her glasses and spoke slowly. "If you expect to solve this case, you'll need to be more observant."

At that instant, two ladies approached the cash register and I let out a sigh of relief. "Catch you later, Lizzie!"

No sooner did I step away from the register when Roger called me over to his table. The two ladies were apparently his customers and now they were purchasing wine.

"Any luck with the investigation?" he asked.

I shook my head. "Everything seems to be moving slowly."

"Funny you should mention that. The same could be said for the first four years of the French and Indian War. At least as far as the British and the colonists were concerned. So many reversals. So many—"

"Oh look! Here come some customers!" I waved my hands wildly, motioning two couples to Roger's table. "You're going to enjoy our wines. This is Roger and he'll get you started."

My God. Theo and Don were right. Fanatic didn't come close when it came to that topic. I walked directly to the bistro, said hello to Fred and ordered a ham, turkey and bacon panini.

"Cammy told us about the request from the sheriff's department. No problem. I gave her our car information. FYI, last place I'd want to drive is in those woods. So many branches and briars. The car would get scratched."

Fred's comment reiterated what I had already concluded about Declan's car.

"Yeah, I know. They're just covering all their bases. It must be in their manual."

Fred laughed and started to make my sandwich. I took a seat at one of the tables and watched the people. A decent number of visitors that would keep growing until the late fall. As I perused the crowd, I thought about what Lizzie had said. About me not being observant. It irritated me to no end. I thought I was fairly observant. Especially at the Peaceful Pines when I noticed the vase with those flowers. Now I was beginning to wonder what I'd missed.

Of course, Lizzie was right about one thing. I never did pursue Stephanie's observation about Elsbeth's car in front of Madeleine's place, but that didn't mean Madeline was the only one who could shed some light on the subject. I grabbed my phone and dialed Yvonne for the second time that day.

"Yvonne? Hi! It's Norrie again. Look, I know I spoke to you a couple of hours ago but I forgot to ask you something. Was your aunt friends with Madeline Martinez?"

"What? Elsbeth friends with one of the winery owners? No way. What makes you think that?"

"Uh, well, I've been asking around and I found out through the grapevine... "—*Gee, how much more lame can I get with this excuse?*— "your aunt's car was often seen at Madeline's place."

"That's ridiculous. Wherever you heard that, it was wrong. Elsbeth never paid social calls. Complaints, maybe, but not social calls. And trust me, her complaints were short and to the point. Like stab wounds. I should know. She had a lot of them. Was that all you needed?"

"Yeah. For now. I was following up on something. It doesn't matter. Remember, whatever you do, don't agree to sell the property. Not yet."

"About that. I should've told you this the first time we talked. The people who made me an offer were willing to let me run the B & B for six months past the sales date. That way, the guests who had reservations wouldn't lose their vacations."

How very considerate of those leeches. "I see. But it's a bad idea. Not while the investigation is going on."

"Like I said, it's not up to me. Not until the will and all my aunt's finances are settled. Of course, nothing is stopping me from signing a pre-agreement."

"What? NO! Don't do that. Baja California's not going to sink into the Pacific Ocean. It'll still be there."

"Oh, I suppose you're right. Anyway, I've got more laundry to do."

"Oh, sure. I didn't mean to keep you."

I tapped the red end-call button and placed the phone on the table. Why would Stephanie tell me about Elsbeth's car being at Madeline's if it wasn't true? Unless Yvonne had no idea. After all, why would she? And another thing about Yvonne—Baja California. I'd watched *Beachfront Bargain Hunt* and, compared to the flood of islands in the Bahamas and the Caribbean, why would anyone want to live in Baja? Then again, Yvonne certainly was strange.

Suddenly the lights began to dim and I realized it was closing time. I got up and headed over to Cammy. She was wiping down her table and looked up when she saw me.

"Hey! Got your message. As soon as I'm done, we can chat. The crew's cleaning up in here and in the kitchen but we can talk in the bistro. It doesn't look as if anyone's in there."

"Great. I'll be at the far end by one of the windows. Plenty of daylight left."

I checked my e-mails, poked around Facebook and did a quick check of the weather before Cammy pulled up the chair directly across from mine.

"So, what's up? The message sounded urgent."

"I need to run something by you, that's all. And I need you to be really open-minded."

"Don't tell me Glenda's gotten to you."

"Yeesh. Nothing like that. We don't need to contact the spirits to find out who killed Elsbeth. I think I already know. What we need to do is to set a trap."

Cammy swallowed hard and clasped her hands together. "I'm listening."

"Declan Roth and his partner from Vanna Enterprises murdered Elsbeth. I can't really prove it but if my plan works, I can get them to admit it."

"Whoa. Slow down. Backtrack. Where's all of this coming from?"

I'd forgotten that as I kept acquiring information, I wasn't necessarily sharing it with everyone I trusted. In this case, Cammy. I took a breath and bit by bit revealed everything I knew. Then I presented my plan. She didn't say a word but her facial expressions kept changing. Like someone who was watching a horror movie. Her last grimace nearly frightened me.

"Come on," I said. "My idea's not that godawful."

"Awful, no. Dangerous, yes. You could put this entire winery out of business with one small mistake."

"I won't make a mistake. I won't sign a thing."

"What about verbal agreements? Sneaky people have a way of taping things without anyone knowing it."

"I'll be careful. Listen, those guys covered up their tracks pretty well. The sheriff's department isn't likely to make an arrest. Sure, all I've got is circumstantial evidence but—"

"I think what you've got is *coincidental* evidence. If there's even such a thing."

"All right. All right. Forget the semantics. Like I said, all I need to do is get them to admit to doing the deed. And what better way than to get them to believe I'm on their side?"

"When? How?"

"First thing Monday morning, I'm going to call Declan and tell him I've thought over his proposal for a mega-winery. He'll be chomping at the bit to meet with me. Then, well, you know. I'll lure him in."

"Geez, Norrie. You'd better watch it. If what you say is true about that company, they'll be doing the luring. Maybe I should go with you. Not that I'm giving your plan an endorsement but if things get out of hand, I could always kick you under the table."

"As much as I relish the thought of a bruised shin, you can't go with me. It might tip them off that I'm up to something. I have to go alone. Don't worry. I'll insist on a very public place and in daylight."

"Okay. Then I'll arrange to be at the table behind yours. Wherever you meet."

"It still won't work. Declan and his partner have been in this tasting room. They'll recognize you."

"Hmm, good point. But I know a few guys they won't recognize—my jerky cousins Marc and Enzo. They're bartenders at my parents' former bar and grill in Geneva. It's their summer job. They're juniors and they go back to college in the fall. They could keep an eye on you."

"I don't know…"

"Well, I do. Let me know the date, time and place and I'll get my cousins over there."

"How do you know they'll do it?"

"Oh, trust me, honey. They'll do it. I have enough dirt on both of them to last a century."

Chapter 18

The barricades seemed to be working in the vineyards. At least that was how it appeared to me when I stepped onto the porch the next morning to enjoy my cup of coffee and one of the muffins I bought yesterday. The visitors weren't traipsing through the rows of grapevines and people were walking in and out of the tasting room. A few people were standing in front of Alvin, and that reminded me of something I needed to do but hadn't gotten around to.

Alvin's pen was a nice-size rectangle off to the front of the building, but it also had a small path around the side that led to his little shack. The fencing was a combination of metal rods and wire mesh. Some of those rods looked like a good kick would knock them over. I wanted to mention it to John, just in case. Then again, Alvin didn't strike me as having a whole lot of energy when it came to knocking down fences. Still, better safe than sorry. I made a mental note to leave a message for John on Monday. One thing that was a relief, Jason made sure to install a motion sensor security system around the pen in case coyotes ventured that way. The high-pitched alarm would scare them off, but someone, mostly likely me, would have to shut it off right away before Alvin went berserk. It was a risk Jason was willing to take. Too bad he didn't wire the rest of the property.

As I sipped my coffee, I glanced across the driveway to that broad swath of area where Elsbeth's body had been discovered. She was found in the new part of the vineyards a few yards from the woods. And Charlie uncovered her plum-colored scarf in those woods. Somehow, this didn't add up. Why didn't her killer dump her in the woods? It would've saved them time and energy, not to mention it was unlikely she'd be found right away.

I took the last gulp of coffee and decided to take a closer look. Theo and Don were adamant I shouldn't go in the woods alone, but this was broad daylight on a warm summer's morning, not the middle of the night. Nonetheless, I pocketed my cell phone, making sure the battery was fully charged.

Charlie, who was fast at work licking his paws, looked up and decided to follow me. I hadn't walked around the far reaches of our property since I was a kid and, even then, I didn't stray too far. Other than the vivid memory I had of seeing Elsbeth's body lying on top of the new irrigation drip system, it was impossible to discern where it had been. Everything was back in place, the broken pipes had been fixed and the burgeoning Riesling vines were no worse for wear.

I stood in front of the spot and took in the surroundings. Woods on two sides and the open area where our other vineyards were. The logging road was directly behind to the west and could be accessed by Billsburrow Road and Rock Stream Road. The other wooded area, to the north, wasn't as dense. In fact, it wasn't really woods at all. Sure, there were trees but the land was mainly brush that consisted of wild berry bushes—raspberry and blackberry. Berries that Francine and I used to pick. As I remembered correctly, there were lots of openings between those bushes and if you didn't mind the occasional scratch, you could reach in and get really juicy berries. Today, however, berries were the last thing on my mind.

I skirted around the edge of the vineyard and walked directly to the brush barrier that separated our property from the land on the adjoining hill—Gable Hill. There was a vast expanse of land that was literally going to waste because the only purpose it served was to provide distance between Two Witches Winery and the Peaceful Pines.

Some of the bushes had gotten thicker over the years and newer branches seemed to poke out everywhere. But others had died and their rotting wood left crumbling pieces on the ground. I stepped over one of those dead bushes and took a good look at the other side of the property. Like ours, there was a worn vehicle path that bordered the woods. Unless the driver was willing to take a chance on unsteady, soft ground, he or she would need to hug the woods. Woods that were laden with overhanging branches and those godawful vines that sprang out of nowhere and grew like crazy.

From the looks of things, the vehicle path had been here forever. It was rutted and had acquired a number of small rocks and even larger stones. Maybe, at one point, the Tyler property was used as farmland, and farmers always had to maximize their space. I could see the Peaceful Pines in the distance and, in that second, I realized Elsbeth's dead body wasn't driven through the woods. It was driven on the vehicle path where I was standing. No wonder the killer didn't dump her in the woods. All they had to do was transport her down to the bushes and then, boom! Toss her onto our newly installed drip system.

In all fairness, they probably weren't aiming to destroy our irrigation piping; they were just in a hurry to lose a corpse. That would explain the blood on Elsbeth's chin and the shoulder of her jacket. She wasn't dead long enough to stop bleeding and she probably sustained those cuts from one of the berry bushes.

Declan wasn't off the hook yet. In fact, he was dangling precariously as far as I was concerned. No wonder his car had to be detailed. I'm surprised it hadn't needed an entire paintjob on the passenger side.

Disjointed thoughts were racing through my mind. Did he kill her first and then get rid of her car, and if so, then Yvonne had to be in on it. Or maybe not. I tried to remember the timeline she gave me. Elsbeth disappeared after dinner. That was around six. Yvonne watched TV afterward in her room and took a shower around nine. Oh yeah. And a pill for her migraine. She wouldn't have heard a thing. And, since it was late at night, the other guests were probably asleep, too, or even if they were awake, they didn't pay any attention to any noises that might've wafted their way. Besides, if they'd known anything, those deputies would've acted on it after they interviewed the guests.

It was quite conceivable that Elsbeth met with Declan and Lucas later that evening and when she returned to the B & B, they killed her, dumped the body in a hurry and, since they had her car keys, drove her car to the Walmart parking lot to make it look as if she'd been kidnapped.

Those two men had to be familiar with her property. Declan told me where they planned on building their lazy river and the Atlantis mega-complex. Real easy for them to skirt the edge of the woods and stash her in my vineyard. Equally easy to pull out a shovel from the trunk of one of their cars and whack her in the head. Heck, they'd didn't even need a shovel. A heavy rock would've sufficed.

I was so deep in thought I hadn't noticed Charlie rolling in something a few feet from me. Suddenly, he shook himself and grabbed whatever it was that made him stop and roll in the first place. It looked like a flattened purse and, for an instant, I was certain it had to be Elsbeth's. Then I took a closer look as Charlie spat it out. Ugh! It was a dead animal of some kind that had dried up and flattened out.

The odor, although not as pungent as the skunk, was enough to make me gag.

"I'm not giving you another bath!" I yelled as the dog darted through the bushes back to our property. Unfortunately, I didn't have a choice.

That hound had gotten used to sleeping with me and no way did I relish reeking of a petrified groundhog, squirrel or rabbit. That was the instant I realized two things–Charlie could very well have gotten that scarf from those bushes and then returned to our property via the woods. Or the scarf could've easily been blown into the woods. No big deal.

My second thought was more unnerving. That rutted road that edged the property also went all the way down the hill. All the way to Gable Hill Winery. What if Stephanie was the killer? Maybe a simple invite for some tea and cake or perhaps a late night dessert wine? Real easy for Elsbeth to drive down to Gable Hill, only to be knocked off by Stephanie and then thrown into our nearby vineyard. Stephanie could then drive Elsbeth's car to Walmart and leave it there. And oh, how very convenient since Stephanie's husband was in Watkins Glen for that overnight with the kids. Yep, it was possible. Stephanie could've called a cab for a ride home. The entrance to Walmart was a regular parking lot for taxis. No one would've been any wiser.

In the back of my mind, I wondered if maybe I shouldn't mention my latest epiphany to Deputy Hickman. Maybe it wasn't such a bad idea to check with local taxi service companies to see who they drove home from Walmart that night. Then again, he explicitly told me to butt out and that was what I intended to do. At least as far as the Yates County Sheriff's Department was concerned.

Aargh. I was really caught between the proverbial rock and a hard place. I decided to go through with my original plan because procrastinating wasn't an option. I had to prove Lucas and Declan were responsible for the murder since they had the strongest motive. And if I was wrong? Then I'd move to the next name on my list–Stephanie's. I'd figure out a way to get her to admit to murder.

My eyes scanned the huge field in front and the vineyards below. Stephanie was right about the location–the gentle slope was perfect for cultivating grapes. In the distance I could see Peaceful Pines and what appeared to be two people walking behind the building toward the edge of the property. No sense calling attention to myself. I followed Charlie's lead and made my way back to our land through the thicket of berry bushes.

I was about to congratulate myself for not getting cut when I felt a small sting on my calf. My jeans had acquired a new rip, rendering them even more fashionable. As for the scrape beneath it, it was too miniscule to worry about. I went back to the house and spent the rest of the day at my laptop. I didn't even bother to check in at the winery. From my vantage point on the porch, Alvin looked well-fed, cars were going in and out of the tasting room parking lot and the only tours taking place were with the college student guides we hired. Groups of ten, and no one in the vineyard rows.

My dinner consisted of canned chicken soup, a bag of pretzels and two apples. I figured one out of the three had to be healthy. I was adamant that *A Swim Under the Waterfall* was going to be delivered to Renee on time and with a minimum of errors. By quarter after seven, I decided if I had to write another line about someone's lips touching someone else's, I would puke. The last thing that had touched my lips was Alvin's spittle and I winced.

In the eight or so years I'd been living in the city, I had a few casual relationships and one near miss. The near miss ended amicably enough, but I wasn't ready for that sort of intimacy and commitment again. Not for a while anyway.

I stepped outside and took a deep breath. It was one of those warm summer nights that made people forget about the last time they had to shovel three feet of snow or scrape the ice off their windshields. I went back inside, made myself a big glass of iced tea and returned to the porch to craft a new screenplay, only this one was for real.

It was imperative I knew what I was going to say to Declan and exactly *how* I was going to say it. I had to convince him that I agreed with the vision he and Lucas shared and that I would be willing to sacrifice Two Witches Winery but only if I got something in return that was more than a monetary settlement. I had to become their third partner.

Line after line, explanation after explanation, I went at my presentation-slash-script as if Renee was standing over my head waving a deadline calendar at me. By the time it was dusk, I thought I had it figured out. I leaned back to enjoy the last sip of my third—or was it fourth—iced tea when a combination of no-see-ums, black flies and mosquitoes attacked my neck, arms and legs. In a matter of minutes, I had become a pincushion for every blood-sucking insect on Seneca Lake.

Apparently the dog was brighter. He'd left the porch a good half hour ago and was now sprawled out on the kitchen floor. I patted him on the head and headed straight for the shower. As the warm water washed over me, I practiced my lines as if I was about to appear on Broadway. I'd promised Theo and Don I'd give the sheriff's investigation some time, but holy geez! How much time did they need? The Fourth of July was coming up in another week and summer always seemed to fly by after that. Last thing this winery needed was to have an unsolved murder looming over us during the fall rush. Nope, I couldn't wait. I had to act.

Of course there was one more teeny little piece of the puzzle I didn't address and I had to admit, it kind of gnawed at me. The Madeline

Martinez–Elsbeth Waters relationship. What the hell *was* Elsbeth doing at Madeline's house? And Stephanie certainly couldn't be mistaken about the car. Not many people drove big clunker station wagons anymore. And Elsbeth's was a hideous shade of dark green, according to Stephanie, who said she had seen it on more than one occasion.

Yep, I'd have to have that chat with Madeline sometime soon. Maybe after my meeting with Declan. I shook the last bit of water from my head and dried myself off. Then I did something I'd meant to do all day but forgot—checked the answering machine for missed calls.

Drat! My parents. I knew I should've gotten back to them sooner. I picked up the receiver and placed the call. "Honest. There's no reason for you to make the drive up here. The sheriff's department should have this solved in no time."

Boy was I becoming one big liar!

My parents told me Francine e-mailed them and was ecstatic about the adventure. Hell, she could've been ecstatic here, too, what with all the bugs that had no problem drawing my blood. Too bad they weren't the Culex aegypti or whatever the heck those were!

I promised my dad I'd let him know if I couldn't handle anything or if, God forbid, another body showed up. Then I called it quits for the night and drifted asleep with Charlie at my feet. It was short-lived. The phone all but exploded in my ear. Don's voice.

"Norrie? Is Charlie inside? Make sure he's inside. The coyotes are out on a hunt. They're screaming and shrieking like mad. I'm surprised they didn't wake you."

No, you did.

"They must've killed something already."

"Uh, sure. Thanks for the heads-up."

Then Catherine Trobert from Lake View phoned. "I hope I didn't wake you. Just wanted to make sure you didn't decide to step outside. There's a pack of coyotes running around and they're screaming their heads off. You should be okay. Make sure your door's locked and your windows are closed."

I wanted to tell Catherine I seriously doubted a coyote was going to open my door with his mouth and let himself inside, but I thought better of it and thanked her.

Then, another call. This one from Yvonne. "Norrie? Is that you? Do you hear that screaming? It sounds like a woman's being murdered behind my house."

"It's not a woman. It's coyotes. They've made a kill. That's what they do. Or, one of them could be in heat. It's a similar sound. I'm not going outside to check. If your guests are still up at this hour, tell them to stay inside."

Thankfully Charlie was still fast asleep on my bed but I didn't want to take any chances. I trudged downstairs and pulled the plastic cover over his doggie door so he couldn't get out. Then I went back to bed and prayed no one else would disturb me.

Chapter 19

"So how will I recognize Marc and Enzo for this covert operation of mine?" I asked Cammy. It was Tuesday afternoon and I was ready to get moving on my plan. I had stopped into the tasting room on my way to the bistro for lunch. There were only so many frozen casseroles or bland sandwiches I could handle at home.

"Real easy. You can't miss 'em. They're your typical college frat boys who think they're God's gift to mankind. Don't get me wrong, they're neat guys and not bad looking, but they're in their early twenties and full of themselves. Both of them are on the tall side with dark hair. Marc's a bit more muscular but, side by side, they look alike, even though one of them is my aunt Angie's kid and the other one is Aunt Luisa's."

"You're sure they're going to be okay with this?"

"Oh yeah. No problem. Just need the time and place. Oh, and it has to be during the day before five. That's when their bartending shifts begin."

"Believe me, it will be during the day. At a heavily populated family restaurant. Got any ideas?"

"Sure. Tim Hortons, Panera Bread or The Bagel Barn on Hamilton Street. Those places all have Wi-Fi and everyone seems to mind their own business. Personally, I'd go for The Bagel Barn. The way it's set up, there's a barrier between the tables with lots of plants. Marc and Enzo could sit on the other side, virtually unseen, but they could overhear you."

"The Bagel Barn it is. I'm going to call Declan the second I get to the house and set up a time for this week. Then I'll phone you so you can let your cousins know. Tell them to look for a woman in her late twenties with auburn hair and freckles. I doubt they'll see my dimple. In fact, I'll make it easier. I'll wear one of our Two Witches T-shirts."

"Done. Hey, you sure you want to go through with this?"

"I'm sure. I think it's the only way I can get those developers to admit to Elsbeth's murder. Make them believe I'm as ruthless as they are."

My call to Declan went fairly well, considering he wanted us to dine at a more elegant spot than The Bagel Barn. I told him I didn't have time for a full sit-down meal but I really wanted to learn more about his proposal for the area, specifically the offer he intended to make for Two Witches. We agreed on Thursday afternoon at two.

Thank goodness I had a screenplay to deal with because I would've spent Wednesday biting off the tips of my fingernails. Other than running into Peter at the bistro on Thursday morning, I really didn't spend any time conversing with anyone. Peter asked again if I'd heard any news about the investigation and I shook my head.

"Not a blasted thing."

"You'd think by now they would've had a lead," he said.

"Not in this county. I think whoever's investigating isn't doing a thorough job."

The instant I said that, I regretted it because Peter wanted to know what I knew and I wasn't about to say anything regarding the berry bushes and my latest theory. I didn't need a new rumor mill to get started. "If they were doing a thorough job, they'd have made some progress by now. It's been almost two weeks."

We left it at that, except for some small talk about the vineyards.

By midday Thursday, the first small wave of panic came over me. What if I couldn't pull it off? What if I couldn't pretend to be callous and greedy? Then I thought about everything we had at stake here. And the other small wineries, too. Last thing any of us needed was to become the next Disneyland. I made myself an iced tea and focused instead on rehearsing my lines for the performance I was about to deliver at The Bagel Barn.

True to her word, Cammy arranged for her cousins to be there. They arrived a half hour earlier than my scheduled meeting time with Declan. I was already seated at one of the tables and made sure no one occupied the one adjacent to it by tossing a sweater on one of the chairs and putting a pile of napkins and plastic utensils in the middle. Marc walked in first, spotted me and went right for the table I'd commandeered. I knew it was Marc the minute he opened his mouth.

"Yo! En-Zo!" he yelled as his cousin walked in the door of the place. "I'm over here! Get me a Coke and one of those pepperoni bagels. I'll pay you as soon as you get over here. Don't want to lose the table."

I sat motionless and watched Enzo approach the counter to place the order. Cammy was right. He was cute. Same with Marc, but these guys

*****

were way too young for me. Not that I even gave that a thought. In front of me was the small coffee I'd ordered and I sipped it sparingly. From time to time, I glanced at the entrance for Declan but I had arrived early.

"Psst!" Marc whispered from behind me. "We've got you covered."

I turned sideways and peered through the leafy plants to respond. "Shh. Thanks. Whatever you do, please don't blow it. The man I'm supposed to meet will be here any second."

"No problem."

I kept my eyes firmly fixed on the door but no Declan. Not yet. I could hear Enzo's voice because it was the one that said, "You owe me seven forty-eight, dude."

People kept streaming in and out of the place and I figured I wouldn't have to wait much longer. Lifting the coffee cup to my lips, I took a long swallow. When I looked up, I was face-to-face with a well-built man in his late forties or maybe he'd just turned fifty, but that would be stretching it. Short-sleeved button-down sage shirt, light charcoal pants and wavy brown hair that didn't have a hint of gray. He moved closer, gave me a nod and smiled. It took a minute but I recognized where I'd seen him before—Port of Call.

He was, in a word, gorgeous. Older, but oh, so good-looking. His hazel-green eyes matched the shirt and I wondered... Contacts? No one's eyes could be that intoxicating. Then I took another look at his shirt – hand-tailored maybe? Quite the contrast from the flaming orange Two Witches Winery shirt I had on. I cringed.

"Miss Ellington? Norrie Ellington?"

"Uh-huh, that's me."

Without asking, he took the seat across from mine and reached out to shake my hand. "Forgive me. I'm Lucas Stilton, Declan's partner. Declan left you a message this morning on your phone. From the look on your face, I don't think you got it."

"No, I, um..."

"He tried your cell phone, too, but it went to voice mail."

Crap. Of all times not to check the answering machine or voice mail.

Lucas went on as if none of this mattered. "Declan got tied up at the last minute. He felt bad about it and asked if I'd step in. I was in the area anyway, so I thought it would be a good time for us to get acquainted. I believe I've already met your sister. Francine, right?"

"Uh-huh."

For some reason, my tongue, my vocal chords and anything else I needed in order to speak coherently seized up. In less than sixty seconds, this drop-dead gorgeous hunk of a man had turned me into a blithering fourteen-year-old. Marc and Enzo must've been watching from between the ferns and potted plants because the next thing I knew, Marc shouted, "Yo! Bro! Tell me again about that babe you met last night."

It was enough of a distraction for me to get my concentration back. Damn it, Stephanie was right. Lucas Stilton's smile could charm the skin off a snake. I hated to think what the rest of him could do. He hadn't even started talking and I'd forgotten the lines I rehearsed last night and this morning.

"Declan told me he showed you our plans for the area. This mega-wine complex we propose would put Seneca Lake on the global map."

He emphasized the word "global" and I opened my eyes wider.

"Oh," he said. "How absolutely crass of me. Let me buy you lunch or, at the very least, another drink. I was so exuberant about our project, I literally forgot my manners. It won't happen again, I assure you. So, what would you like? I haven't eaten so please order something. I don't want to be dining while you sit there with nothing but a cup of coffee."

"Um, fine. That would be nice. I'll have a toasted salt bagel with cream cheese and this time, an iced tea. I'm pretty much coffee-d out."

Lucas walked to the counter and Marc whispered between the plants. "Don't let that old dude talk you into anything."

Yeah. Real easy for you to say. I kept my voice low. "Don't worry, I've got it under control."

Just then Enzo made some sort of a chortling noise and I looked away. Lucas returned to our table with our drinks and told me the bagels would arrive in a few minutes.

"That's great. Thank you."

Lucas stretched his arms back. *Terrific. Now I can add broad chested to his list of physical attributes.* Then he leaned forward and looked directly at me. "It wouldn't be as if you or your sister were losing anything. Quite the contrary. Our offer to buy your winery is a generous one. You could open another such business along one of the other lakes, or you could join our venture by retaining your name and running a small winery kiosk inside our mega-plex. Of course, the wines would be produced by our company, not your existing one. Am I getting too far ahead for you?"

"No, I'm galloping along quite nicely."

"Good. Good. I understand that for the duration of a year, the business operations and all legal decisions are yours. Is that correct?"

I nodded. "It is."

At that second, the server placed our bagels in front of us and I caught a breath. I took a small bite out of the soft dough and took a closer look at Lucas's face. Some small crow's feet but my God! This guy was off the charts. So what if he was a good ten or fifteen years older than me. It didn't stop all those celebrities like Calista Flockhart or Shania Twain. Of course, I seriously doubted they met their future husbands while wearing a garish T-shirt and consuming a bagel.

Off to my left I heard Marc and Enzo coughing. It quickly put a stop to any ridiculous daydreams that flooded my mind. I was here to keep the family business intact and that was exactly what I intended to do.

"Mr. Stilton, I'm not interested in selling our winery and walking off into the sunset. What I have in mind is a proposal that would make all of our lives richer."

"Please. Call me Lucas. And go on. I'm listening."

"Okay, Lucas. Here goes. No one knows this winery business better than the people who've been running it for decades. From soil acidity to nuances in the fermentation process, we're familiar with it. What I'm proposing is to become your third partner."

At that moment, Enzo gasped, with Marc quickly covering for him. "That's what he said, man. Those exact words. What a horse's ass."

Lucas looked up and turned to the potted plants that separated our table from Cammy's cousins. "Next time we'll have to dine at a more refined place. Or a quieter one."

I took a breath and reiterated what I'd said. This time without my feet tapping on the floor. "The sale of Two Witches would provide enough equity for me to become your business partner. The top portion of the hill with only the house would more than get me in the front door."

"Get me in the front door?" Where did I come up with that idiotic cliché?

I'd watched enough TV dramas and written more than a few of my own to know what my next move should be. I picked up my glass of iced tea slowly and as I sipped, I kept my eyes wide open and fixed on his.

"You caught me by surprise, Miss Ellington. This wasn't at all what I expected. Was Declan aware of your intentions?"

I shook my head. "No, that's why I wanted to meet with him today."

"I see."

Lucas paused and didn't say anything for what seemed like an eternity. Meanwhile, I continued to sip my tea and take small bites of my bagel.

"You've made an interesting proposition, I must admit. Have you given it serious thought?"

"I wouldn't be here today if I hadn't. Your vision and Declan's will open an epicurean gateway to the east that will rival anything that's been done in the last decade. Finger Lakes wines will be world-renowned. I don't want to sit back and watch it unfold when I could be at the helm with both of you." *Whew! That was one line I remembered.*

"You do realize we take risks and we sometimes take actions that others might not understand."

Like murder? This might work after all. I've got to make him trust me. "I'm well aware of that. All great businesses have been known to be ruthless. But with good branding and even better PR, the public tends to forget."

"How right you are, Miss—"

"Norrie. And I hope you'll consider my proposal."

Lucas reached out to shake my hand again. "Let's meet again, you and me. Unless, of course, you're more comfortable with my partner."

"My first introduction to your company was with Declan and I feel it's only right to continue working with him. I hope you understand." *And I hope you understand I can't have anyone undressing me with their eyes or any of their other body parts, for that matter.*

"I do. You've given us quite a lot to think about. I'll be sure Declan reaches out to you by the weekend."

Like clockwork, Lucas's phone went off and he turned to excuse himself. I took another sip of my iced tea and glanced at the potted plants. No ruckus from Cammy's cousins.

"That was my office," Lucas said. "I'm terribly sorry. I've got to rush off. Please, stay and enjoy your drink. It was a pleasure."

"Likewise."

I didn't take my eyes off him until he'd exited the restaurant. Then I leaned on the table, making sure Marc and Enzo could hear me. "Holy Crap."

"Hold that thought for a sec, will you? I want to see what kind of car that dude drives."

Marc got up from his seat and thundered over to the bank of windows in front of the restaurant. He was back in less than a minute. "Nothing like seeing a Series 7 Beemer up close and personal. Cool color, too. Sort of a cross between black and gray."

I stood and leaned over the plants. "So he's gone?"

"Yep. You can get your brain back now."

"Hang on. I'll join you at your table."

I walked around the cluster of tables, made a right turn and sat down with Marc and Enzo. "What do you mean by that?"

Marc rolled his eyes and his entire head. "It was like watching someone sell their soul to the devil. And, by the way, the guy's not all that. If you get my drift."

"Yeah," Enzo said. "He's old. Must be in his mid-forties."

"Listen, guys, I'm not selling anything to Lucas Stilton or his partner. I'm trying to make them *think* that's what I'm going to do so I can get information out of them."

Enzo looked at his cousin and then at me. "That's what Cammy told us but if you want the truth, it looked as if you were about to cave."

"That bad, huh?"

They both shook their heads.

"I won't be as gaga with Declan," I said. "Honestly, I don't know what came over me. It was like Lucas—"

"Had you in some weird spell or something?" Marc asked. "Because he's just a dude. Get over it."

"You're right. I've got to make this work."

I thanked Cammy's cousins and offered to pay them for their time but they adamantly refused, saying something about Cammy whooping them upside the head if she got wind of it. They also offered to run interference at my next encounter and I agreed. Granted, it was like having Abbott and Costello on my team, but I couldn't afford to be choosy.

Chapter 20

I kept kicking myself the entire drive back to the house, following my less-than-stellar performance at the bagel place. Regardless of his impression of me, Lucas Stilton took the bait. Now all I needed to do was make sure I got what I needed from those men at Vanna Enterprises.

My stomach churned by the time I got in the door, and I was drenched from perspiration. Even my palms were sweaty. I was dying to tell Cammy how it went, or *didn't,* in my case, but it was midafternoon and the tasting room would be full. I couldn't pull her away. Same deal for Don and Theo. They wouldn't be pleased, but the way things were going with the official investigation, I seriously doubted those deputies would come up with anything.

The red light was blinking on our answering machine and I clicked the button to play the messages. The first was from Madeline Martinez calling to remind me of the next winery women's meeting in another week to discuss the "Sip and Savor" event and the second was from the bank that held our loans for the winery equipment.

Fearing the worst, I called the bank first and spoke with the loan officer, who'd initiated the call. Stewart McKinley assured me nothing was wrong but wanted to let me know there had been an inquiry into our finances from an outside source.

"Are you planning to refinance or take out another substantial loan, Miss Ellington?"

"What? No. Of course not."

"Hmm, that *is* odd. Credit checks like the one that was made regarding your business usually occur when the owner plans on a major purchase. I notified you because if that were the case, we'd like to be the bank you continue to do business with."

"Yes. Sure. Can they do that? Look into our finances?"

"Banks and lending companies can certainly check your credit. I hate to say this, but no one's information is totally safe from prying eyes. Anyway, we'll be on the lookout, should anyone try to establish credit in your name. Fraud's become very common these days. If you don't already have a credit monitoring service, I suggest you get one."

"I, er, uh…"

"There are many reputable ones. Experian. TransUnion. LifeLock, Equifax. Pick one if you don't already have one."

"I will. I will. Thanks, Mr. McKinley. I appreciate your call."

I was seething the second I got off the phone. Then again, what did I expect? That Lucas Stilton and Declan Roth would accept any deal of mine without thoroughly scrutinizing my assets? But damn. I didn't expect Lucas to go all nuclear a half hour after meeting with him. Well, there was at least one good thing about my meeting—he took me seriously.

With a good hour to kill before the tasting room closed, I turned on my laptop and picked up where I left off with my screenplay. If anything, it got my mind off Elsbeth's murder and whatever strange and dangerous attraction I felt for Lucas. At a quarter to five I called it quits and walked to the tasting room.

Three little girls were sticking their hands between the mesh opening to pet Alvin and he seemed to be enjoying every minute of it. He rubbed his nose against their hands and licked them. The girls giggled and ran off when they heard someone calling for them. I moseyed over to Alvin and reached my hand into the pen to pet him as well. Instead of rubbing against it, he snorted and stomped a foot.

"What don't you like about me? Never mind, I don't need a full explanation."

Alvin stomped again and I heard a voice behind me. "Having goat troubles?"

I turned.

Peter had a small wheelbarrow of hay with him. "Maybe if you fed him, he might feel differently."

"I'll take a raincheck. Everything going all right?"

"Seems to be. Since we put up the barriers, the visitors aren't walking all over our vineyard rows. How are you doing? I imagine this is the last thing you expected when you came onboard."

Peter unlatched the gate and rolled the wheelbarrow into Alvin's pen. The goat immediately started chomping on the hay.

"I'm doing okay," I said. "How come you got stuck with Alvin duty?"

"It's all part of the operation. If I wasn't feeding Alvin, I'd be doing something else. There's never a slowdown when it comes to managing a vineyard. Even in winter. That's the worst. The winter pruning. Sometimes it feels as if our fingers are going to fall off from frostbite. Even with heavy gloves."

I nodded and Peter continued to talk as he threw hay around Alvin's pen.

"Of course, the worst risk isn't to our fingers, it's to the grapevines. If the temperatures drop too low for the plant to tolerate, we get winter injury."

"Winter injury?"

"Freezing damage might be a better word for it. It can totally kill the vines or the buds. That's why wineries carry crop insurance."

Crop insurance. Did we have crop insurance? Francine never said anything about it. I nodded again and muttered "yeah."

"Sometimes I close my eyes and wonder what it would be like to manage a vineyard in a warmer climate. Like California."

"Didn't you used to work for a big winery there? I think Francine mentioned it." *And I saw it on your application.*

"Uh-huh. When I got out of school."

"Then why the Finger Lakes? Why did you relocate here?"

Peter stopped tossing hay and wiped some strands of hair from his brow. "I suppose I couldn't resist growing wine in a region that has so much untapped potential."

And growing your resume? "That's it? Potential?"

"More than that, I suppose. This region is the testing ground for scientific research. I want to be on top of things, not grunting along."

The second he said the word *grunt,* that was exactly what Alvin did. He let out a huge grunt and rubbed his head in a fresh pile of hay.

"See, even the goat agrees."

"Oh my gosh," I said. "It's closing time and I've got to catch Cammy. It was nice talking to you."

"Same here."

As I raced into the tasting room, I wondered if those were the lines Peter used when interviewing with Francine and Jason for his position as assistant vineyard manager. It didn't matter. I had more pressing things on my mind.

Lizzie was cashing out when I walked through the door. I walked right toward her. "We have crop insurance, don't we?"

She looked up from the computer and took a step back. "Norrie. Hi! What did you ask? Something about crop insurance?"

"I figured you'd be the one to know since the bills for the business land on your lap. So, do we have it?"

"Yes. We've got coverage and endorsements to cover all sorts of issues. Only they're referred to as exposures. Did you want to see the policy? It's in your sister's files."

"Uh, no. The topic came up and I wanted to be sure we were covered."

"You can relax. Your sister and brother-in-law made sure to purchase a comprehensive policy. So, now that the issue of insurance is settled, how's your sleuthing going?"

"I'm working on a new strategy. I'll let you know."

"There you are!" came Glenda's voice from across the tasting room. "I wondered when I'd ever get a chance to talk to you. Have you had time to mull over my suggestion about a ritual cleansing or the séance? That malevolent spirit of Elsbeth's is never going to leave this place unless we intervene."

"Smudging, no. But séance, yes. But only after hours and outdoors. Preferably, as far away from the tasting room as you can get."

Glenda bobbed her head up and down and tapped a foot on the floor. "I'll begin the preparations right away. It's not something one can do haphazardly."

Of course not.

"It will have to take place where her body was last seen," she went on. "Remnants of her spirit linger on tangible objects or, in this case, maybe the soil."

"No! Not the soil! You can't go in the vineyard. Absolutely not. Maybe her spirit can sort of waft its way over the irrigation piping and into a clearing."

Glenda clamped her lips together and crinkled her nose. "We'll make it work. We'll have to use a stronger incantation than I originally thought."

"Good idea. A stronger incantation. By the way, have you seen Cammy?"

"She's in the kitchen," both women said at the same time.

"Thanks and have a good evening. Oh, and Glenda? Make sure I know when this conjuring of the dead is taking place. I don't need any surprises."

"Don't worry. Since it involves the entire tasting room staff, everyone will be informed."

As I approached the kitchen door, I heard Lizzie saying, "Since when does it involve all of us? It's hard enough dealing with the living."

Cammy had just finished stacking a rack of clean wineglasses on the table when I walked into the kitchen. "I did it," I said. "Only it wasn't Declan. His partner showed up instead. I'm surprised I can still function."

"What? Did that SOB threaten you? Coerce you? I told you it wasn't a good idea. Did my cousins show up? Geez. What did they do?"

"Marc and Enzo were great. Sophomoric, but great."

"That's because they are sophomores, technically. They start their junior year in two months. It can't come fast enough for my family. Well, what happened?"

I pulled a chair over to the table and motioned for her to sit. Then I relived every single detail that took place at The Bagel Barn. When I was done, Cammy stared at me. Mouth wide open but wordless.

"Why are you looking at me like that?"

"Because I want to remember you before you get chewed up and spat out. Norrie, that guy is a wolf. There's no other word for it. He'll beguile you and render you and your family penniless if you continue with that idea of yours. Clearly, you're no match for him. How long were you with him? A half hour? Forty minutes maybe? And look how he got to you. What are you going to do if you're with him at a fancy restaurant? One with mood music and dim lights."

"It won't happen. I won't let it. From now on, I'm only meeting with Declan. And I won't be alone. Marc and Enzo said they'd be my backup."

"Oh, brother. So, now what?"

"Now I wait for Declan to call. I guarantee it'll be in less than forty-eight hours. Those guys want to move and they want to move fast. Francine and Jason may be gone for a year, but Rosalee's only got four weeks. They'll want to wrap things up, trust me."

Cammy rubbed her hands together then crossed her arms. "Have you thought about what you're going to do if they tell you they were the ones responsible for knocking off Elsbeth? If you go to the sheriff's' department, they'll only deny it. Then there'll be a target on your back."

"Aargh. I hadn't thought of that. I guess I'll have to figure out how to get a confession out of them that I can prove. Whatever you do, don't say anything to Lizzie or she'll insist I read the entire Nancy Drew mysteries again."

"Better that than communicating with the spirit world if Glenda gets her way."

"Um, yeah. About that. I gave her the green light for her séance. Might as well get it over with. She said she'd let me know when she had it planned."

"Boy, this conversation just keeps getting better and better."

Both of us laughed and got up from the table. Cammy turned off the lights and we exited out the building through the tasting room. As she locked up, I said, "At least I think I bought Yvonne some time. Lucas and Declan will be so busy with my proposition they'll hold off on pressuring her. With Elsbeth dead, there's no hurry."

"You've got a point there."

Cammy walked to her car and I debated whether or not I should saunter over to the Grey Egret and tell Theo and Don face-to-face what I had done or slither back to the house and phone them. I took the coward's way out and went home.

"You did what?" Theo asked when I got him on the phone.

"I know. I know. Don't get too upset. I'm still beating myself up over it. And before you say another word, you have no idea what it's like to be inches away from someone as mesmerizing, as tantalizing, as beguiling as Lucas Stilton. He could make a diamond turn back to coal."

"Uh, I may have some idea. Although, Don's attributes don't go as far as being able to manipulate geological changes."

"Theo. I'm dead serious. It was like that scene in *Damn Yankees* where Joe Boyd sells his soul to the devil. Stephanie Ipswich warned me about Lucas Stilton, and she was right."

"Aside from the fact the guy all but turned your thought processes into mush, did you make any headway with your plan?"

"Yes. That's the good news. He believed me. He honestly believed me. I'm certain of it. I'm wagering Declan Roth will have a contract for me to sign by the beginning of the week. Then I move to phase two."

"Phase two? I didn't realize you planned this fiasco in phases."

"Well, I did. And it's not a fiasco. Phase two is the stalling process. I'll keep mulling over the contract, making little revisions here and there, all the while wearing them down until they finally relent and admit to killing Elsbeth to further the gains of Vanna Enterprises. I'll insist on knowing the truth before I sign anything."

"And once you know the truth? That could put you directly in harm's way."

"You sound like Cammy. That's exactly what she said. Only not as eloquently."

"Norrie, this isn't a game. This is scary business. Please. Don't make another move until we've had time to talk."

"Don't worry. The only move I intend to make is to get my screenplay done."

"Good. Keep it that way."

I honestly tried to concentrate on my writing but unfortunately, all I could think about was Lucas Stilton and how he made me feel. I took a breath, opened a new file on the laptop and wrote down every single thing. If nothing else, I'd have plenty of fodder for my romances.

Chapter 21

I was positive I'd hear from Declan by the weekend or, at the very least, by Monday but five days had gone by and nothing. It was Wednesday morning and I was getting edgy. Maybe Lucas saw right through me and decided to try another tactic of his own. To make matters worse, Lizzie called the night before to ask if I was interviewing people properly.

"You have to be direct, you know. Exceedingly polite, but direct. Nancy Drew always got straight to the point with refinement and charm."

If Nancy Drew were a real person, I would've reached out to strangle her. "I can't just blurt out an accusation. I'm sleuthing, not interrogating."

"You won't get anywhere if you're too afraid to ask the real questions."

I thought about what she'd said and wondered if maybe it wasn't time for me to confront Madeline Martinez. After all, Stephanie was certain she'd seen Elsbeth's ugly green wagon in front of Madeline's house on more than one occasion.

You're not going to upstage me, Nancy Drew.

I decided to phone Madeline, but the landline began to ring before I could place my own call. I took a breath and picked up.

"Good Morning. May I please speak with Miss Norrie Ellington?"

The voice sounded fairly young and professional. A telemarketer maybe? I was about to give her the brush off when she continued.

"This is Abigail Blake from the legal firm of Armstrong, Patel, Smolowitz and Tarrow. I'm calling from our New York office on behalf of our client, Vanna Enterprises."

Holy Cannoli. What the heck did I get myself into? "Yes?" My voice sounded tenuous and shaky.

"Mr. Stilton and Mr. Roth directed our firm to prepare a partnership contract for you. They were quite insistent that it take top priority. I'm calling to let you know you'll be receiving a FedEx delivery sometime today with the preliminary contract. You'll need to review it with your attorneys. We've also made arrangements with one of our lawyers to peruse said contract with you. Mr. Arden Grant from our satellite office in Rochester will be calling to arrange that meeting."

I was still trying to get over my last meeting. Naturally, I froze at the thought of finding myself sitting across from another Lucas Stilton. I grabbed my laptop off the couch and immediately went to the search engine.

"Does your firm have a website, Miss Blake?"

"Certainly. It's apstlaw.com."

My fingers flew across the keyboard, and I stared at their home page. Impressive. Offices in New York, Chicago and San Francisco, with satellite offices in those same states. I immediately went to the ribbon on top of the page that listed their attorneys and pulled up a profile and photo of Arden Grant. He looked to be in his fifties, bald with a large nose and hairy eyebrows.

"Miss Ellington, are you still there? Miss Ellington?"

"Oh, sorry. My phone slipped. Mr. Arden Grant, you said?"

"That's correct."

"Fine. When will he be contacting me?"

"Expect a call later today or first thing tomorrow. If I can be of further assistance, please don't hesitate to call. All of our contact information will be in the package you receive."

"Thank you. Have a nice day."

It wasn't as if I hadn't expected to be offered a contract. I mean, that was exactly what I had proposed to Declan, well, Lucas, actually. But I'd expected Declan to show up with it and leave it for me to look over. Not some bigshot attorney for a huge firm. I felt as if things were snowballing around me.

I couldn't very well call the lawyers Francine and Jason had on retainer for the winery because I really wasn't going to go through with this charade. I was merely creating a ruse, in exchange for information. Last thing I needed was to incur large legal fees over nothing. Instead, I did the next best thing. I changed out of my pajamas, washed up, fed the dog and powerwalked my way down the hill to the Grey Egret's tasting room.

Theo and Don both had customers at their tables but as soon as they saw me, they exchanged glances and Don came over to where I was standing. "I'll be done in a jiffy. Theo and the rest of our staff can pick up. You look as if you've seen a ghost."

"Humph. That would be good news."

"Uh-oh. There's juice in the kitchen. And cookies. Help yourself. I'll be right in."

I poured myself a glass of apple juice and took one of the large oatmeal raisin cookies on a platter by the sink. A few minutes later, Don walked in and I told him about Abigail Blake's phone call.

"My God, Norrie. This is really getting out of hand. Theo told me about your meeting with Lucas Stilton last Thursday, but I never expected things to go so far."

"No kidding. I thought I'd be dealing with Declan, not his attorneys. Oh my God! What have I done?"

"Calm down. Have some more juice. Let me think for a minute."

I took another sip of juice while Don popped a cookie in his mouth. When he was done, he reached for my hand and gave it a squeeze. "Okay. From what you've said, all this attorney is going to do is to meet with you to go over the contract. That's it, right?"

"I think so."

"Fine. Fine. Theo can go with you. He was pre-law at Union College before he changed his mind."

Just then, Theo walked into the kitchen. "I heard the words 'Theo' and 'pre-law.' This isn't sounding good."

Don explained my predicament and Theo looked absolutely stricken. "Pre-law. That was eons ago. I don't remember anything and even if I did, it wasn't that much to begin with. That's like asking a pre-med student to perform open-heart surgery."

"No, it's not. You can act. If it's one thing you're good at, it's acting. Sit there and pretend you know what you're doing."

Oh God. This is going to be a worse catastrophe than when I met with Lucas.

Theo studied my face and didn't say anything. He got up, poured himself a glass of juice and gulped it down. "Guess it's our only recourse, huh?"

Don and I nodded.

"All right." Then Theo looked at me. "Here's our strategy. We let the Vanna Enterprises's lawyer spell out the contract. Then we tell him we'll be reviewing it for any revisions, modifications or clarifications. If you can think of other words, we'll throw those in as well."

I got up and gave Theo a huge hug. Then I did the same with Don. "I can't thank you enough. I'll let you know as soon as Arden Grant calls me. Oh my gosh! What if he wants *his* office to call *your* office?"

Theo furrowed his brow and narrowed his eyes. I hadn't seen him look so intent. "Don't say anything about having your lawyer attend the meeting. When Arden arrives, you can simply introduce me. Tell him you thought it best to have your attorney present."

"Where? Where present?"

"At your house. No reason to meet at a restaurant or worse yet, at their satellite office. Insist he meet at your house."

I nodded and muttered, "My house…okay, my house."

"You'll be fine, Norrie," Don said. "Concentrate on the big picture and you won't get unhinged. It's too late to turn back now."

"Got it. Thanks again. I'd better let you get back to work. I'll call."

I walked back up the hill slowly. My hands were still shaking from the brief conversation I'd had with Abigail Blake, but my pulse wasn't racing like it was a half hour ago. Small consolation. It was a quarter to eleven and I hadn't eaten anything except oatmeal raisin cookies. I breezed through our tasting room and waved at Cammy, Lizzie and Roger.

Fred had his back to me at the bistro and I called out to him, "Hi there! Good to see you. I'm starving as usual."

"Wow, you must be. This is early for you. What can I get you?"

"Bacon and cheese panini with tomato."

"Done."

I sat down at one of the tables when Cammy came rushing over. "You walked through the tasting room so quickly I didn't get a chance to talk to you. You got another floral delivery. It came about a half hour ago. The guy said he went to the house but no one was there and he didn't want to leave the flowers wilting on the porch. He also thought Charlie might eat them."

"More flowers?"

My face went from slightly warm to nearly hot. *If the card is signed Lucas, I might as well pen my obituary.*

"Did you look at the card? Did you see who they were from?"

"No, of course not. That's private business. The flowers are in the kitchen. Day lilies, tiny little orchids, asters and mini carnations. Your admirer went all out."

"I'll bet he did."

"Fred!" I shouted. "I'll be right back."

I charged to the kitchen and didn't let out my breath until I took the card from the small envelope. It read:

Sorry I missed our meeting and the bombshell you dropped on Lucas. We'll talk as soon as I'm back in town. Maybe by then we'll have something to celebrate. Lunch next week? Declan

Cammy hovered over me and wouldn't budge. "Are you all right, Norrie? You've been staring at that note without saying a word. Declan Roth again?"

"Uh-huh. He's out of town but the note didn't say where. Listen, I may have gotten us in deeper than I expected, but it'll be all right. I've got a lawyer. Sort of."

By the time I was done bringing Cammy up to speed with the phone call I got from Abigail Blake, Fred knocked on the kitchen door to tell me my panini was getting cold.

"No worries. I'll be right there." I gave Cammy a sheepish grin. One I'd perfected in middle school. "Like I said, I have a lawyer."

As if my day wasn't jarring enough, I had a surprise visit from Deputy Hickman about an hour after I'd returned to the house with the floral arrangement. The kitchen was beginning to resemble the waiting room at my dentist's office. Too bad Grizzly Gary wasn't intimidated.

When I opened the door and invited him inside, motioning to one of the chairs at the kitchen table, he shook his head and stood perfectly still. At least he closed the door behind him leaving the hot air outside where it belonged. Unlike the winery, with its state of the art air-conditioning, our house was limited to a few ceiling fans and one portable one.

"Good afternoon," I said. "Are you here to tell me you caught Elsbeth's killer?"

His voice was loud and monotone. "The case, I'm afraid, is still open. I stopped by to inform you that the results from the tire markings were inconclusive. And, our analysis of Ms. Waters's vehicle failed to yield any results."

"So, that's it? You're going to shove all the paperwork in a file, put it in a box and mark it Cold Case?"

"Certainly not. We intend to re-question some of the winery owners and certain staff members who might have had strong motives to murder her."

I immediately thought of Stephanie and the way in which Elsbeth had cheated her out of the Tyler property, but I didn't say a word. Deputy Hickman took out a small notepad and flipped through some pages.

"Precisely what time was that flight your sister and brother-in-law took to Costa Rica?"

"I thought I gave your department that information. You're not suggesting they had anything to do with killing that old battleax, I mean...oh, what the heck. Elsbeth *was* a battleax. Francine and Jason took an early morning flight out of Rochester on a Friday. Elsbeth's body didn't arrive on our doorstep, so to speak, until the following day. Well, the night before, I suppose, but my family was already in Costa Rica. You can verify this with their airline."

"Not necessary. I need to be absolutely certain the information we took during our initial investigation hasn't changed."

"If you're looking for someone with a strong motive, try Vanna Enterprises. Those developers were anxious to buy her property."

"We've already questioned them, if you must know. It's been my experience that these types of murders tend to be personal, not business related. That's precisely why we intend to re-visit our conversations with the wineries."

Well, pooh for you. "Will you please let me know if you find out who did it? We've had to put barricades in front of our vineyard rows because the tourists are clamoring to see where the body was. It's cost us time and money. I seriously doubt anyone who owns a winery on these hills would stoop so low as to dump a body in one of their neighbors' vineyards."

"And again, Miss Ellington, that's why I tell you, in all sincerity, leave the investigating to the professionals. Don't think I haven't been aware of what you've been up to."

Oh my God! Not the Lucas Stilton deal?

He squinted and gave me an ugly stare. "It just so happens I was at Wegmans the morning you had that nice little chitchat with Mrs. Marbleton from Terrace Wineries. Together, the both of you could pen a crime novel."

"I can't help it if people bring up the subject."

"Then change it! Anyway, I've got other stops to make. Have a nice day."

Ah-hah! The real reason for his visit. To warn me to stay away. "Wait! Before you leave, are any of our employees on your revisiting list?"

Deputy Hickman perused his notepad and gave his head a shake. "Not at the moment."

He flung the door open wide and hot air rushed into the room for the second time that morning.

Maybe his investigation was crawling at a snail's pace but mine certainly wasn't. The entrapment plan I'd devised, for lack of a better word, was about to go full swing. I figured the least I could do, in order to prepare for my meeting with Arden, was to Google some sample partnership documents. An hour and twenty minutes later, I wanted to scream from the highest rooftop. Limited partnerships. Voting requirements. Cost sharing. Nondisclosure agreements. Joint venture agreements. LCC's. Maintenance of accounting. The list was endless.

I stood, opened the fridge and poured myself a large orange juice. I was in over my head, but that didn't mean I was about to drown. After all,

I wasn't the one presenting the contract, Arden Grant was. All I needed to do was sit there poker-faced and pray Theo retained something from those undergrad classes of his.

The only good news, albeit temporary because things had a way of changing in a blink, was the fact none of the Two Witches' employees were suspects. Not with Elsbeth's murder, anyway. But I was certain it was Declan's car I saw in front of the winery. Too bad I couldn't tell who he was arguing with. Or which of the men said, "Like hell you will."

Franz, Alan and Herbert usually called it quits for the day around four, unless something really demanded their attention. I looked at the clock on the microwave. If I hurried, I could get to the winery lab before they were gone.

In spite of the heat, my feet moved quickly as I ran down the hill. There was only one car left in their parking lot and it was Franz's. The Volvo. I slowed down and took a breath before opening the side door and announcing myself.

"I'll be right there, Norrie," Franz called out. "Feel free to sit at any of our desks."

Their small office area looked as pristine as it did when Herbert first led me through there on my way to the lab. I pulled out a chair and was about to sit when Franz came in.

"Is everything all right? Have you heard anything about the case?"

"Yes and no. In that order. What about you? The lab? The fermentation or whatever else is going on?"

"All of our processes are running smoothly and I've selected a few competitions for us to consider. Is that why you're here?"

The competitions. Damn it. I forgot all about them. "Franz, I trust your judgment on that. Select the ones you feel will give us the most exposure and you can go ahead and enter them. Just don't go overboard. See Lizzie about the paperwork and fees."

"Thank you. And thank you for trusting my judgment. Was there anything else you needed?"

"Sort of. A curiosity thing, really. Can you tell me what Declan Roth from Vanna Enterprises was doing at our lab about two weeks ago?" *I'm out on a limb here. It better have been Declan Roth.* "It was when I'd just arrived. I saw his car and I believe I heard him arguing with someone. Was that you?"

"I wasn't aware you knew Declan Roth. He and his partner, Lucas Stilton, have made offers to a number of winemakers in the area. When I told him I wasn't interested, he insinuated he'd find a way to discredit our wines. I told him in no uncertain terms, it wouldn't be in his best interests."

"Wow. I'm glad you set him straight."

"For now. I'm afraid he might make an offer to Alan, and I would hate losing him. He's a very talented winemaker."

"Hopefully it won't come to that. Those developers don't even have a winery yet."

"True, but they have enough money to pay the existing winemakers decent salaries to sit back and wait while the wineries they worked at scramble to find replacements. It's a nasty tactic. Winemakers can't just walk in the door and start working. They're usually groomed, and that takes time. Each winemaker has his or her own preferences regarding the winemaking process. Winemaking is a science *and* an art. We're not flipping burgers here."

"I know. Listen, I'm sure you've talked with Alan, but I'll have a word with him, too, during the week."

"Good idea."

"Thanks, Franz. I didn't mean to keep you. Have a nice afternoon."

I cursed Declan and Lucas under my breath all the way up the hill. So what if they were smoking hot. And in Lucas's case, downright combustible. They were unscrupulous, conniving and ruthless. All the more reason to put my plan in play.

Chapter 22

Abigail Blake kept her word. The FedEx delivery was at my doorstep before five and Arden Grant called me the next morning. Charlie had finished gobbling up his kibble and was halfway out the doggie door when the phone rang.

"Miss Ellington? I hope I didn't wake you. This is Arden Grant from Armstrong, Patel, Smolowitz and Tarrow. I trust you received the documents."

Compared to the APST documents, *War and Peace* looked like a dime novel.

"Uh, yes. Yes, I did. Thank you."

"I was hoping we could set a time to meet. I'm at your disposal. I have strict instructions from the firm to meet with you as soon as possible."

"How does Monday sound?" *And it better sound good because Theo and I are going to need the next four days to prep.*

"Monday would be fine. Would you care to meet at our satellite office in Rochester or—"

"If you don't mind, I'd just as soon we meet here. At my house. It's much more private and we won't be interrupted."

"If that's your preference, I can certainly accommodate you."

We settled for ten in the morning because I knew it would be a slower time in the tasting rooms and Theo's absence wouldn't be missed as much. Most of the tourists headed back to the cities on Sunday nights and the locals usually started their tasting later in the week. I gave Arden explicit directions to Two Witches and told him not to listen to his GPS.

"The county roads are quicker and not heavily trafficked," I said. "Those GPS systems aren't happy unless they direct you through at least one major thoroughfare."

He thanked me and said he looked forward to making my acquaintance. I think I said something similar, but what I really meant was I hoped he could look forward to my award-winning performance.

I immediately called Theo to let him know about the meeting and to ask if he wouldn't mind perusing the contract documents that APST sent over.

"I can't cook," I explained, "but I can call Joe's restaurant and have them deliver the best pizza and wings ever. You and Don can come by after work."

"Anything but anchovies and pineapple. Did you start to read the contract?"

"Yes. I got as far as 'in consideration of the mutual covenants made.' Then I gave up. This is worse than when I bought a multi-handset answering machine for my apartment in New York. That time I got as far as 'Congratulations on your purchase of your new cordless digital answering system.' After that, the instructions might as well have been written in hieroglyphics."

"Okay. Don't stress yourself out. We'll take a look tonight."

As things turned out, Theo was the one who got totally stressed. He and Don arrived forty minutes before the pizza. We sat around the table and tried to make sense of Vanna Enterprises's partnership agreement.

At one point Theo exclaimed, "Good God! I don't even think Sheldon Cooper could figure this out!"

That was when I knew I was in trouble. Real trouble. "I thought all we had to do was sit and listen."

Theo's head bobbed up and down and his eyes glazed over. "True, true. In theory."

"In theory?" I was starting to panic.

"We should at least have some idea what they're offering."

Don leaned across the kitchen table and moved some papers around until he found what he was looking for. "Ah-ha. Here's a table of contents. At least we'll know what's on each page. I'll start reading aloud and we'll see how that goes."

It didn't. Don went down the list, including partnership name and purpose, capital contributions and accounts, waivers, transfers and liabilities. I rubbed my hands together and then moved them up my arms. "I'm lost. Totally lost."

"Maybe we should pick a topic and see how it reads. How about capital contributions?"

Theo and I both shrugged.

"Go ahead," I said.

"The capital of the partnership shall be tantamount to the aggregate amount of capital contributions made to it by its partners."

"What on earth does that mean?" My voice modulated between a croak and a whine.

Theo put his hand on my shoulder and winced. "It means you have to cough up the same amount of equity Lucas and Declan did. In this case, your property and your business."

"Oh, *that*. Okay, fine. That's what I want them to believe."

"Look, Norrie," Don said. "As long as you don't sign anything or verbally commit to it, you'll be fine. The only thing that lawyer is going to do is make sure you understand the ramifications of entering into a partnership with those developers."

All of a sudden Charlie got up from his dog bed and raced outside.

"The pizza delivery must be here," I said. "Hold on, I'll get the door."

Theo and Don gathered up the documents and put them back in the FedEx box. Two minutes later, a giant pepperoni and mushroom pizza with a side order of hot wings was spread out on the table. Joe's restaurant even included paper plates and napkins.

"Call it sacrilege," I said, "but I went to the store and got us some beer to go with the pizza. Real beer and O'Doul's."

"I know you're convinced those two men were responsible for the murder," Don said in-between bites of pizza, "but have you exhausted any other leads?"

"Not really. I intend to, if this doesn't pan out. The trouble is, my other suspect is one of the winery owners and I'd hate to think she was the perpetrator."

"Who? Why? What do you know?"

"Stephanie Ipswich had a real good motive for giving Elsbeth the axe."

Don all but choked on his pizza. I went on to explain about the rutted road that bordered Gable Hill Winery all the way past the Peaceful Pines and how it led directly to the edge of the property where the berry bushes separated our vineyards from the land that Elsbeth owned.

I then presented my theory about how Stephanie could've lured Elsbeth to her house, had tea and crumpets with her, walked her back to the car, knocked her in the head with something and shoved the body over to the passenger seat. "Because, remember," I said, "Elsbeth's car was an old clunker. The front seats weren't separated like they are today. Next, Stephanie could've driven her to the edge of the property, opened the car door and given Elsbeth a good shove."

"You think Stephanie would've been strong enough to drag a dead body?" Theo asked.

"She wouldn't have to drag it far. And Elsbeth was on the thin side."

Don reached for another pizza slice. "Dead weight is dead weight."

"Not if Stephanie used a tarp and slid the body," I said.

"All conjecture, I'm afraid."

With that, he took a bite of the pizza.

"But you have to admit, *good* conjecture. Anyway, I don't want to go there until I follow through with the plan I already have in place."

Don swallowed and cleared his throat. "You mean the disaster waiting to happen?"

"Huh? You said yourself I'll be fine if I don't commit to anything verbally or on paper."

"True, but this still worries me."

Then he turned to Theo. "Make sure she doesn't go near a pencil or pen."

We were down to our last piece of pizza and it went to Charlie.

"Francine's really going to kill me. I think I'm spoiling that dog."

Theo agreed to be at my house no later than nine-thirty on Monday. That would give us time for a quick run-through. We agreed to let Arden do most, if not all of the talking, with one exception.

"The guy has to believe we're not blithering idiots," Theo said. "Here's the deal—every so often one of us should ask, 'Can you repeat that, please?' or 'Would you expound upon that?' We can also say, 'We need some clarification.' Furrow your brow, Norrie, and look intent."

Don bent his head into the palm of his hand and groaned. "Heaven help us. You're not directing a play, Theo."

"Um, in a way, he is," I said. "Plus, it's a good stalling technique."

Truth be known, I was petrified but I refused to waver. At least Arden Grant wasn't about to intimidate me with his good looks. Come Monday, I'd be intense and direct.

* * * *

It was difficult to concentrate on my screenplay the following day. I was absolutely restless and nervous as hell. I got up from the table, walked to the counter where I'd placed the contract and began leafing through it. That only made things worse. I came across words I didn't recognize, phrases I didn't understand and paragraphs that made no sense.

By mid-morning I gave up on both endeavors and walked to the bistro for lunch. Cammy, Roger and Sam were all inundated with wine tasters, and I gave them each a quick wave as I walked by.

"I'll have a turkey, bacon and avocado panini, Fred," I called out to his back. In a split second, he spun around, only it wasn't him, it was a young woman about his height with longish dark hair tucked behind her ears.

"Hi there! You must be Norrie. I'm Emma, Fred's wife. I wondered when I'd get to meet you. Seems we keep crossing paths."

She reached over the counter and gave my hand a shake. Like her husband, she looked as if she were still in junior high.

"It's nice to finally meet you," I said. "Things have been really crazy around here."

"You're telling me! First the body in the vineyard, then those crazy tourists looking for the crime scene and now a return visit from the sheriff's department to question everyone again."

"What?" The tiny bristles on the back of my neck started to move. Deputy Hickman made it clear none of our employees were on his re-questioning list, so why was he bothering them? "When? When was he here?"

"Just a little while ago. He wanted to know if any of us had heard any scuttlebutt about the other winery owners or their employees having it *in* for Elsbeth Waters. I told him I didn't even know the woman but, from what I'd heard, I was glad I never made her acquaintance."

"And that's it? Rumor mongering?"

She shook her head and whispered, "Between you and me, I don't think their investigation is going well. Maybe Glenda will have better luck."

Glenda? Oh no. Now what? What else can she want besides a smudging and a séance? "Glenda?"

"It's her day off but she stopped in this morning to ask if I'd take part in the conjuring of Elsbeth's spirit on the Fourth of July. After dark. I thought Glenda had your permission."

"Oh, *that*. Um, yeah, she does. I didn't know she'd settled on a date. And the Fourth of July? That's unusual."

"Not according to Glenda. I guess there's a lot of energy in the air that night and Glenda believes it will attract Elsbeth's restless spirit. Plus, we don't have fireworks on this lake. Only in Branchport on Keuka Lake and Ithaca on Cayuga. Sure, people will shoot off their own spinners and Roman candles, but that's minor."

"What else did Glenda say?"

"Not much. I was the last employee she had to track down. Everyone in the tasting room and bistro will be there. Unfortunately, Franz and Alan are going to a wine symposium in Syracuse, but Herbert said he'll come. He told Glenda his academic advisor would never believe it. John plans to send Peter because he needs to have someone make sure no one walks down the rows or, worse yet, those little aisles where the plants are right next to each other. I'm really running off at the mouth, aren't I? I'm not getting Glenda into any trouble, am I?"

"No, no. I told her she could do this. It's just so…so…"

"Weird. I know. Anyway, you must be starving. One turkey, bacon, avocado panini coming right up."

I plopped myself in a chair, propped my elbows on the table and leaned my head into the palms of my hands. It felt as if I had entered an alternate reality. I closed my eyes for a second when, all of a sudden, someone tapped me on the shoulder and I jumped.

"Norrie! I didn't mean to startle you. It looked as if you were taking a catnap. Cammy said you'd be in here. She's got a full table of customers."

"Madeline. Hi. Can I get you anything to drink?"

"No thanks. I'm only here for a few minutes. I'm making the rounds to all the wineries participating in the 'Sip and Savor.' I'm dropping off the flyers for your tasting room. Didn't they turn out great? Miller Printing does a marvelous job."

She handed me a large stack of colorful flyers with a photo of scrumptious hors d'oeuvres paired with glasses of wine. "We might as well start getting the word out early. It'll give the tourists something else to think about other than a murder. That's all they seem to mention when they stop by Billsburrow Winery for a tasting."

"Geez."

"Still no news on the Elsbeth case, huh? I just came from the Grey Egret and the boys informed me things were moving at a snail's pace."

"Yeah, about that…Did you know Elsbeth well enough to wager a guess at who might've killed her?"

"Me? I hardly knew her. Now the niece, well, that's a different story."

"What do you mean?"

"That poor girl. Indentured servants were treated much better than she was. I met Yvonne a few months back when I was waiting for a prescription at Wegmans. We got to talking and I told her she could feel welcome to stop by and visit with me at my house. Believe it or not, she took me up on it. Usually on Saturday mornings on her way to the transfer station with the weekly trash and recyclables. I don't know what excuse she gave her aunt, but she visited sometimes for over an hour. Like I said, the poor thing. Imagine living with such a shrew as Elsbeth."

Oh my God! It isn't Elsbeth and Madeline who are chummy. It's Yvonne and Madeline. Stephanie got it wrong. "Wow. Those were long visits. Yvonne didn't strike me as much of a conversationalist when I met her."

"She isn't. But she's genuinely interested in the winery business and picked my brain on all sorts of topics. I imagined she wanted to know more about the topic so she'd have something to tell her guests at the B & B."

"Really? She was that interested?"

"I know it sounds hard to believe, but it's true. She wanted to know about cultivating a vineyard and the entire winemaking process. I'm certainly no expert on enology or viticulture, but I was happy to tell her what I've learned over the years running Billsburrow Winery. And, of course, I told her what every winemaker knows."

"What's that?"

"Great wine depends on four things—the grape, the climate, the soil and the winemaker. In that order."

"Hmm, I'm still trying to wrap my head around Yvonne being so interested in the wine business. The last time I spoke with her, she wanted to get the heck out of here and fast!"

"I'm not sure what that poor girl is going to do. The legal process surrounding her aunt's death is certainly going to eat up her time. Not to mention she's got to run the B & B. Oh, I also dropped off some of our flyers there so guests who are visiting might decide to make a return trip later in the summer. That would help Yvonne with bookings, too."

"Good idea."

"Oh my gosh. I've been gabbing forever. I simply must be on my way. I've got two more stops to make and Catherine Trobert will chew my ears off. It was nice talking with you, Norrie. I hope the sheriff's department can reach some closure on the case."

"Me, too. Thanks for dropping off the flyers and visiting. Oh wait. One more thing before you go. Are those developers still pressuring you? I haven't heard much more about that."

"I wouldn't call it *pressuring* as much as I would *ferreting.*"

"Ferreting? I'm not sure I know what you mean."

"Kind of like digging or poking around for answers. Needling might've been a better word but ferret comes to mind when I think of them. You see, Billsburrow Winery isn't top on their acquisition list as far as wineries and land go. However, Lucas Stilton must've found out I was dining at the Port of Call not too long ago and made it a point to catch me off guard."

So it was her. This day is jammed with all sorts of surprises. "What did he want?"

"He offered to compensate me rather nicely if I would use my influence on Yvonne to get her to sell that B & B. How he ever found out I know her is beyond me. Needless to say, I was quite polite, after all I was in a public place. I declined his offer rather diplomatically, I think."

"How did you do that?"

"I told him if he ever approached me again in a public place, I'd scream bloody murder and people would think he touched me."

"Whoa. Did it work?"

"I'll say. And of all times for my husband to be in the men's room!"

Madeline smiled and left the bistro. She waved to our tasting room staff before going out the door. So much for a Madeline-Elsbeth connection. At least I was able to definitively cross Madeline off my suspect list. No surprise. Her name was way, way down at the bottom.

Chapter 23

I approached the full-length oak mirror for the third, and hopefully, last time in the past twenty minutes. I tried to decide which outfit would convey a sense of professionalism and knowledge. Arden Grant would be at my door in less than an hour and I was nervous as hell.

The breezy sundress made me look like a wide-eyed ingénue and worn jeans with a top—*any* top—made me look as if I was prepared to pave the driveway, not enter into a partnership agreement. I finally reverted back to the one pair of tailored slacks I owned and a short-sleeved ecru blouse my mother would've considered stylish for any occasion. Naturally, the top belonged to Francine.

To make the outfit complete, I borrowed gold stud earrings from Francine's jewelry stash and selected a gold-plated chain that draped nicely over the blouse. I ran my fingers up and down the chain and stopped the second I heard a knock on the door. It was Theo.

"Got your act together?" he asked as I let him in. "Curtain opens in half an hour. Here, Don made us banana bread with chocolate chips. Two loaves. We'll be sure to offer Arden a big slice."

"Thanks. All I had this morning was a glass of grape juice. If you don't mind, I'll eat my slice right now. I'm starving."

Theo and I dove into the bread as if it was our last meal.

"I don't know if I'm ready for this," I said.

"You will be. By the way, you look great."

"Same for you. You didn't have to put on a shirt and tie."

"I sure did if I wanted to convince the guy I was your lawyer and this meeting meant billable hours for me."

Theo got up from the table and looked out the window. "Showtime. Your guy's getting out of his car. He's wearing a peach-colored button-down shirt with a geometric tie. In case you wanted to know."

All of a sudden, my heart beat faster and, without realizing it, I had clenched my jaw.

Theo noticed immediately when he turned away from the window. "Hey, he's a paid lawyer, not the Attorney General. Get a grip."

"You're right." I walked to the door and opened it before Arden Grant had a chance to knock.

"Good morning. Come on in, Mr. Grant. I'm Norrie Ellington. Allow me to introduce my legal counsel, Theo Buchman."

"Nice to make both your acquaintances," Arden said. "I didn't realize you brought your legal advisor or I would've printed an additional copy of the contract. I'll make sure our office e-mails you another one today."

I smiled and pointed to the kitchen table. "That's all right. We'll share the one I have. Before we get started, would you care for some coffee? We also have fresh banana bread with chocolate chips."

Arden looked as if I'd offered him access to the United States Treasury. "I haven't had homemade banana bread in years. Did you bake it yourself?"

"No, a friend of mine made it."

I cut Arden a gigantic slice and popped a Dunkin' Donuts K-cup in the Keurig. "I'll get a coffee for you too. Make yourself at home."

"This is delicious. Simply scrumptious. By the way, was that a Nigerian Dwarf Goat I saw on my way up the driveway? I grew up on a small farm a few miles south of Syracuse. Anyway, my family had goats and one of them ate the embroidered Black Knight logo off of my school's baseball cap. By the way, those goats tend to spit, you know. If you weren't aware of it."

"Oh, I'm aware of it. The goat's name is Alvin and he showed me that trick when we first met."

"We appreciate you driving to Penn Yan to meet with us," Theo said.

"Not a problem. Frankly, I was glad to get out of the city and away from my desk. Well, I suppose we might as well get started. As you probably surmised, Vanna Enterprises has a tremendous amount of clout when it comes to my firm. Between you and me, if they said jump, the partners would drag out a trampoline."

In that instant, Arden Grant went from the intimidating clout I expected to a down-to-earth normal human being. He explained every aspect of the contract using language that actually made sense. Theo and I only had to ask him to repeat something once. We hadn't reached the point of "clarify" or "expound."

"This contract is a learning experience for me, too," he said. "It was originally supposed to be presented by Eleanor Tavish, but she developed an unsightly rash from something she ate or touched and it put her out of commission for a while."

The way he pronounced her name made me think he was gloating inwardly at Eleanor's demise.

"Anyway," Arden went on, "this partnership agreement is a bear. It's a three-pronged piece of legalese that treats the transfer of your property as the capital contribution. That means the business, of course, with all of its assets and the property itself. We'll need a complete financial disclosure before anything can be finalized. Naturally, Vanna Enterprises will provide you with their financial disclosure as well. Beyond that are the usual stipulations and considerations. We'll go through those in a moment if you'd like, but something puzzles me. Perhaps you can explain."

I nudged Theo under the table with a light kick to his ankle.

"We'll do our best," he said.

Arden gave him a nod. "Vanna Enterprises has agreed to enter into this contract regardless of whether or not your winery is a liability. That means they're willing to forgive and take on your outstanding loans and other financial obligations. Listen, this isn't any of my business, and Eleanor certainly would be hush hush on the matter, but it's been my experience that when one party is willing to do something like that, they have an ulterior motive. I'll put it bluntly. Lucas Stilton and Declan Roth want that contract signed no matter what. They're willing to make you, Miss Ellington, a full equity partner. So I ask, what's really in it for them?"

"You don't know?" I asked.

"For lack of a better explanation, I'm the contract courier."

"Hold on. You'll need another cup of coffee and more banana bread."

I then proceeded to spill out the entire Atlantis-Disneyland dream the developers had nurtured.

Arden's jaw dropped and he slapped both of his hands on his cheeks. "Oh no. It sounds like Euro Wonderland all over again."

"You mean that giant European theme park in Lichtenstein? They own *that?*"

"Sure enough. The very one. Once those two get an idea that takes hold, there's no stopping them. Listen, I don't mean to dissuade you. I could lose my job. So, this part of the conversation never happened, understand?"

"Uh-huh. Absolutely."

Arden looked around, as if he half expected someone to be spying on us. "Let me reassure you, first, that as a full-equity partner, you stand to make quite a bit of money. I emphasize the word 'quite.' However, Lucas and Declan haven't had a solid track record when it comes to bringing on other partners."

"What do you mean?" Theo asked.

"They had a silent partner for the Euro Wonderland venture and when I say 'silent,' I mean 'silent.' The man was found dead in his apartment in Paris shortly after he helped to bankroll their project. Then there was the partner in San Francisco. A middle-aged woman who helped finance one of their upscale malls. She was found dead in her residence as well. In both cases, the deaths were ruled natural. Miss Ellington, two Latin phrases apply here—*caveat emptor* and *caveat venditor.* Let the buyer beware and let the seller beware."

My hands shook slightly and I became a bit lightheaded. "You mean—"

"Precisely. Review that contract carefully. Scrutinize it. You won't find any issues with it, I can assure you. My firm does impeccable work. But it's not the contract I'd be concerned about if I were you. Needless to say, I've said enough."

"Thank you. Really. Uh, er, when do they expect a response?"

"According to my notes, Declan Roth plans on securing the contract from you. You're on his time schedule."

Terrific. Just like Sidney Carton's wait time for his turn under the guillotine. "Can we contact you if we have any questions about the contract?"

"Of course. My name and information are on the cover letter, but let me give you my card. It's got my cell phone in addition to the office number."

I got up from the table, shook his hand and walked to the counter where Theo had put the second banana bread. "Hold on a moment before you head out. You should have this for your ride home or whenever."

I unrolled some aluminum foil and wrapped it over the existing plastic wrap. "It'll keep better this way."

"Wow. That's very nice of you. Are you sure?"

"Perfectly sure."

Theo shook Arden's hand as well. "We genuinely appreciate your candor and honesty. Don't worry. The conversation we had won't go beyond this room."

"Thank you. I wish I had time to stop by your winery for a tasting, but maybe it'll give me an excuse to drive back here again. Some days I feel as if I'm tethered to the office."

Theo and I walked Arden to the front porch and watched as he turned the car around and drove away.

I stood motionless for what seemed like minutes but it was only a few seconds. "My God. Did you hear what he said? That makes three dead people. Oh my God!"

"Worse than I imagined. I knew you shouldn't've gotten yourself into this. Thank goodness for Arden. He seems like a really decent guy. If you weren't going to give him the other banana bread, I was."

"Yeah. Imagine if that Eleanor woman showed up instead. You do realize it's too late for me to back down now. I've got to see this through. Especially now. Not a single doubt in my mind Lucas and Declan were responsible for Elsbeth's death."

"Norrie, do you have a plan for your next meeting with Declan? At the very least, we can peruse the contract and find things we want changed. It'll buy you some time."

I rubbed my hands together and stared out into the vineyard. "You got that right. Every second I have with Declan counts. I have to convince him I'm as ruthless as he and his partner are in order to get him to admit to the murder. Did that contract have a nondisclosure clause?"

"It did. Vanna Enterprises is covering their tracks. How did you know about nondisclosure clauses?"

"*Fifty Shades of Grey.*"

"Say no more."

"Guess now it's a waiting game."

"I don't think you'll have to wait too long. From what Arden said, the partners at Vanna Enterprises are eager to get their plan going. I can give that monster of a contract another look this evening after work."

"I really owe you big time. Arden said he's having his office e-mail me an additional copy. I'll go through it when it arrives. It's not that intimidating now that Arden went through it."

"Good deal. How about we touch base with each other tomorrow?"

"You've got it! Want to sit down for another cup of coffee?"

"I'd love to but our tasting room will be filling up. I'll grab the contract and be on my way."

"Hey, before I forget, please give Don a hug for me. It was his banana bread that got Arden to open up with us."

"I knew I married that guy for a reason."

In spite of consuming three slices of Don's delicious bread, I was still hungry when it got to be a quarter to one. I found a foil packet of tuna, added some mayonnaise and dried dill and made myself a sandwich. I was still under Renee's writing schedule and didn't want to lose any precious time by walking down to the bistro and getting caught up with the goings-on in the tasting room. I'd do that tomorrow when Cammy and Glenda would both be in. I needed to focus on my work today.

At a little past three, the phone rang and I grabbed it. It was John.

"Is everything okay?" I asked.

"Yeah, we're about done for the day but I've got a question for you. Any reason someone from the Experiment Station, at least I think it's the Station, it could be someone from Cooperative Extension, well, anyhow, do you know why they would be taking soil samples? Some of the workers spotted a guy with a soil probe at the far left of the property. By the time they reported it to me, he was gone."

"A soil probe?"

"It looks like a golf club but it works like an auger. Goes into the ground and pulls up a thin dense linear sample. We're continually testing for pH and chemical elements like potassium, calcium, boron, but why would someone else be doing that on this property?"

"I don't know. Did they cause any damage?"

"Nah. Nothing like that. Listen, don't worry about it. I'll make sure to alert my guys to tell me if they see any more suspicious goings on."

"Thanks. Catch you later."

Soil samples. It had to be Vanna Enterprises. Chomping at the bit. I knew firsthand that soil really mattered when it came to growing grapes. Oddly enough, the soil from one winery in the Finger Lakes could differ widely from another only a few miles away. Something about glacial action and debris when the Finger Lakes were formed. I had to admit, I didn't pay much attention to it in my geology class in high school or when my father pontificated about it at the dinner table. Francine, on the other hand, all but took notes.

Maybe Vanna Enterprises was making sure they got the "good soil" since they were about to take the property in exchange for a new partner. Suddenly, that got me thinking. If they could take me on, could they get rid of me?

In a half panic, I phoned Theo and got my answer. They would have to buy me out. It was clearly spelled out in that mammoth document. He suggested I write down any of my concerns or, in this case, genuine fears and we'd go over them tomorrow. That being done, I went back to *A Swim Under the Waterfall*, but I was beginning to feel as if I'd be the one getting soaked.

My plan had to work. I had too much at stake. To add to my stress, the Fourth of July was only a few days away and I had to brace myself for that fiasco in the vineyard. God knows what Glenda had planned.

When I went to bed that night, my mind was overwrought with smudgings, ghosts and thoughts of selling my soul to the devil.

Chapter 24

"Miss Ellington! Miss Ellington! Wake up!"

For a second I swore it was *déjà vu*. The yelling outside my bedroom window and the pounding on my door. At least it was daybreak and I recognized the voices—Travis and Robbie, our vineyard workers.

Please do not tell me you found another dead body. Why can't anyone ever find buried treasure instead? "What? What is it? Who died?"

Travis and Robbie quickly exchanged looks as they stood at my front door.

Finally, Robbie spoke. "John and Peter aren't here yet, but John told us to let him or you know if we saw anything suspicious."

I cinched the belt to my robe and brushed the hair from my face. "What did you see?"

"They're in the lower left vineyard now. Surveyors. Two surveyors from Carson and Minolo. Their truck is parked off the driveway. Are they supposed to be here?"

"I didn't hire them but I'm about to find out. Thanks for letting me know."

It took me less than five minutes to pour out kibble for Charlie and slip into jeans and a top. I was out the door and down the driveway like nobody's business.

"Hey!" I shouted from across the lower part of our road. "What are you up to?"

The two lanky men who were standing near a tripod stopped what they were doing and approached me. They looked to be in their late thirties or early forties. Both had that day-old Brad Pitt growth on their faces.

"I'm Ray Shultz with Carson and Minolo. This is Hank Watts. We've been assigned to survey this property."

"From who? Who assigned you? I didn't and I'm the owner, Norrie Ellington."

"We've got a work order here from our company." Ray fished in his pocket to pull out a piece of paper. He handed it to me and shrugged at his partner.

"I didn't authorize this," I said. "Give me a minute."

The property information was correct and it looked as if they had acquired it from the assessor's office. I read the order again and felt my face get warm. It was contracted by Lucas Stilton. He was moving fast.

"There must be some mistake," I said. "You have to leave now."

The last thing I needed was for John to find out Vanna Enterprises was surveying our property. This way I could tell them it was a mistake. After all, they hadn't gotten started when Travis and Robbie saw them.

"But—"

"If we need your services, we'll contact you."

"Miss Ellington," Hank said, "our company has a tremendously long list of clients who need their properties surveyed. If we don't do it today, it could take weeks."

"I understand. You've got to leave now. Right this minute. Our vineyard crew will be arriving any second and they need absolute access to the property."

Ray nodded and motioned for Hank to remove the tripod.

My heart was beating a mile a minute as they loaded their truck and took off.

A few minutes later, Peter's white Toyota pulled up beside me. "Studying the vineyards again?"

"Actually, there was a mix-up with some surveyors. They got the wrong address."

"Hmm, that's ironic. For surveyors. They should've just used their own coordinates."

"Doesn't matter. I straightened it out."

"Want a ride up the hill?"

"You don't have to take me all the way to my house.. You can drop me off in front of one of the buildings. I'll head home from there."

"Sure?"

"Yeah. This way I can say I got my morning exercise."

Peter reached his hand over the passenger seat and slid a stack of books into the middle console. I glanced at the titles—*Vines and Wine, Soil Sampling Techniques* and *Spanish for Beginners.* Interesting choices. Peter was probably trying to learn Spanish since we hired a number of migrant workers in the fall to assist with the harvest. In fact, that was probably the language tape playing in his truck the first time I met him.

"Well, here we are," he said. "It'll only take me another minute to go all the way up the hill."

"Thanks, but this is fine. Tell John I said hello."

I closed the truck door behind me and glanced at the rear windshield. A faded decal from SUNY Cobleskill was barely legible along with a smaller one that looked like a helmet. On the rear bumper was a dog-eared oval sticker that read I (heart) PY. His truck must've been older than I thought because the Penn Yan Chamber of Commerce had changed that sticker design eons ago. The new ones were everywhere, including our tasting room and, if I remembered correctly, even on the brochure table at the Peaceful Pines. Yep, everyone loved Penn Yan.

I waved at Peter and walked back to the house, fuming. How dare Lucas Stilton send surveyors when I hadn't even signed that contract. Not that I ever *was* going to sign it, but what did they know? I took a breath, composed myself and popped a K-cup into the Keurig. There was no way I'd be able to go back to sleep.

It was imperative I came up with something to stall the contract process but what? Even Theo had to admit the document was flawless. I paced around the kitchen for the full minute it took my coffee to brew. Then I spent another minute adding the right amount of sugar and cream. Lots of both. It was going to be one of those days.

The instant I swallowed the first sip of coffee, it hit me. Vanna Enterprises would need to spell out exactly what my obligations would be as a partner. They seriously didn't expect me to work for them, did they? And what about the current employees at Two Witches? I couldn't very well leave them out in the lurch. At least as far as Lucas and Declan thought.

In the five minutes it took me to finish my coffee, I had already come up with additions and clarifications to the contract. I bit my lip and opened a clean page in Microsoft Word. No sooner did I type the words Contractual Additions when the phone rang. It was too early for the tasting room crew, but Franz sometimes arrived at the break of dawn, not to mention the vineyard workers.

I picked it up on the second ring. "Hello?"

"Norrie, It's John. We need to talk."

The four worst words in the English language. I rubbed my temples and took a breath. "What's up?"

"You tell me. I stopped at the gas station to grab a cup of coffee on my way in and ran into Carson and Minolo's surveyors. I overheard them talking about having to reschedule Two Witches Winery. Norrie, what's going on? Are Francine and Jason planning on selling the property and the business?"

There was no sense fabricating something. Besides, I was too overwrought to come up with an excuse he'd buy. John had been with this family since before I was born. He'd see right through me. "It's a long, complicated story."

"Give me the abbreviated version."

He was absolutely quiet at his end of the line while I explained in detail how I planned to get a confession out of Declan by dangling the winery in front of him like some sort of jewel.

"So you see," I went on, "there's really nothing to worry about."

"Nothing to worry about! Are you kidding? And they already drew up a preemptory contract?"

"Like I said, I'm not signing anything. I'd never do that. No matter how many dead bodies show up in our vineyard."

"You'd better be right, Norrie. One wrong move and it'll mean financial ruin for your family and unemployment for the rest of us. By the way, were Lucas and Declan aware that the winemaker and vineyard manager have retirement plans from Two Witches?"

"Um, no, but they will be. Not that it matters. None of this matters. It's simply a ruse."

"All right. I'll try to catch you later. If not, tomorrow. If you must know, this ruse of yours is scaring the hell out of me. Did anyone else see those surveyors?"

"Peter. But I told him the surveyors made a mistake. Oh, and Travis and Robbie."

"Geez. I hate lying. Let's hope none of them bring it up."

My hands were sweating when I got off the phone and my heart was beating faster than usual. What had started out as a ploy that would only involve a few people was now turning into a genuine convoluted mess. I had to move things along before everything imploded.

For the next two hours and forty minutes, I wrote a complete addendum to the contract. That included the time I needed to agonize over it. I clarified my role as a silent but voting partner and spelled out the financial remuneration for all of the employees at Two Witches. I even added a clause that stated Vanna Enterprises would assume the retirement obligation for the two managerial positions at the winery. All in all, it would've made a decent screenplay under the nebulous category of "drama," had I written it in dialogue.

"It's got the right legal jargon," Theo said when I read it to him.

"Good enough for me. Style is everything."

I was positive Lucas and Declan would tell me to pound salt, but it gave me a decent starting point for the conversation I knew I was going to have with Declan sometime during the week. After all, Arden did say Declan planned on securing the contract and I was on his time schedule.

Satisfied with my revisions, I rinsed off, slipped into clean clothes and walked directly to the tasting room. That ridiculous séance of Glenda's was creeping up on me, and I had to speak with her.

Cammy waved me over as soon as I walked in the door. "Where've you been hiding? I feel as if we haven't spoken in ages. Did Declan call you?"

"Not yet but he will. I met with their attorney. Well, one of them. Arden Grant. And Theo was there as my legal consul."

"Theo from the Grey Egret?"

"Uh-huh."

"He has a law degree?"

"Not exactly. Anyway, I think Arden Grant is on our side."

"Okay. Let me know when you're going to see Declan so I can round up Marc and Enzo again. I think they really enjoyed going undercover, so to speak."

"I will. Listen, I've got to talk with Glenda. I really need to know exactly what she has planned."

"Good idea. Tell her to send her customers to my table. I'll cover for her."

Just then, two blondes, who looked more like teens than legal-age drinkers, approached Cammy's table.

"Hi and welcome! Do you mind showing me your driver's licenses?"

"I told you we should do this more often," the shorter-haired blonde said to the other. "This is the only place where we look young."

They both held out their licenses and beamed. Twenty-two years old. No wonder they looked young.

"Do you have Zinfandel? I love pink Zinfandel," the other one said.

Cammy went on to explain that Zinfandel wasn't grown in the Finger Lakes but we had similar wines they might enjoy. I gave her a thumbs-up and walked over to Glenda's table.

Glenda was bent down, returning some bottles to the small fridge underneath her tasting room table. All I could see were waves of turquoise and purple hair woven into her natural gray color. When she lifted her head, I noted the red lipstick was now a deeper shade of mauve and the hoop earrings had been replaced with what looked like coiled snakes.

"Norrie! Finally! I was hoping you'd stop in. We're all set for the séance. Actually, it will be more of a conjuring than a séance, although I will be casting a protective circle. It's not an evocation. We certainly don't want to invite evil spirits, although Elsbeth isn't exactly what one would call benevolent."

"So, let me get this straight. You and the tasting room crew, along with Emma and Fred from the bistro and Herbert from the winery lab will be going up to the vineyard area where Elsbeth's body was discovered and then what?"

"First, a purification ritual. We'll light sage and lavender sticks to purify the air."

"Don't drop them on the ground. We don't need to purify by fire."

"Understood. Then I'll lead the chanting of the souls. It's an ancient summoning call that sounds somewhat like animals keening."

Terrific. Just what every winery needs.

Glenda looked unfazed. "This particular summoning builds and builds with intensity until the spirit, in this case Elsbeth, is loosened from the tethers that bind her and is released into our realm, albeit temporarily. Then, at that point, we will thank her and ask her to tell us or show us who was responsible for her death."

"Uh, not to sound pedantic, but how exactly is she supposed to do that?"

"Oh, you'd be surprised. Spirits have their ways. It might be as simple as a gust of wind that carries the aroma of someone's perfume. Or if, heaven forbid, it was one of us, they might start to choke or cough without stopping. With spirits you simply never know."

"Okay. Just don't go near the vineyard rows or aisles. You'll have to conduct this conjuring or séance a few yards away. And I think Peter may show up to make sure everyone keeps off of the Riesling vines."

"I understand. That's why it's so important we do a full crescendo of the chanting of the souls."

And if we're lucky, maybe someone's backyard fireworks will drown it out.

"You will be there, of course, won't you?"

I did a mental eye roll and nodded. "I can't make any guarantees, but I'll see what I can do."

"It's our last chance, Norrie. Keep that in mind. Elsbeth's spirit is slipping farther and farther away. The energy from the Fourth of July won't last past that evening."

I don't know if any of us will last past that evening...

I told Glenda how much I appreciated her efforts and made a beeline for the bistro. Nothing like a decent panini to bring things back to reality.

When I got back to the house, I took a cool shower and focused on my screenplay. Charlie was happily snoring from his dog bed and, for a few minutes, I actually felt a sense of bliss. That ended abruptly when the phone rang.

"Miss Ellington...Norrie, it's me, Declan. Hope you're doing well. I've been tied up with business for the past few days, but I heard everything went well with Arden Grant."

"Um, yes. It did. He's very nice."

"He informed us you brought along your legal consul and that was a smart thing to do. I trust you've had a chance to review the contract in depth?"

"I did. I mean, we did."

"And?"

"Uh, it was direct and to the point."

"So, you're all right with it."

"Not exactly."

"What are you saying?"

"The contract fails to explain mý role as a partner and doesn't address the current employees at Two Witches. It will need revision."

There was silence at his end of the phone and I held my breath.

Finally, Declan spoke. "Would you or your attorney fax me your revisions and I'll have Armstrong, Patel, Smolowitz and Tarrow incorporate those changes. Unless, of course, it's something we simply cannot do and I'll let you know. You have our fax number, don't you?"

"Yes. I have all of your business information."

"Wonderful. How about this? You get that fax to us this afternoon and you and I can meet to discuss everything at dinner later this week."

"Dinner? At night?"

"Of course at night. My schedule is packed, and I won't have time during the day for a lunch meeting. I'll make it easy on you. I'll make reservations for us at Belhurst Castle. That's only three or four miles from Two Witches."

"I know where it is. It's a major landmark around here." *Not to mention one of the most expensive, highly rated restaurants on Seneca Lake.*

"Let's make it the day after tomorrow. Eight o'clock?"

"Um, sure. Eight would be fine."

"Then it's settled. Belhurst at eight. I look forward to seeing you again."

"Likewise." *Likewise? Why do I always wind up saying things I don't mean when I talk to him?*

The day after tomorrow. Boy, Vanna Enterprises certainly had their lawyers on a short leash. For the rest of us in the real world, these things took weeks. Sometimes months. I printed my addendum to the contract and raced down the driveway to use the office fax machine.

Cammy and the crew were finishing up in the tasting room when I walked in. I motioned for her to join me in the office and I closed the door behind us.

"I don't suppose Marc and Enzo can make it to Belhurst Castle on Thursday night? I'm willing to pay for their dinners if they don't go overboard."

"They'd be punching each other on the arms for something like that, but it's a work night for them and impossible to find substitutes."

"Yeah, I sort of figured as much, but I thought I'd give it a try."

I told her about my call from Declan and the addendum I was about to fax.

"What about Theo and Don?" she asked. "It wouldn't look that unusual for them to be going out to dinner at Belhurst."

"Maybe, but I don't want to take that chance. Worst case scenario, I can always excuse myself to go to the ladies' room and call them."

"Make sure your phone is charged. By the way, are you copacetic with Glenda's glimpse to the world beyond?"

"Yeah. Might as well get that over with. Next thing you know, Lizzie will want to teach me Morse Code."

"Huh?"

"It's a Nancy Drew thing. Trust me, you don't want to know."

If Vanna Enterprises worked at breakneck speed to incorporate my addendum into the partnership contract, God knows what else they were capable of doing. I figured I'd get one step closer to learning on Thursday night and, with any luck, eke out a confession from Declan. Or so I thought.

Chapter 25

"You sure you have our number on speed dial?" Theo asked.

It was seven thirty on Thursday and I was on my way to Belhurst Castle.

"I do. I'm all set."

"Remember, whatever you do, no matter what he says, don't sign anything. Not even the dinner receipt if you're charging it to a credit card. Make him pay."

"Whoa. That didn't even cross my mind."

"Call us the minute you get back. I don't care how late it is. Okay?"

"I will. Don't worry. And thanks."

Francine and Jason were right. Having Theo and Don on my side felt darn good. Cammy, too, for that matter. I drove slowly to Belhurst Castle, my eyes drifting across the road to Seneca Lake. A few sailboats were making their way to shore, although the sun wouldn't set for another hour. If the weather held out for the Fourth of July, the lake would be filled with boats and partygoers.

The winding road that led to Belhurst Castle looked like something out of a fairytale with its tall pine trees and smaller deciduous ones. The structure was once a private residence built in Romanesque Revival style with towers, arches and bays. The neat thing I remembered about it was the fact it was a speakeasy during Prohibition. Rumors abounded that it was part of the Underground Railroad, although that couldn't be proven. Still, it was listed in the National Register of Historic Places. The last time I was there was for my senior class prom. Yikes. Ages ago.

Declan was waiting for me in the formal lobby and we were both escorted immediately to our table overlooking the lake. I ordered tonic water with lime and fidgeted nervously hoping Declan would start the conversation.

"You look lovely tonight, Norrie."

Francine will be glad to hear that. It's her teal sheath. A tad shorter on me due to our height difference, but what's a little leg among friends? "Thank you. You don't look so bad yourself." *And that suit must cost some people a month's salary.*

"Well, you'll be relieved to know we can incorporate your addendum wishes into the contract. Armstrong, Patel, Smolowitz and Tarrow will be FedExing you another copy. You should receive it sometime tomorrow morning. I thought perhaps we could meet at one of the banks so our signatures can be notarized. I'll call you after noon to make those arrangements."

Okay. Good news. Bad news. He didn't bring anything for me to sign tonight but, unless a major earthquake hits the Finger Lakes tomorrow, I'm going to be in deep trouble.

Given how fast he was moving, I had to get that damn confession out of him. My stomach began to tighten. I'd better order something light.

"I'll have the herb-roasted chicken salad," I told the waiter.

"You sure that's all you want?" Declan asked. "You're making me feel guilty. I'm ordering prime rib."

"The salad's fine. It's got walnuts and grapes. All sorts of neat tastes."

"If that's what you'd like…"

I took a sip of my drink and looked Declan straight in the eyes. "I'm on your side, now. Nondisclosure agreement and all."

"You won't regret your decision. This move will catapult you into a whole new life experience."

"I actually like the one I have."

"You asked to be a silent partner, but should you decide to change your mind, our attorneys have written language to address that."

I clasped my hands together and folded over my fingers, leaning my head into the table. "I hope the language was clear to include remunerations for my sister and brother-in-law."

"It was and it does. Stop worrying and enjoy your meal. The artisan breads are scrumptious."

I reached for one of the butter pats and hoped Declan didn't catch the slight tremor in my hand. This wasn't as deadly as my lunch with Lucas Stilton, but it was getting close. Declan talked a bit about his plans for the mega-winery and I nodded politely, trying to figure out exactly what I was going to say that would make him crack.

Our meals arrived and we ate quietly, sticking only to small talk. When the waiter cleared the table and took our coffee orders, I clenched my teeth, swallowed and reached my hand across the table, giving Declan's a quick squeeze. Judging from his expression, I caught him completely off guard.

"As I was saying about the nondisclosure agreement, I know I'm completely bound to keeping everything confidential." I emphasized the word "everything."

Declan didn't say a word.

"I understand that, in your business, certain decisions have to be made in order to ensure the growth of your company. Ruthless decisions, at times. Please note, I'm not entering into this lightly. I'm prepared to accept those decisions and those actions. When barriers stand in the way, sometimes they have to be removed, even if it means doing something that, well, shall we say, goes against the human conscience."

Hmm. *The human conscience. I think I used that expression in one of my screenplays.* Kisses in the Snow? *Oh, what the hell.*

"Anyway, Declan, I wanted you to know how I felt. How I'm prepared to act. That Atlantis vision of yours will bring so much joy to so many, what does it matter that one less person is part of the picture? It had to happen to make all of this come together. She had to be done away with. It's the details I'd like to—"

"My God!" Declan rubbed the nape of his neck and it looked as if all the color had suddenly drained from his face. "You planned this all along. How could I have been so blind? So dense. To not see it. To not realize it. My God, Norrie! You're the one who killed Elsbeth Waters to make it easier for us to acquire that property. You must've known the niece would be a pushover."

I opened my mouth but nothing came out. Okay, maybe a few garbled syllables but nothing coherent.

Declan kept on talking. "It was no secret Vanna Enterprises wanted that property, as well as Two Witches, in order to establish our mega-winery-entertainment center. And you figured out how to become a part of it. A full-fledged partner. It would've meant millions for you. Oh my God!"

He paused for a moment to swallow some water while I stared at him, unable to utter a sound.

"This deal is totally off the table, Norrie. I'm not getting into bed, so to speak, with a killer."

I finally got my voice back and I tried to keep it low. "A killer? Look who's talking. What about your silent partner for Euro Wonderland? And the other one? The woman from San Francisco who bankrolled your mall? Just for the record, my attorney"—*whoever that may be*—"did his homework."

"Well, he got the answers wrong. Gerhardt Weimer died from complications of congestive heart failure and Patrice Vandermark suffered a stroke. My partner and I are twenty-first century businessmen, not nineteen-thirties racketeers. Sure, we may be ruthless when it comes to contracts and legal matters, but murder? That's unconscionable."

"If you say so. Then how do you explain my brother-in-law getting that grant all of a sudden? I know, for a fact, Lucas Stilton made a formidable donation to Cornell University's philanthropic fund with the monies earmarked for one project and one project only—insect research in Costa Rica. He had to know it was Jason Keane's forte."

Declan shook his head and made an annoying tsk-tsk sound. "Wrong again. You probably didn't know this, but Lucas was a twin. When he and his sister were fourteen, their parents took them to Costa Rica for a vacation and an opportunity to see the rainforests. His sister contracted Dengue fever, only a serious version—Dengue Hemorrhagic Fever. She died from it and he never got over her death. He contributes millions to research in order to find a cure."

Everything felt as if it was spiraling around me. I still had one more dart to toss his way.

"Then how do you explain Rosalee Marbleton's sudden sweepstakes win and subsequent trip to Alaska? She didn't even remember buying a ticket. Her property would've completed the package for you."

"You got me on that one. Alaska, huh?"

"She's there now."

"Well, I had no idea."

By now small beads of perspiration were forming on my forehead and my foot was tapping uncontrollably under the table. Then something dawned on me. "Your car! Why would a new Mercedes have to be detailed? I'll tell you why. Because it was used to transport a dead body across a rutted makeshift road so you could dump it in our vineyard. There are all sorts of vines and bushes alongside that road. Enough to scratch and mar the finish."

"Nice try, but wrong again. I made the mistake of parking my car at the Monroe County Fairgrounds to catch a car show. That'll never happen again. So much dust and dirt and small pebbles wreaked havoc on the finish. Oh, and, for your information, Lucas and I alibied out. We were in the Bahamas during the time of Elsbeth's murder. Atlantis, to be exact. We both wanted our project to outdo that one."

Suddenly, our waiter appeared. "Can I interest you in any desserts to go with your coffees?"

No, but a hari-kari knife is beginning to sound inviting.

"Just the bill, please." Declan's voice was devoid of any emotion. Then he turned to me when the waiter walked off. "Like I said, Norrie. It's over."

I must've been in shock because nothing was processing. Declan stood, put a wad of cash on the table and walked out. I sat there stunned, the delicate coffee cup shaking in my hand.

When I finally focused, I pulled out my cell phone and sent a text to Theo and Don. It read:

He pointed the finger at me. Do you know any real lawyers?

Less than three minutes later, my phone vibrated and I answered.

Theo sounded calm but concerned. "Drive straight here. It'll be okay."

As I walked out of the gracious dining room in Belhurst Castle, I wondered if I'd ever see the place, or any other restaurant, for that matter, ever again. Knowing Declan Roth, he wasn't going to waste any time accusing me of murder. Then again, maybe he'd simply toss it up as a business deal gone sour and forget about it. Either way, the pressure would be off for the other wineries since Vanna Enterprises wouldn't be able to have their choice piece of property.

Unfortunately, I was no closer to finding Elsbeth's killer and, for all I knew, I was one step closer to my own demise. Don opened the front door to their house without me knocking. He must've been looking out the window.

No sooner had I stepped inside than I started bawling like a baby. It was uncontrollable. I sobbed and shook, scaring the daylights out of everyone. Myself included.

"I'm so sorry," I said. "I don't even remember the last time I cried."

"That's okay," Theo said. "Sit down. I'll make you some tea."

"Thanks, no. I can't eat or drink another thing. It was awful. Awful. I botched up everything."

For a second it felt as if something tickled my neck and then, without warning, a huge long-haired cat jumped in my lap and bumped my chin.

"Wow," Don said. "It usually takes Isolde months to warm up to new people. She must really like you."

I stroked the cat's silky fur and relaxed long enough to relive every single detail of my dinner experience with Declan. When I was finally through, both guys came over and gave me hugs.

"It'll be all right." Don said. "Chances are, Declan won't want to call attention to himself and get involved with this matter."

"You think so?" I tried to sound hopeful.

Theo grimaced. "Hate to be a buzzkill, but I'm not so sure. No sense worrying about it tonight. All it really means is we're back to square one when it comes to finding Elsbeth's real killer."

"What if I do get arrested? Then what?"

"Calm down," Don said. "We'll get a good criminal lawyer and make sure we have lots of bail money. But seriously, I don't believe Declan will lift a fingernail to accuse you."

"I hope you're right. I really, really do."

Chapter 26

Again with the pounding on the door at the break of dawn, only this time it wasn't accompanied by Travis and Robbie's voices. I reached for clean undergarments in my drawer, slipped a top over my head and threw on some jeans. The pounding was relentless.

"I'm coming! I'm coming!"

Charlie bounded down the stairs and went straight for his food dish. I poured the kibble automatically before I opened the door.

Deputy Hickman stood pokerfaced as he spoke. "Miss Ellington, you'll need to accompany me to the sheriff's station in Penn Yan for questioning regarding the murder of Elsbeth Waters."

"That's ridiculous. Absolutely ridiculous. I didn't even know her until I got here."

"But you *were* acquainted with her, were you not?"

"I only met her on two occasions when she came into our tasting room. Well, once in the room. Once in the parking lot, if you want to be specific. Are you arresting me? Because if you are, I need to call my lawyer."

Or the winery owner from down the road who'll have to suffice.

"At this juncture in time, I am bringing you in for questioning. That's all I'm at liberty to say at the moment."

"Fine. Let me comb my hair at least and put on some shoes. You can grab a seat at the table. Don't worry. It's not as if I'm going to make a run for it."

I trounced back upstairs, brushed my teeth, put on some sunscreen tint and combed my hair, but not before sending Theo and Don another text.

Hauled into the sheriff's station in PY. Wait till you hear from me.

It didn't make sense for one or both of them to drive over there if I was going to be released a short while later.

I locked the door behind me and followed Grizzly Gary to his car. "Are you going to cuff me?" I was half kidding.

"You're only being questioned at this time. Sit in the back, if you will."

It was a ten minute drive to the Yates County Sheriff's Office, officially titled the Yates County Public Safety Building. The structure was a gray nondescript flat-roofed building that had all the charm of a boxcar. The interior wasn't much different.

We skirted past the glass-enclosed window that separated visitors from the safety personnel. Next, we headed past a number of small cubicles until we reached Deputy Hickman's office. Francine's work spot at the winery looked like the Taj Mahal compared to his tiny office space.

Deputy Hickman walked around his desk and sat, pointing for me to take the only other chair in the room. A small uncomfortable one that faced his desk.

"Miss Ellington, it is my sad duty to inform you that you are now considered a person of interest in the murder of Elsbeth Waters."

"You could've mentioned that at my house, you know."

"And risk having you bolt out of there?"

"Where? Where would I bolt?"

Deputy Hickman ignored my question. "Our office received some very recent evidence that points directly at you."

"Fine. And what exactly would *that* be?"

Without wasting a second, he took out his iPhone and placed it on the desk. Seconds later I heard my own voice. Only the words had been edited. *"When barriers stand in the way, sometimes they have to be removed, even if it means doing something that goes against the human conscience. What does it matter that one less person is part of the picture? She had to be done away with."*

"Like I was saying, Miss Ellington, you're a clever woman. I wouldn't put anything past you."

"First of all, that *human conscience* bit came from a screenplay I wrote, and second, this is entrapment. That dirty son-of-a-gun. That sneaky, lowlife you-know-what. See? I can't even say the word. You think I could kill someone? If I'm guilty of anything, it was trying to get Declan Roth into admitting he was responsible for the murder. And yes, before you say another word, I know. I know. I should've kept out of it, but I didn't."

"Speak slower. I'm getting this all down."

Unless Deputy Hickman aced a shorthand class back in the sixties, I didn't know how or what he was getting down on that pad of his but I didn't say a word about it. Instead, I told him every single detail about my scheme and the rationale behind it, including the car detailing, Jason's sudden grant, thanks to Lucas Stilton's generous donation, and Rosalee Marbleton's sudden sweepstakes win. He looked at me as if I had just stepped off a spaceship.

"Oddly enough, I believe you, Miss Ellington, but that scheme of yours had to be the most ill-conceived, downright dangerous plot I've ever heard. For your information, our department, in conjunction with the Monroe County Sheriff's Department in Rochester, scrutinized and verified the whereabouts of Lucas Stilton and Declan Roth, on and before the time of Elsbeth's murder. And not only that, but our investigators looked into any possible contacts those two might have had in order to execute a murder. And you know what? Clean as a whistle. They may be unscrupulous businessmen, but they're not killers."

I rubbed my temples and groaned.

"You were right about one thing, though. Rosalee Marbleton didn't win any sweepstakes."

"I knew it. It was those developers, wasn't it?"

"No, as a matter of fact, it wasn't." Deputy Hickman's voice reeked of exasperation. "It was Rosalee's children. My wife happens to be friends with one of the daughters. Rosalee would never have accepted money from them to go on that trip of a lifetime, so they worked with a travel agent in the area and came up with that sweepstakes idea. Now, are you satisfied? And now, do you understand why these investigations should be left to the professionals?"

Ouch. "Uh-huh."

He had one of the younger deputy sheriffs drive me back home and warned me again to keep out of his investigation. I called the Grey Egret the minute I got in the door.

Don's relief was overwhelming. "Don't know about you, but that took ten years off my life. One for your near arrest and nine thinking about what your sister would do to us. Hold on a second…"

His voice trailed off and then I heard, "Theo, you can stop looking up criminal attorneys in Rochester."

"I'm so sorry for putting you through this. Honestly. I thought I was doing the right thing."

"It's okay. Try not to think about it. We'll catch up later, all right?"

"Sounds good."

I made myself a cup of coffee and paced around the kitchen. Charlie, who had gone back to sleep in his bed, looked up once in a while.

"This really bites, you know," I said to the drowsy hound. "Really, really bites. I suppose I should break the bad news to Yvonne, since there's no way Vanna Enterprises is going to buy her property now that Two Witches is off the table. She might've stood a chance while Lucas and Declan thought they had a deal going with me, but that shriveled up fast, huh?"

The dog began to snore and I made myself another cup of coffee.

"Yep, bye-bye to Yvonne's dreams of relocating somewhere in California. Or was it Baja California? Anyway, it was someplace without snow. Guess she better not get rid of her winter wardrobe."

I looked at the clock on the microwave—9:51 AM. Yvonne was probably done with breakfast at her B & B and maybe it wasn't such a bad idea after all if I paid her a visit. It would also give me an opportunity to snoop around a little more at her place. Snoop, not investigate. There was a subtle difference.

Only one car was in front of the Peaceful Pines when I got there, and the driver was backing up. Connecticut license plate. Tourists, for sure. I knocked on the door and Yvonne opened it almost immediately.

"Hi, Norrie. What brings you here?"

"Have you got a minute? There's something I wanted to talk with you about."

"Sure. All the guests have taken off for the wine trail, so come on in."

"I'm not going to be long but I needed you to know something. Remember a while back when you told me you'd had an offer on this property from a larger wine company? Well, I hate to say this, but Vanna Enterprises won't be buying up the wineries on these hills. They needed Two Witches but, er, they changed their mind and don't want anything to do with us. Well, *me*, to be exact. Long story. I'm really sorry, Yvonne. I know you didn't want to spend the rest of your life running this B & B."

She crinkled her nose and shrugged. "Vanna Enterprises? They weren't the ones who wanted to buy our property. It was Stephanie Ipswich and her husband from Gable Hill Winery down the road."

My God! The second suspect on my list is Stephanie. Stephanie with the tea and crumpets, and tarp to drag the body.

"Norrie, are you all right? You look as if you've seen a ghost."

"What? No, I'm fine. I was taken by surprise, that's all. I was positive it was those developers who wanted your property."

"Nope, it was the Ipswiches, and I plan to take them up on it as soon as this miserable estate is settled. Things move so damn slow around here. And still no arrests regarding my aunt's murder."

"An arrest might come sooner than you think. You never know. Anyway, I should get going. Have a good day."

I was out the door, in my car and back to my kitchen in record time. With every other possibility exhausted, it all boiled down to the one person who had the big three—motive, means and opportunity—Stephanie Ipswich. I was dying to share this revelation with Theo and Don, but it was Friday and they'd be swamped in their tasting room. Besides, I had plagued them enough for one morning. It could wait. Especially since I was without a plan. Maybe I'd bother them after Glenda's wackadoodle séance, or conjuring of the dead, or whatever she'd planned for the Fourth of July.

Oh my gosh! The Fourth of July! That was tomorrow night. I had told Theo and Don about it, but neither of them wanted to participate in Glenda's summoning of the dead.

"Call if you need us," Don had said when I first broached the topic. "But I seriously doubt you'll run into any problems. Not with the dead, anyway."

The rest of the day and the following morning I tethered myself to the house and refused to leave until I had made some headway with my screenplay. I was still steaming over the fact Declan had accused me of murder and worse yet, called the county sheriff. I tried to dismiss it as I dove into my writing. Thankfully, screenplays didn't require intense grammatical scrutiny like novels or short stories. As long as the characters were compelling, the dialogue flowed, the storyline was tight and the interest level high, I was in business. The only break I took was to double check the séance timeframe with Cammy and grab an aioli burger at our bistro.

"You just missed Peter and Herbert," she said. "They left a few minutes ago after lunch. Doesn't matter, I'm sure you'll see them tomorrow night."

"Yeah, with bells on."

* * * *

On July Fourth, Glenda insisted everyone meet in front of the new Riesling vineyard, aka Elsbeth's near final resting spot, at exactly eight forty-nine, the official time of the sunset.

"The spirit forces will be the strongest between eight forty-nine and nine twenty-four, when the twilight hour ends," she had told everyone. Not that I wanted to participate, because, believe me, I didn't, but I felt as if I should at least make an appearance as the crowd gathered. I felt sorry for the staff at Two Witches since they'd already put in a full day and now had to return to our winery a few hours later because one of them was certifiable.

Charlie trotted beside me as I walked toward the infamous spot. The sun had just started to set and cast a pinkish hue on the horizon. Up ahead, closer to the Riesling vineyard, I saw Cammy, Lizzie, Sam, Fred and Emma. Oh, and Glenda. It was impossible not to notice Glenda. She was decked out in a long purplish robe circa nineteen sixty-nine Woodstock and small flowers were pinned to her hair.

"Hey, Norrie! Hold up!" came a voice. I turned.

Herbert quickened his pace and caught his breath when he reached me.

"Thanks for doing this," I said. "It's really above and beyond any of your responsibilities."

"My advisor said the same thing when I told him. That was before he doubled over laughing and asked me again for the name of the winery."

"Oh, geez."

"Relax. This'll be a hoot." He turned back for a second when we both heard a car pulling into the tasting room parking lot.

"That must be Roger," Herbert said. "Let's hurry before we get caught up in the French and Indian War. He had me tied up for a full forty minutes once going on and on about William Shirley's expulsion of the French settlers in seventeen fifty-five. After listening to him, I wanted to be expelled as well. Come on, we'd better put some distance between us and him."

"Hello there!" Glenda called out as we approached. "Our circle is almost complete. I believe that's Roger heading toward us. Isn't that him?"

"Looks like him," Cammy said. "Good. Maybe we can get this over with so I can get off my feet."

Glenda ignored her remark and waved Roger over. "I believe we're all here, except for Peter. I thought I saw him earlier."

"You did," Cammy said. "He showed up and went back down the hill to check the barn for his wallet. He thought it either dropped out of his pocket down there or maybe even by the bistro when he had lunch." Then she turned to me, "I hope you don't mind, but I loaned him the key to the tasting room and gave him the alarm code to get inside, in case the wallet fell out in there. Must not be his week. Fred had to chase after him a few days ago because he left his baseball cap on one of the tables. You know, that black one he always wears with the red knight on it."

I was half listening but something caught my attention. *Black cap with a red knight.* Where had I seen something like that before? Oh yeah. That faded decal on the rear windshield of his truck. Then, something else hit me. It was as if I was spinning a Rubik's cube and every algorithm fell into place.

"Um, you'll have to excuse me, everyone. I need to take care of something. I'll be back. Get started without me. You don't want to miss the spirit forces while they're at their strongest."

"She's right," Glenda said. "We must begin. Quickly now. Form a circle. We'll start with a soft incantation chant I'll teach you. Everyone should be holding a sage and lavender incense stick. I'll pass around my barbeque lighter. It's much safer than the smaller ones. Once your stick is lit, hold it in the air."

The sky was getting darker and the air more humid. What was it with the Finger Lakes? Every night the same thing–an invitation for every insect to come out and suck blood. The gravel underneath my feet made a soft crunching sound as I raced to the tasting room. It was dark. That meant Peter was still in the barn somewhere, looking for his wallet. I had time.

I unlocked the front door and walked inside, latching the screen door behind me. Alvin must've been in his little hut because I didn't notice him on my way inside the building. I hurried to the office and unlocked the employee records file with the small key that was now a permanent fixture on my keychain.

It took me all of three seconds to pull out Peter Groff's file. A copy of his high school diploma, along with his degrees from colleges, was staring me in the face, but it was the high school that mattered. Tully, to be exact, a small hamlet outside of Syracuse and home to the black knights. I remembered Arden Grant saying something about it because it was his hometown, too. And he wasn't the only one.

Too bad I didn't have an eidetic memory or it would've saved me some time. I immediately Googled Tully Central High School Alumni and was hit by a number of sites, each one with a list according to the graduating year. I found Peter's year and clicked the site. Then I scanned the names and bit my lip. Yvonne Finlay. Just as I thought. It was Peter's baseball cap on the rack by her B & B door the first time I was in the Peaceful Pines. And, as for Yvonne? It was all starting to make sense.

The last time I had seen her name was in a Syracuse newspaper dating back from the time she was sentenced for embezzlement. She graduated with the same high school class as Peter. Everything was beginning to jell. I wondered why on earth someone like Peter Groff would leave California to work as an assistant vineyard manager in Penn Yan. And his explanation when I asked him a while back was really vague. Now it made sense—he wanted to be near Yvonne. Yvonne and Peter. Peter and Yvonne. My God! Her necklace. The rotating letters in that heart. It wasn't Penn Yan she loved, it was Peter. When that B & B guest, Cheyanne, mentioned "the couple," it had to be the two of them.

I could hear Lizzie admonishing me now. "Nancy Drew would've figured this out weeks ago. Without the drama."

Well, piss on Nancy Drew. I wasn't doing too badly myself.

Outside, the incantation circle was getting louder and louder. Elsbeth's spirit could save herself the bother. I knew who her killer was.

Chapter 27

I pushed Ctrl+P on the keyboard and waited for the information to print. Then I picked up the phone and dialed the Yates County Sheriff's Office. The call hadn't connected when I heard the latch on the screen door opening and closing. Instinctively, I stood, dropping the receiver.

"Norrie? Are you in here? It's me, Peter. I think I might've left my wallet in the bistro."

"Peter, I…"

He stepped inside the door of the office at the same instant the paper rolled off the printer and onto the floor. He snatched it up and read it before I could get there. The look on his face was one I recognized. One I always used in my screenplays—betrayal. The look of betrayal. Actually, a combination of furrowed brow, a grimace and jaw clenching.

"So, you figured it out." His voice was softer than usual and slower. "It wasn't supposed to go down the way it did, but things happened."

"If it was an accident, I'm sure the deputy sheriff will understand."

"It wasn't an accident. Not all of it."

My heart was racing and my hands felt sweaty. With only the screen door closed, I heard Glenda's séance getting louder and louder. Keening sounds. Moaning sounds. At one point, something that resembled yodeling, but I wasn't sure. What I *was* sure of, was the fact I needed to get the hell out of there but Peter was blocking the door.

"It makes sense, you know," I said. "Elsbeth stood in the way of your future with Yvonne. I could understand why you and Yvonne—"

"She didn't have a thing to do with this. NOT A DAMN THING! Understand?"

I nodded. "Uh-huh."

"Yvonne took the fall for me. Sacrificed her career for me and got a felony record to boot. The only reason she siphoned monies from that department store was to help finance my college expenses. In case you haven't figured it out, there aren't too many millionaires living in Tully."

I wasn't about to give him a lecture on scholarships, grants and student loans. He'd made his own choices and was about to make another one. He reached into a back pocket and grabbed a pruning knife. Nasty little sucker—serrated teeth on a wide-curved blade. I stepped back, bumping into the desk. Outside, the chanting had reached a fever pitch. The moans echoed everywhere and there was some sort of awful trilling sound. At that instant, two things happened.

Peter lunged toward me with the knife, and Alvin broke through the screen door into the foyer. The noise was enough to startle Peter long enough for me to grab hold of one of those Dowitcher paperweights. I jabbed the bill into his upper thigh and made a run for it.

"You witch!" he yelled. "Think a little blood's going to stop me?"

Alvin was now in the tasting room, knocking into chairs. It was only a matter of time before he'd find the racks with our wine bottles. I heard crashing sounds but ran instead to the front entrance where I screamed my lungs out. It was pointless. That infernal caterwauling from Glenda's incantation made it impossible for anyone to hear me.

I was just about out the door when Peter grabbed me by an ankle and pulled me to the ground.

"What are you going to do?" I asked. "Stab me right here?"

He poked the pruning knife into my side and told me to stand. "We're going to walk nice and slow to my truck." He prodded me along.

I screeched as loud as I could but Peter pasted his hand across my mouth. I tried biting it but all I managed to do was nuzzle his hand with my lips. Ugh. Then, out of nowhere, Alvin charged into us from behind. It took Peter completely off guard and he lost his balance. I managed to sidestep the goat and paste myself against the door frame. Then I screamed again. Louder this time.

My scream must've hit a lull in the séance because the chanting had stopped. Unfortunately, the blasts from Roman candles and assorted fireworks pounded my ears. The lake-goers, the neighbors and the tourists were all celebrating the Fourth of July.

I didn't bother to turn and see if Peter was behind me. I ran down that driveway as fast as I possibly could. Granted, it was a longer distance to Theo and Don's, but why run uphill? That most definitely would've slowed me down.

Suddenly, I was all but blinded by red-and-blue lights. An emergency vehicle. And it was headed straight up our driveway. *Dear Lord, had someone complained about Glenda's little spirit fest in the vineyard?* I ran directly toward the car and waved my arms. "Someone's trying to kill me."

My mind was so intent on getting away from Peter that I hadn't realized I was being followed. Apparently, the entire entourage from the vineyard either heard my screams or saw the emergency flashers. Behind me, I could make out voices. Voices I recognized—Cammy, Lizzie, Glenda, Sam, Roger, Herbert, Emma and Fred. And they were all yelling at once.

The flashers gave off enough light for me to turn and see them. And that wasn't all I saw. Alvin had made his way into one of the vineyards and was now happily chomping on some vines. *Dear God, will this nightmare ever end?*

"Don't worry!" Sam shouted. "I'm wearing a belt. I'll get it around Alvin's neck and lead him back to his pen. Hopefully he didn't break the gate, only knocked it over. Was that why you were screaming? Because of that goat?"

Sam didn't wait for my answer. He took off after Alvin at the same instant as Deputy Hickman got out of his car.

"Dispatch got your emergency call but couldn't make out what was going on. That's why I'm here. So, Miss Ellington, what brings me out to your winery on the Fourth of July?"

By now, everyone had crowded around me and they all began to speak at once.

"Elsbeth Waters's spirit has emerged from the dead."

"The dwarf goat got loose."

"The conjuring séance worked."

"Did you hear our incantation?"

"Damn fireworks are too loud."

"Elsbeth's ghost is among us."

"That goat's gonna cause a lot of damage. Did Sam catch him?"

Deputy Hickman crossed his arms and said two words—"QUIET EVERYONE!" Then he looked directly at me. "You haven't answered my question. This better be good."

"It is," I said. "Peter Groff tried to kill me. I was calling your office for help."

Just then, another vehicle pulled up behind the deputy's car and my two buddies from the Grey Egret came racing over.

Don was practically out of breath. "We heard the commotion! My God, Norrie, what's going on?"

"The killer... He—"

A few yards away, Sam shouted. "I've got him. I'm taking him back now."

"Sam caught the killer?" Theo yelled. "Shouldn't someone help him?"

"The goat," Roger groaned. "Sam corralled Alvin. God knows where Peter Groff has gotten off to. Very similar to a situation back in seventeen fifty-five when—"

"Enough!" Deputy Hickman exploded. "There are far too many of us to stand in the middle of a driveway at night and discuss the whereabouts of an alleged killer." Then, to me, he said, "Miss Ellington, perhaps we can all take a seat in your tasting room and work this through."

What followed next was one of the longest nights of my life. First, my recounting of the events that led me to the revelation that Peter was the one responsible for Elsbeth's murder. Then, my blow-by-blow description of what had taken place in Francine's office. Then, the Alvin fiasco. I think the incantation noise scared the living daylights out of the poor goat. And finally, the realization that none of us had any idea where Peter Groff had gone. I imagined he got into his truck and exited from one of the seasonal dirt roads that connected to the vineyards.

The tasting room crew remained to clean up the outrageous mess Alvin had made. Fortunately, he only broke a dozen or so bottles of wine and those were our blends, not our most expensive varieties. Theo went outside to help Sam repair Alvin's fence or gate or whatever it was that the goat had broken.

"I'll go to Home Depot tomorrow," Don offered, "and get you a replacement screen door. This one is totally shot."

Deputy Hickman took copious notes and notified his office to put out an all-points bulletin on Peter Groff. He also directed someone to pay a little visit to Yvonne, shouting, "I don't give a rat's patootie if it *is* the Fourth of July. Send someone over there!"

"I'll need a complete written statement from you, Miss Ellington, but it can wait until tomorrow."

All of a sudden, Glenda stood and grabbed the deputy by the wrist. "There's something you should know. Our séance worked. We conjured Elsbeth's spirit and she led us directly to her killer."

"I'll be sure to make a note of it," he replied, not batting an eyelash.

It was well after two in the morning when our employees left the building and I followed Grizzly Gary out the door. Theo and Don were right behind me, making certain I set the alarm.

"Are you sure you're going to be all right?" Theo asked. "What if Peter comes back?"

"He won't," Deputy Hickman stated. "Or he's dumber than I thought. We'll have a sheriff's car posted in front of the house tonight until we catch him."

I should've conked out the minute my head hit the pillow, but I was too wired. Instead, I made myself a cup of tea and snuggled with Charlie on the couch, taking catnaps throughout the night.

The next morning I called Franz and John to let them know what had happened. Franz took it in stride and said he'd notify Alan, but John was absolutely beside himself.

"I'm stunned," he said. "Speechless. Peter was the last person I'd ever suspect of doing such a thing. I can't even imagine how he could kill someone."

"Me either. Maybe we'll find out when the sheriff's deputies catch up to him. Meanwhile, he's at the receiving end of an all-points bulletin."

As things turned out, it was the Monroe County Sheriff's Department who managed to nail Peter at the airport a few days later. He had a one-way ticket to Loreto, Baja California, with a stop in Los Angeles. I imagined he planned for Yvonne to join him once she sold the B & B. I found all of this out when Deputy Hickman stopped by my house at some obscene time in the morning. I was barely awake when he knocked on the door.

"I came by to inform you that Mr. Groff has been apprehended and is no longer a threat to you or your winery."

"Great." I ran my fingers through my hair, hoping it would flatten down. Thankfully I was awake enough to have thrown on a decent T-shirt and jeans.

"I know I've admonished you on numerous occasions, Miss Ellington, for interfering with deputy business, but I must admit, your sleuthing led to an arrest."

"I should've figured it out sooner," I said. "It was so obvious. The way Yvonne used Madeline Martinez to learn about running a winery. That was Yvonne's plan. Along with Peter. To have their own winery in Baja California. And the Spanish tape Peter had in his truck, along with his book for beginners. All of it escaped me. So, how did he do it? How did he kill Elsbeth? You can't leave me in the lurch. I caught a killer, after all."

"No need to whine, Miss Ellington, I'll try to be succinct but, keep in mind, until a jury can prove him guilty, Peter Groff is innocent. Under arrest and behind bars, but innocent until proven guilty."

"I get it. I get it. Sit down. I'll get you some coffee. And a muffin. Just tell me."

Deputy Hickman made himself comfortable at the kitchen table and took a breath while his K-cup brewed. Charlie sniffed at the guy's boots for a few seconds and then ran out his doggie door.

"Mr. Groff was adamant it was not a planned murder but nevertheless, he did admit to killing her."

I know. I know. Get on with it.

"According to his statement, Elsbeth Waters had been particularly demanding of her niece, who, as you know, turned out to be Mr. Groff's girlfriend. Until he could establish himself financially, Mr. Groff was resigned to working at your winery, with Yvonne doing the same at her aunt's bed and breakfast."

I nodded once.

"On the morning of her murder, Elsbeth had slapped her niece on the face for failing to use softener sheets in the dryer."

That woman really was a witch.

"Yvonne told Peter about the incident and he, in turn, called Elsbeth, saying it was of dire importance that he speak with her but it would have to wait until late evening since he was working and had other obligations. He led her to believe he would notify the authorities about domestic abuse if she refused to meet him."

"Then what?" I asked.

"Peter didn't want to meet in anyone's house or place of work so he arranged to speak with her after dark in row twenty-six at the Geneva Walmart Supercenter. He picked that row because he had parked there before and knew the pole light wasn't working. He didn't want anyone to see him confronting Elsbeth. What he didn't realize was that someone had shot out the security camera at that location as well."

"So that's how Elsbeth's car wound up at Walmart and the forensic team was unable to find anyone else's fingerprints in it except hers and Yvonne's."

"Exactly. As per Mr. Groff's confession, Elsbeth approached his truck and they began to argue. He said she was particularly vicious, pointing a finger in his face when she wasn't jabbing it on his shoulder."

"Yeah. I can see that happening."

"The two of them were perpendicular to the truck bed. At one point, Elsbeth jabbed him so hard that it enraged him. He reached behind and snatched one of the round point shovels he had in his truck. She turned away and, in that moment of fury, he whacked her in the back of the head. He never expected it to kill her. But the blow did."

"Yikes."

"She fell over so that the upper half of her body was leaning into the truck bed. Panicking, Mr. Groff was able to wield his weight and shove her into the cab of his truck. He quickly threw a tarp over her and left the parking lot."

"I think I can figure out the rest. But why dump her body in our vineyard? Geez. Couldn't he have found another place?"

"It was dark. It was late. Mr. Groff didn't have the leisure to scout around. He was familiar with the side road on Gable Hill. It was far enough away from the Ipswich house that no one would see him driving up to where the road ended and your property began."

"So that's how he did it. He must've used his tarp and dragged her through the clump of bushes until she wound up where we were installing that new irrigation drip system. That's how her chin got bloody."

I didn't want to tell the deputy I had envisioned this scenario before, but with Stephanie as the killer. "Um, what about Elsbeth's bag? And her cell phone? And her glasses?"

"If you'd let me finish, Miss Ellington, I'm getting to that."

I got up and plunked another K-cup in the machine. "Have another muffin. More coffee's on the way."

"Thank you. Now, as I was saying, Mr. Groff removed those items and stepped on her phone to put it out of commission. When he got back to his house, he put them in a trash bag. Didn't even bother to see if her purse had money in it. The next morning was Transfer station day for Yates, Ontario and Seneca Counties. He arrived at work well before dawn and slipped that small trash bag in with the winery trash from Two Witches. He then drove it to the Tri-County Transfer and Recycling center on Pre-Emption Road, getting back in time to go up to the Riesling vineyard with John."

"Wow. That was kind of serendipitous for him, huh?"

"The timing was in his favor. I'll give you that much."

Deputy Hickman took a sip of his second cup of coffee and finished off another muffin. "By the time our investigation was underway, that evidence was already buried somewhere in the landfill. I trust this satisfies your curiosity."

"It does."

"Good. Because I'd appreciate it if you didn't say anything to anyone until an official report is released."

"You have my word."

Lucky for me, I didn't have to wait long. The next morning the entire story was plastered all over the front page of *The Finger Lakes Times*. The headline read, "Assistant Vineyard Manager Charged with Murder," and the story must've mentioned Two Witches Winery at least half a dozen times. I felt like burrowing into a small hole and never coming out.

Chapter 28

The next few days were a blur. All of the winery women, except for Rosalee, who was still somewhere in Alaska, called to see how I was doing. At least that was what they said, but I knew better. They wanted the full scoop on the murder and went straight to the horse's mouth—mine.

John removed the temporary barrier Sam and Theo made for Alvin and repaired the giant gap in the goat's pen. He also installed the new screen door Don had picked up. Poor John was still reeling from the fact his assistant killed someone.

"It's going to take me a long time to get over this one, Norrie." He put the final bolt into the screen door to the tasting room.

"Hey, Peter had all of us fooled. I missed so many clues. Like the fact he was always asking me if I'd heard anything about the investigation. Peter was almost too interested. Not to mention, one of the B & B guests told me how much they liked the couple who ran the place. I never figured the guy was our own employee. Listen, I don't suppose I could talk you into staying on a bit longer until we find and train another vineyard manager, can I?"

"You didn't even have to ask. Of course I'll stay. And I'll get started right away with the search. By the way, do your sister and brother-in-law know about any of this?"

"Nope. They're still pretty much off the grid. Just as well. They'll find out soon enough."

Although I called my parents with the news, I was relieved there was no phone service to reach my sister. I did, however, send her an e-mail on the off-chance she'd actually receive it. It was brief and to the point, without going overboard.

"Everything's great. We're hiring a new assistant vineyard manager. There were issues with the last one and his littering in the Riesling section."

In spite of all the chaos, I was actually able to make headway on my screenplay and knew I'd meet Renee's deadline. Only one thing gnawed at me and I had no alternative but to take care of it.

I got up early on a Thursday morning, grabbed a quick cup of coffee and drove to Penfield. Declan's office to be precise. I really owed him and his partner an apology. Of course, he owed me one, too, but, in fairness, he probably thought I was a murderess. Especially after my performance at Belhurst Castle.

The receptionist recognized me and told me Mr. Roth would be with me in a few minutes. I wasn't quite sure what I was going to say to him, exactly, but I had a general idea. He stepped out of his office and had a really sheepish look on his face.

"Hi, Norrie. I guess we both kind of stepped in it, didn't we? I'm really sorry if I—"

"You don't have to be. I played a good role in this as well. Hey, at least the real killer was apprehended."

"Very true. So, I suppose that whole deal about you wanting to be our third partner was just a fabrication, right?"

"Yeah. It was and I'm really sorry for leading you on. Listen, I know you and Lucas are looking for a spot for your mega-winery. Have you ever considered Waneta Lake? It's virtually untapped. It borders Steuben and Schuyler counties, where lots of small wineries are just getting started. It's worth a look."

"Hmm, that does sound promising. Thanks for the tip."

"Well, anyway, no hard feelings, I hope." I reached out my hand and he did the same.

"None whatsoever. Good luck, Norrie."

"Same to you."

* * * *

The next day I got a call from Godfrey Klein, the entomologist at the Experiment Station. His voice was brimming over with enthusiasm.

"Miss Ellington? Norrie? I have wonderful news. Amazing news. We've just gotten word from one of the field agents in Costa Rica that your brother-in-law came across a new sub-species of the Culex aegypti. You know what this means, don't you?"

Yep. Better buy another bottle of DEET. "Not really."

"It means Jason Keane's grant may be extended past the original year."

"What? Extended?"

"I know. I know. We're all buzzing with the fantastic news. I can only imagine your reaction."

Seriously? In a million years, I don't think you can.

"Miss Ellington? Are you still on the line?"

I wasn't sure what I said because my mind had gone numb. The only thing I remembered was scooping out a gigantic bowl of triple-chocolate ice cream and shoving it into my mouth. I was so intent on inhaling the stuff I didn't hear Charlie come inside.

He plopped something at my feet and, for a minute or two, I struggled to figure out what it was. Flat. Hairy. Icky.

"Oh yuck! A dried-up, dead thing. Geez, Charlie." I stood, tore off a paper towel from the roll by the sink and scooped it up. "This better be the last dead thing that shows up for a long, long time."

The dog looked at me with those expressive brown eyes as if to say, "I wouldn't bet on it."

If you enjoyed *A RIESLING TO DIE*
don't miss
CHARDONNAYED TO REST by
J.C. Eaton
in September 2018

In the meantime, turn the page for a preview of J.C. Eaton's other series,

BOOKED 4 MURDER
Book #1 of A Sophie Kimball Mystery
Available at your favorite book stores and e-tailers.

Chapter 1

"I'm telling you, Phee, they were all murdered. Murdered by reading that book."

I tried to keep my voice low, even though I felt like screaming. I had gotten the full story last night, but apparently that wasn't enough.

"That's insane, Mother. No one drops dead from reading a book. Look, can we talk about this later? I'm at work."

"Then you shouldn't have answered your cell phone."

She was right. It was a bad habit. One I had gotten used to when my daughter was in college and had all sorts of would-be emergencies. Now it was my mother in Arizona who seemed to have a never-ending supply of issues—the plumbing in her bathroom, a squeaky garage door, the arthritis in her right hand, a bridge player from her group who was cheating, and trouble keeping her succulents alive. Today it was some bizarre story about her book club. I glanced at the bottom of my computer screen for the time and decided to let her speak for another minute or so.

"Like I was saying, all of us in Booked 4 Murder are going to die from reading that book. There's a curse on it or something."

"Honestly, Mother, you can't be serious. We went through this last night. Minnie Bendelson was eighty-seven, overweight, diabetic, and had a heart condition! Not to mention the fact she was a chain-smoker. A chain-smoker! Edna Mae Langford fell, broke her hip, and died from complications of pneumonia. And she was in her eighties."

"What about Marilyn Scutt? She was only seventy."

"Her golf cart was hit by a car going in the wrong direction!"

"That wouldn't have happened if she wasn't engrossed in that book. That's what I'm telling you. She died from that darn book. And now I'm petrified. Of course, I've only read up until page twenty-four. I was in the middle of a paragraph when I got the call about Edna Mae. That's when I stopped reading the book."

"Good. Read something else."

"I'm serious, Phee. You need to fly out here and find out how that curse works."

"How on earth would I know? And once and for all, there is no curse."

"You can't say that for sure. You need to investigate. With your background, that shouldn't be too hard."

"My background? What background?"

"Well, you work for the police department, don't you?"

"In accounting and payroll! I have a civil service job. I'm not a detective."

As if to verify, I picked up the placard in front of my computer. It read, Sophie Kimball, accounts receivable.

"You come in contact with those investigators every day. Something must have rubbed off by now. You've had that job for years."

"Look, Mother, I promise I'll call the minute I get home from work, but I can't stay on the phone. Do me a favor. Stop reading those books for a few days. Turn on the TV, listen to the radio, or find something other than murder mysteries to read. Maybe a good cookbook."

"Who cooks in Sun City West? This is a retirement community. I'm going out with friends for dinner. Call me after seven your time."

"Fine. And stop thinking about a cursed book."

My finger slid to the red End button just as Nate Williams approached my desk. He had been a detective in this small Minnesota city for close to two decades and was counting the days till his retirement. At sixty-five, he still looked youthful, even with his graying hair. Maybe it was his height or the way he sauntered about as if he didn't have a care in the world.

"What's this about a cursed book? Some new case and they called your department by mistake?"

I tried to ignore his grin.

"No curse. Unless you consider wacky mothers a special variety. Come on, hand over your receipts for processing. I'll make a quick copy for you. The machine's right here."

"So, what's with the cursed book? Sounds more interesting than the stuff I've got on my docket."

"Well, if you must know, my mother is convinced that she and her book club are going to drop dead from reading some ridiculous novel. She started in with me last night and wouldn't quit. Now she's calling me at work."

Nate took the receipt copies and let out a slow breath. "And you don't believe her?"

"Of course not. It's just her overactive imagination. When my father was alive, he kept her in check, but he passed away when they moved out west years ago. Now it seems she and her friends have nothing better to do than speculate on all sorts of stuff—the government, health care, economics, immigration. . . . You know, the usual things that retired people talk about."

"Hey, I haven't even turned in my retirement letter, so no, I'm not part of the geezer gossip group yet."

"Oh my gosh. I wasn't referring to you."

My face started to flush, and I quickly turned toward my desk to hide my reaction.

"Take it easy. I'm only kidding. So, what gives? What's this book club death threat all about?"

"Gee, Nate, you sound more and more like a detective each day. Quick, pull up a chair and I'll fill you in. I've got a break coming in a few minutes. Might as well put it to good use."

Working in this department for so many years, one of the perks was having my own office. Granted, it was tiny, just a desk, computer, and copier, but it was fairly private if you weren't bothered by the hallway traffic and constant interruptions. Nate had stopped by at a good time. Most of the workers were already making their way to the coffee machine for a fifteen-minute respite.

"Want me to run and get you a cup of coffee before we start?" he asked.

"Nah, I'm fine. You're the one who's going to need a cup of coffee or something stronger when you hear this lunacy."

"I'm listening."

"There are about fifteen or so members in my mother's book club, and every year they give the librarian at Sun City West a list of their choices for murder-mystery reading. To avoid arguments, the librarian selects a different book from the list for each month and makes it a point to acquire some copies for the library."

"Hmm . . . he or she isn't in the club, I presume?"

"Correct. It's a she, but that's all I know."

"Okay, fine. So this book came as one of the suggestions from a book club member?"

"Uh-huh. It was part of the original list for the year."

Nate rubbed the bottom of his chin and leaned in. "What makes your mother so sure the book has anything to do with these deaths? From what I overheard, and believe me, I wasn't trying to snoop, it sounded like they were all unrelated."

"Three of the women died within days of each other and, according to my mother, each received a cryptic e-mail a few days before."

"What kind of e-mail? What did it say?"

"'Death lurks between the lines.'" I couldn't tell if Nate was trying to stifle a laugh or clear his throat.

"Astounding. Sounds like a take on those old nineteen eighties urban legends where someone gets a mysterious videotape, they watch it, and within days they die."

"You think someone is trying to scare a bunch of old ladies?"

"I don't know what to think. But you were right. Your mother should stick to reading a cookbook or something."

"She never went near one when I was growing up, and she's not going to start now. Frankly, the only thing that's going to stop my mother from dwelling on this is if I fly out there and make a fool of myself investigating."

"Listen, kiddo, you'd never make a fool of yourself, no matter what."

"I don't know the first thing about investigating. I'm no detective."

"The heck you're not! The way you track down and verify receipts, hold everyone accountable for monies spent, and triple-check every bit of documentation that comes across your desk? If that's not detective work, then what is?"

"You know what I mean. What does my mother expect me to do even if I fly out there? Take out a pencil and paper and start acting like Sherlock Holmes?"

"Nah, he'd use an iPad by now."

"You do think this is absurd, don't you?"

"Yes and no. Coincidental deaths maybe, but not that e-mail. Keep me posted, Phee. By the way, what's the name of that book?"

"It had a strange title. *The Twelfth Arrondissement.* Whatever that means."

"It's a neighborhood in Paris."

"How on earth do you know that?"

"You'd be surprised at all the irrelevant facts I know. But this one is firsthand. I lived in Paris for a year when I graduated from college. Couldn't figure out what to do with the rest of my life and thought I'd take a crack at studying art. Needless to say, that dream evaporated and here I am."

"Yes, here you are!" came an unmistakable voice that bellowed down the hallway. "I was looking all over for you, Williams."

"Be right there, Boss. Gotta run. Remember, Phee, if anything turns up, give a holler."

"Sure thing."

I clicked the Refresh button on my computer and waited for the screen to adjust. Of all the crazy things. Why would the book club be reading about some neighborhood in Paris? It didn't sound like their usual cozy mystery. Then again, there was nothing cozy about this.

As hard as I tried, I couldn't stop thinking about that bizarre book and my mother's irrational fears. They plagued me the entire afternoon. I mean, who in the twenty-first century, other than my mother, her book club friends, and my mother's sister, Aunt Ina, would believe in curses? The only saving grace was that my aunt wasn't in the book club. She lived in the East Valley, miles from Sun City West. Compared to her, my mother was the epitome of rational thinking.

Once when my cousin Kirk and I were ten or eleven, we were having lunch with our mothers at some restaurant after a horrid morning of clothes shopping for school. Kirk accidently spilled the salt shaker and my aunt went berserk.

"Quick! Kirk! Take a pinch of salt and throw it over your left shoulder."

"I'm not gonna do that. I don't want salt all over my neck. It'll itch."

"If you don't throw it over your shoulder, you'll be cursed with bad luck. Pinch that salt and throw it."

Kirk refused, forcing my aunt to lean over the table and throw the salt for him. Unfortunately, she knocked over two water glasses in the process, both of them landing in Kirk's lap. What followed next was one of those memorable family moments they tell you you'll be laughing at ten or twenty years later.

In a rush to stand up, Kirk toppled backward, knocked the chair over, and landed on the floor.

"See, I told you," my aunt said. "Next time you'll listen to me."

Was *The Twelfth Arrondissement* my mother's spilled salt shaker? I tried dismissing it from my mind till the moment the workday ended and I set foot in my house.

Chapter 2

I barely had time to put my bag on the counter and kick off my shoes when my phone rang. The voice in my head screamed, *LET THE ANSWERING MACHING GET IT,* but I didn't listen. I grew up in a household without an answering machine and you had to race to the phone or forever wonder what you missed. Old habits die hard.

"Phee, thank goodness you're home."

"We agreed I'd call you later this evening, Mom. I just got in."

"Thelmalee Kirkson is dead. Dead. This afternoon at the rec center pool. It was awful."

"Oh my gosh. Did she drown?"

"Drown, no. She doesn't even swim. I mean, *didn't* even swim. Just sunbathed and read."

"Heart attack?"

"No, bee sting. Out of nowhere. She got stung and died from anaphylactic shock before the paramedics could get there."

"That's awful, Mom. I'm so sorry. She was in your bridge group, wasn't she?"

"No, that's Thelma Morrison. Thelmalee was in my book club. When the fire department finally removed her body from the lounge chair, do you know what they found?"

Before I could catch a breath, my mother continued. "They found that book. *The Twelfth Arrondissement.* Facedown on the small table near her chair. She only had a few pages left. So you see, it *was* that book. It's put a curse on us!"

"For the last time, Mother. There is no curse. No book curse. This was a horrible accident. A fluke."

"Four perfectly fine book-club members dead in such a short time is not a fluke or a coincidence. Sophie Vera Kimball, you need to fly out here and investigate. I don't want you to get a phone call from my friends, or worse yet, the Sun City West Sheriff's Posse telling you that your mother is number five."

"I think you're overreacting. Besides, I can't just up and fly to Arizona."

"Knowing you, Phee, you've got plenty of vacation and personal days. I'm right, aren't I? Besides, you can get away from that awful Minnesota weather and enjoy the sunshine out here."

"The weather's fine in Minnesota. It's September, for crying out loud. You'll see me in December. Liked we planned."

"December is too late. Call me tomorrow to let me know what flight you're on."

"Mother, I am not—"

Drat! She'd already hung up, and I wasn't about to call her back. I took off my blazer and slacks, and slipped into my favorite worn jeans and an old sweatshirt. Then I grabbed some leftover lasagna from the fridge and popped it into the microwave. No sooner did I press the Start button when the phone rang again.

Unbelievable. Is there no stopping her from driving me insane?

I debated whether or not to answer and decided to let the machine get it. Nate's voice was loud enough to drown out the sound of the microwave. I quickly picked up the receiver.

"Sorry, Nate. Couldn't get to the phone fast enough. What's up?"

"Thought I'd give you a head start, kiddo. I looked up that book, and I have to say, it's really obscure. I mean, on the Amazon ranking list, it's got a really high number, and that's not good. Plus, it's not even listed with Barnes & Noble. No one's heard of it. No one's reading it. Except for your mother's book club."

"Who's the publisher?"

"It's self-published and copyrighted with the author. Also an unknown. So unknown the name didn't come up on Google."

"You didn't have to go through all of that trouble on my account. Honestly, my mother is just being overly dramatic about this. Although . . . she did call a few minutes ago to tell me another book club member died. She was stung by a bee and died of shock at the large recreation center pool."

"So that makes what? Four? Four deaths in less than a month with all of the people having a common relationship? If you ask me, maybe you should fly out there to investigate."

"Oh, come on. I don't have the slightest inkling of how to go about something like that."

"Want me to rent an old noir movie for you? It's really quite simple. You interview, or in your case, talk with the people in the book club, library patrons, and witnesses who were there when one of the women died. Start to put together bits of information that seem to lead up to something. You know, follow the clues. Like I told you earlier today, you already know how to conduct an investigation."

"Nate, you don't really believe there's a curse related to that book, do you?"

"Logically, no. Then again, was it a curse that killed those archeologists who uncovered King Tutankhamun's tomb, or was it a coincidence?"

"I think it was a virus. Dust spores. Maybe you should be the one to fly out there and commiserate with my mother."

"Thank you, no. But I'll do one better for you. Do you remember Rolo Barnes who used to work in the IT department for us?"

"Rolo Barnes? The guy who looked like an black Jerry Garcia?"

"That's the one."

"Of course I remember him. Made payroll a nightmare for me. He refused to have direct deposit and insisted that his paychecks be even-numbered only. Boy did that guy have his quirks. Why?"

"Because no one knows more about cyphers and codes than Rolo. And, he owes me big-time for a matter that I'd rather not discuss. Anyway, I downloaded the e-book version of *The Twelfth Arrondissement* and sent it to him. He'll check to see if there are any codes or messages embedded in the text."

"Boy, things in your office must really be boring if this is getting your attention."

"I wouldn't say boring, more like routine. And honestly, Phee, what detective wouldn't want to sink his or her teeth into a good old murderous curse."

"One who lives in this century and not the Middle Ages. Anyway, thanks for doing some of the legwork. If I do decide to hop a plane, you'll be the second one to know."

No sooner did I hang up the phone when the buzz of the microwave made me jump out of my skin. I half expected to turn around and see my mother standing there offering to pack my suitcase. Now I was the one getting unnerved. I was positive my mother was being totally irrational about this. Or was she? Nate certainly didn't dismiss it, and he'd dealt with all sorts of bizarre situations. Still, my mother lived in a senior community and well . . . the likelihood of someone passing away wasn't unusual, even if the cluster of deaths was.

I hated thinking about getting old and at approaching forty-five, I still considered myself years away from middle age. I had no gray hair and still looked decent in a two-piece swimsuit, although I shied away from thongs and bikinis.

I ate my dinner quickly, threw on a light jacket, and headed out for a quick walk before it got too dark. The river side of Sibley Park was only a few blocks from my house and strolling down the trail that bordered the water always seemed to help me unwind. The maples, elms, and oaks were starting to show the first signs of autumn, but the spruces and pines held steadfast to their greens and blues. In another few weeks they would be the only ones with any color left. Soon I'd need a heavier jacket. Then a polar fleece one. And then . . . Ugh. The heavyweight down coat that wouldn't come off until April. If I was lucky.

I had to clear my head, but, unfortunately, the walk wasn't working. All I succeeded in doing was giving myself more time to think about death, curses, and my mother's perpetual nagging. She wouldn't give up. When I returned from the park and turned the key into the front door, the annoying beep sounded from my answering machine.

Not my mother again! I swear I'll have the landline disconnected.

I glanced at the clock on the microwave: 8:37 p.m. Almost a quarter to six in Sun City West. I pushed the button on the phone and sure enough, my mother's voice exploded like a cannon.

"One more thing, Phee. I know you think there's no such thing as curses or hexes, but I wanted to remind you about the summer when you were eight. You may not remember it, but I do.

Of course she remembers it. The woman must have an eidetic memory. She probably remembers everything I did or said. Yeesh.

I took a long breath as her message rambled on. I expected the machine to cut her off, but it didn't.

"The water pump went out on the car and cost us a fortune; then the dryer broke and was beyond repair, so your father and I had to shell out money we didn't have, and then that rotten storm swept through Mankato and the tree in front fell, taking our bay window with it."

I recalled the tree falling into the front window but pulled up a blank as far as the car and dryer were concerned. What any of this had to do with unexpected deaths in Sun City West was beyond me.

"For six weeks, we were jinxed. That was the only explanation. And you know when it ended? Well, I'll tell you when it ended, Phee. It ended with the tree. That was the third thing. Jinxes always come in threes. But this is different. This is a book curse. A curse! God knows when it will end. We've already had four. And that's why you have to come out here and figure it out. Four dead women aren't figments of my imagination. And you don't want your mother to be number five. Understand?"

I understood all right. The curse had reached me. Across the phone lines and into my living room. My mother would nag, demand, and whine worse than a fourteen-year-old girl whose cell phone was confiscated by the vice principal. Dinnertime or not, I pushed the Redial button on the phone. She picked up before it even finished ringing.

"So, did you make those reservations?"

"No, Mother, I didn't make reservations. I'm sorry those ladies passed away, but there's no such thing as a book curse. Only Wes Craven could have come up with something like that."

"Who's Wes Craven? Don't tell me he's someone you're dating."

"I'm not dating anyone, Mother. And never mind about Wes Craven. He was a director of horror films who passed away."

"I'll bet he was reading that book. Well, are you coming or not?"

She'd gotten me so rattled I mumbled the four possibly worst words in the world: "I'll think about it."

Meet the Author

J.C. Eaton is the wife and husband team of Ann I. Goldfarb and James E. Clapp. Ann has published eight YA time travel mysteries.

Visit their website at www.jceatonauthor.com.

Printed in the United States
by Baker & Taylor Publisher Services